identity him

BY D. ANGLIN FACEY

WTL INTERNATIONAL

IDENTIFY HIM

Published by
WTL International
930 North Park Drive
P.O. Box 33049
Brampton, Ontario
L6S 6A7 Canada
www.wtlipublishing.com

978-1-927865-89-7

Printed in the U.S.A.

To Gabby and Jeff,
my cornerstones

PROLOGUE

A small moan forced its way up past Senator Barrington J. Welch III's throat as he read the note:

In case you don't know what this is, let us explain. It is called a DNA fingerprint. They tend to be pretty good at identifying a specific person. This one belongs to you, Senator Welch. We went the extra mile and paid for the most detailed test available, so there is no mistake.

His eyes glazed over. He could not read the rest of it. His life as he knew it was over.

CHAPTER ONE

There was a skeleton on the bed. It spoke.

"Darling! How nice of you to get here so quickly. And how is my favourite writer?"

Jessica stared in confusion.

"Mom?"

She sounded just like her mom. She was propped up in bed with a book, just like her mom on a rainy afternoon, but the woman in the hospital bed looked nothing like her mom.

Her mom was five feet, two inches tall, with one hundred and thirty pounds spread over her short frame. Her hair was a thick sable cap that she wore in a simple bob. The woman on the bed was five feet two inches of skin stretched taut over bones, with hair so thin you could see her scalp. She slowly maneuvered stick legs over the side of the bed and patted the space beside her.

"Come here, love. Come sit with mommy," the skeleton said in her mother's voice.

In the back of her mind, Jessica recognized the statement as one from childhood. She walked forward, intending to lower herself gently to the bed, but ended up collapsing into a sobbing heap on her mother's neck. Her mom laid her head on hers and held her close. When she was cried out, her mother pointed to a door in the corner.

"Bathroom's through there," she said quietly.

Jessica stared at her reflection in the mirror. Her eyes were puffy, her nose red, her face blotchy. Less than twenty-four hours ago, everything had been fine in her world. One phone call had changed that. She closed her eyes and thought back to her last conscious moment before the phone had rung.

She closed the laptop, fell face down on the couch, and was asleep before she could congratulate herself on finishing the article ahead of schedule. She had pushed herself, and now exhaustion wrapped her in its warm cocoon.

The telephone's ringing seemed to come from a long, long way, and she fumbled for it as she struggled out of sleep. She glanced at the clock. 3:21. AM or PM? Dark, so AM. She grabbed the phone. No one called her at 3:21 AM.

"Hello?" It was a cautious, questioning sound.

"Miss Kaene? Jessica Kaene?"

"Ye-es?"

"My name is Brandon Knight, and I'm your mother's neighbour. She has just been taken to the hospital, and she wanted me to let you know," said a cultured voice.

"What's wrong? Was there an accident?" Jessica asked, coming awake in a hurry.

"No, not an accident, but she wants you to come," the unknown voice told her.

"Of course. Flights. I have to call and find out what time . . . " she trailed off, trying to organize her mind.

"I took the liberty of checking. You have a reservation on Delta Airlines, leaving Hartsfield-Jackson Airport at 9:45 AM. I'll meet you at Pearson International."

"9:45! Is that the earliest flight?"

"No, but it's the first direct one. You'll get here at almost the same time as the earliest, and you'll have a bit more time to arrange things at your end. If you could clear yourself for a few weeks, it might be best. I'll see you in a few hours, Miss Kaene."

Only after hanging up did she think about the facts. She didn't know this man, so how would he recognize her? He hadn't said what was wrong with her mother, and he'd neglected to mention which hospital. She sat, immobile and numb. Maybe she'd just had a very realistic dream.

A near-cold shower removed all lingering traces of sleep, and for a moment, she wished she drank coffee. The stimulant would have been welcome. She made a list of all the things she had to do before heading to the airport and started working through them.

She sank into a cramped seat at the very back of the plane. It had been close, getting to the airport on time. She had spent two precious hours fine-tuning two articles that weren't due for another three weeks, but with them out of the way, she had no immediate obligations. Freelancing had some merits, after all.

It was a pity she'd been too befuddled to ask the obvious questions last night. She figured a 3 AM trip most likely meant an emergency call at the North York General Hospital, the one closest to her mom's house. Of course, if mom had been lucid enough to call a neighbour, she probably wasn't critical. She was only forty-two, not old enough to have any of the problems associated with age.

Jessica managed to nap during the two-hour flight and was firm in believing that it wasn't too bad when she walked into Terminal 3 at the Toronto Pearson International Airport. She looked around at the waiting faces and strode to a row of seats. She lowered her overweight bag and was rotating a weary shoulder when she heard her name.

"Miss Kaene? I'm Brandon. I'm stopped, not parked, so let's hustle. I'll take the shoulder bag, and you haul the wheelie."

Before she could acknowledge the greeting, he grabbed the bag, took two steps, and stopped abruptly. She watched in bewilderment as he shook the bag.

"Is there a problem, Mr. Knight?"

"The name is Brandon, and I'm just wondering if I've finally found someone with the guts to put a false bottom in her bag. You know, to hide things like weaponry and contraband from the authorities. That seems a more reasonable explanation than the clichéd bricks," he answered, giving the bag another shake.

She felt her lips twitch, and the unexpected smile eased some of the tension she'd convinced herself she wasn't carrying. She took the time to study her companion as they headed onto Highway 401. He was of mixed heritage, but what the mix consisted of eluded her. His skin was a light honey tone, as though he had a permanent tan. The dark brown eyes were almond-shaped and ringed with lashes that women have been trying to buy for centuries but have never quite achieved. His hair was too low cut to give any real clue, and he had no facial hair. Not as in clean-shaven. He had no facial hair.

"So, do I pass inspection?" he asked, amusement tingeing his voice.

Her face warmed.

"Sorry, I didn't mean to stare. Just trying to guess your ancestry," she said.

"My mother was half Mexican, half white, and my father, half black, half Chinese. I like to think I got the best of the four races!"

"And what qualities would those be?" she asked.

"I'm sure if you think hard enough, they will come to you," he replied with a grin.

She knew they were avoiding talking about her mother and decided to let him get away with it. After all, he had gone out of his way to meet her, and she would know in a few minutes, anyway. She leaned back in the plush leather seat and closed her eyes. He must be pulling in some serious money to afford the Mercedes Coupe, which couldn't be a year old. She wondered what he did for a living but thought it rude to ask. He kept up a steady stream of white noise chatter, and she pegged him as one of those people who could talk to anyone, anywhere, on any subject. A talent she often abhorred but was glad of this morning.

She opened her eyes when he stopped to take a ticket from the dispenser at a parking lot entrance, vaguely alarmed because she wasn't sure where they were. She looked around as he hustled her across the lot. Her heart tripped.

Sunnybrook Hospital? He hurried her along, talking about her lack of proper clothing. September in Atlanta and September in Toronto were sometimes very different. She'd always relied on her mother to show up at the airport with a jacket if it was colder than expected, and she had come with that unconscious expectation.

He pulled her into the hospital entrance, and after many twists and turns, stairs and long corridors, they arrived at a bank of elevators, and he punched the button for the fifteenth floor.

"15A, Room 21," he said as he reached for her hand. He unclenched her fist and wrapped her fingers around a business card. They stopped in front of a door, and he turned to her.

"I'll be downtown all day and can get back here pretty quickly. Call me if you need me. I can be a sounding board or a punching bag. I've got strong shoulders, and I come equipped with various absorbents, from hankies to Kleenex. I know everywhere to eat, and I'll do pick up or delivery. I'll hold onto your luggage and come take you home when it's time."

He dropped a casual and gentle kiss on her forehead and turned back the way they had come. She pushed open the door, and her life changed forever.

Five minutes in the bathroom where she washed her face, cried some more, and washed again. Then she started getting angry.

"What were you waiting for to tell me, Mom?" she demanded as she re-entered the room.

"The right time?" her mother grinned at her, and Jessica marveled that she could find humour in the situation.

"And the right time was 3:21 this morning?"

Her mother laughed. "No, dear. The right time would have been tomorrow. There were a few things I had planned to do today, and then I was going to call and ask you to come home."

"What's wrong, and when did you find out?"

"Just after you left in the spring. April tenth, to be exact."

"What happened?"

"Remember I'd been feeling a bit under the weather while you were here? That had been going on for a while." She paused, frowning slightly.

"The problem was that I didn't have any major symptoms, I just felt sort of generally unwell. My stomach ached after eating, but only sometimes. I had a minimal appetite, so I was losing weight. Since I'd been trying for years to lose weight, I was quite happy at first. But then it became a bit more than I wanted, and I was tired all the time, irritable. Just little nagging things, but nothing that could be pinned down.

"Then, after you left, I started having more eating problems. The stomach pains were a little worse; I'd throw up almost every time I ate, which caused some really dramatic weight loss.

"From the beginning, the prognosis wasn't good, but I wanted to wait and see if there were any treatment options worth looking at before I brought you back. We looked and tried some experimental treatment, which didn't work. There's nothing they can

9

do. It seems there is cancer somewhere, but we don't know exactly where.

"We know it has spread to my liver and lungs, and they did a liver biopsy that said it was likely from some place in my gastrointestinal tract. But they haven't found a tumour anywhere.

"They started treating it like pancreatic cancer, and tried some chemo, but my system couldn't tolerate it. Massive diarrhea and vomiting. Plus, they said only a small number of people get hair loss, but I'm clearly in that small number because I only did two treatments, and after the second treatment, I started shedding, and it has not stopped."

"What happened last night?"

"I had a bit of a stomach ache after dinner. It was a very light meal, and usually, if I lie down on my side and pull my knees up, the pain goes away. Last night it didn't, and it just kept getting worse. By three in the morning, I knew I couldn't deal with it at home anymore. So, I called Brandon, and he and his co-hab came over."

"Who is he?"

"He's my accountant, among other things."

"Why didn't you tell me as soon as you found out?"

"Because you would have dropped everything and come home, and you were in Austria at the time. You had been planning that trip for a long time, and I wanted you to focus on what you had gone there to do. No one, least of all me, expected the severe reaction to the few treatments I agreed to, so I thought you'd get back in time to be with me while we worked through the options. Problem is, we don't seem to have any options right now."

Jessica had a million questions but realized her mother was getting tired. She was also very concerned about having left the house without making her bed, and in what she considered a state of chaos, so to ease her mind, Jessica agreed to go and clean up. She stopped by the nurse's station to find out who to speak with about her mother's condition, then called Brandon.

He took one look at her red, puffy face, swollen from crying, and hauled her into his arms. He said nothing, just held her, and then gently put her into his car.

Every corner of the townhouse reflected her mother. There was a deacon's bench in the small foyer, and she idly wondered how the name came about. It seemed like a somewhat useless piece of furniture, and there had to be better places for storing scarves and hats and other outdoor accessories, but her mother was proud of that bench. She had taken a continuing education course in woodwork and had made the bench herself. It was a tad lopsided, but you had to look closely to notice it.

Dried flowers in coloured dishes, potpourri, scented candles, and a four-foot stuffed bear they had won at Canada's Wonderland years before. The bear lived in the family room corner and had a more extensive wardrobe than hers. Today he was wearing burnt-orange pants and an olive and orange shirt. His gaudy outfit was topped by an orange cap with olive green trim. Her mom must have hunted long and hard for the matching cap.

She thought of the number of courses her mother had taken: cake decorating, macramé, woodwork, auto mechanics, archery. Every year something new came up, but only two had stuck.

11

Ballroom dancing and cake decorating. All the courses were with the Toronto District School Board Continuing Education Program and cost very little.

After taking introductory, intermediate, and advanced ballroom dancing, she'd started private lessons. Although she no longer needed lessons, she still paid a membership fee to the dance studio for the privilege of having somewhere to dance. More often than not, she taught beginners for a few hours each month, which covered her fees. Every Thursday night, she'd go out dancing with the group and often attended competitions with them.

The dancing, she said, was for fun and exercise. The cake decorating she did for profit. She couldn't bake, so she teamed up with a friend who could bake but not decorate. They managed to build a business that brought in more than her medical records job did, and after two years of trying to keep up with the demands of the business, she gave up her job to run the business fulltime.

In a round of manic activity, Jessica cleaned the house thoroughly, then eased her aching body onto the daybed. Once again, the phone woke her, and once again, it was Brandon.

"I won't tell you to shine, but surely you must rise. You have half an hour before your chariot departs for the city. You've got doctors to talk to, I hear, so shake it, babe," said Brandon's voice.

No greeting and no goodbye. She blinked slowly as the odd wakeup call washed over her. She would have to pry a bit more information about this man from her mother. He was definitely on the far edge of strange.

Half an hour was more than she needed, and as she waited on the steps, she realized that she had no idea which house was his. She was busy scanning for a Mercedes Coupe and didn't note where the Jeep came from. It muscled its way to her gate, and a fashionable blonde popped out.

"Hey! I'm Reena. All set?"

This was delivered while legs squeezed into skin-tight denims conquered the few feet to where Jessica stood.

"You look shocky. I take it Brand didn't tell you I'd be driving you in?" the vision asked.

Reena proved to be a fountain from which a ceaseless stream of words flowed, and Jessica wondered how a conversation between her and Brandon worked. Did they draw straws to see who got to talk?

"Tell Lanni I'll see her in a few and call Brand if you need anything. One of us will swing by to take you home," she said, as Jessica stepped out in front of the hospital. Before she could reply, the car peeled away from the curb. She really could take the bus home, but why turn down a freely offered ride? She fortified herself with deep gulps of icy air before putting on her cheerful face to meet her mother.

"I'm sorry, Miss Kaene. There is nothing else that we can do. We can keep her comfortable with pain control, but that is the extent of our usefulness at this point. She had agreed to be part of a clinical trial, but she wasn't responding to the treatment, and decided that the resulting discomfort wasn't worth it."

Jessica stared at the doctor. His face was kind, his eyes tired. She'd waited until he finished his rounds to talk to him.

"She wants to go home," she informed him.

"I wouldn't recommend it, Miss Kaene. Your mother is going to need nursing care that you cannot provide. She is going to need increasing doses of morphine. If she takes too much, it will depress her respiratory system. She is going to lose all mobility soon. She needs to be where she'll get the care she'll need," he responded.

"No disrespect intended, Dr. Kent, but if she is dying, I think what she needs is what she wants. You've just told me that your care is not going to keep her alive. So, she will either die in your care or doing what she wants. Either way, she'll be dead. She wants to go home," she insisted.

He gave her a card.

"Come to my office at 2:15 this afternoon. I'll see what I can do."

When Jessica returned to her mother's room after speaking with the doctor, she found her putting down a copy of Jane Austin's "Pride and Prejudice."

"I still think someone should have given Wickham a good thrashing," she declared.

Jessica laughed. This was an ongoing argument that had started when she first read the book. It had been a birthday present from her mother when she turned sixteen. It was one of her mom's favourite books, and they had spent hours talking about it.

"Mom, he got to live with Lydia. Don't you think that was punishment enough?"

The argument continued through the morning, between nursing visits, bathroom runs, tests, medications, lunch, and I.V. adjustments. They argued the merits of Mr. Darcy, Mr. Collins' manners, and how Charlotte managed to live with him. By the time they got to Mr. Darcy's aunt, Lady Catherine de Bourgh, it was 2 PM, and her mother was falling asleep.

Leaving her to nap, Jessica headed for Dr. Kent's office. He was on the phone, and she sat in the tiny reception area to wait. She looked at the reading material on the wall. Leukemia. Hodgkin's Lymphoma. Multiple Myeloma . . . so many cancers, so few treatments.

He waved her in as he hung up the phone and handed her a folder.

"Before you decide to take your mother home, Miss Kaene, I'd like you to read the information in this package. Take it home and read it carefully. If, after you're done, you still want me to do so, I'll discharge your mother."

"Dr. Kent, I know you don't think it's the right thing to do, but this is not about what we want or recommend. Would you say that her life will be significantly shortened if she goes home?"

"Not at all. Here or there, I'd say three to six weeks is what we are looking at. There is a really good hospice that we could get her into. She might prefer it to the hospital, and you wouldn't have to worry about home care. The choice of location will determine the degree of pain control that will be available to her."

"I think she should be the one to make that decision."

"That's all right, for as long as she's able. The palliative care team has seen her, and they can help organize home medication. She may be given a morphine pump so she can self medicate, but at some time in the next few weeks, she's going to become only semi-conscious. She won't be aware enough to operate the pump."

"I'll bring her back when being home can no longer give her any satisfaction, which it won't if she's not aware of her surroundings. I appreciate the information you've given me, and I will read it tonight, but regardless of what it says, I'd like to take my mother home as soon as possible."

He silently reached behind him and pulled out another folder. He extracted a sheet and gave it to her.

"Here's a list of the things you'll need to have in place before she gets there. I'll make sure the paperwork is ready whenever you are."

Clutching her pile of life-changing information, Jessica eased her way into her mother's room, trying not to awaken her, and stopped. There was someone sitting by the bed. She looked at them, puzzled. They had their eyes closed, and he was murmuring to her. Some kind of meditation? Should she advance or retreat? Before she could decide, he opened his eyes.

"Jess, this is Pastor J.C. James. JC, my daughter, Jessica."

A pastor? They'd been praying?

His greeting was casual, his leave-taking even more so. The ease and camaraderie between them indicated a friendship, not a hospital chaplain visiting a dying patient.

"But he isn't the chaplain, love," her mother said when she mentioned it. You're right. He's a friend. Actually, he's Reena's uncle, and I've known him for a couple of years. He says his mission is to rescue Reena from a life of sin, so he comes to see her, and she brings him to see me."

"Ouch! That can't be too comfortable."

"You would think so, but he is surprisingly pleasant. Reena likes him, and that's why she lets him come by. In fact, she invites him over if too much time goes by between visits. She first brought him to see me, she said, to give him another soul to save, and give me unlimited cake orders!"

"Did it work?"

Her smile was vague and a little dreamy.

"Yes, I'd have to say it worked." She closed her eyes and slipped into sleep, wearing the same dreamy smile. Jessica wondered if it was the soul-saving or the cake orders that had worked.

CHAPTER TWO

"I met your uncle today," she told Reena on the drive home.

"JC? He's a decent sort. Poor Grandma is still trying to get over his defection. She thought he'd be Pope one day."

"You're Catholic?"

"Grandma is. She says JC always took religious things more seriously than her other children, so she thought he'd become a priest. She was totally ticked off when he took on a different church."

"He joined another church?"

"Yeah. He turned protestant. Grandma can't stand it, but the rest of us don't mind. He doesn't beat you over the head with it, you know; it's just a part of who he is. He's fun, though, so I hang with him sometimes."

"He and Mom seem pretty chummy," Jessica said hesitantly.

"JC's chummy with most people, but he and your mom are good friends. He's friendly but has only a few close friends. He says pastors have the same need to talk about problems as other people, but they have to be more careful who they talk to. According to him, your mom is a Venus flytrap for information. It goes in—it never comes back out!"

The stream of chatter flowed over her, and Jessica let her mind wander to the things she had to do. She had only glanced at the list, but from its length and complexity, she didn't see how she'd get everything together in time for it to be worthwhile.

"Jessica? You're home!" There was a thread of amusement in Reena's voice. Jessica looked around. Sure enough, they were parked in front of her mother's house.

"What's on your mind?" Reena asked.

Jessica started to fob her off and then noted the caring on her face.

"Mom wants to come home," she said baldly.

"Oh. She's feeling better then?"

"No. But she wants to come home anyway."

"What did the doctor say?"

"He says it's ill-advised. He gave me a bunch of stuff to read, and a long list of things I'd need to get before she could come."

"Can you get them?"

"With enough time, I'm sure I could. I'm just not sure I can do it in time."

"What do you mean?"

"Three to six weeks—that's how long he thinks she has left."

"Three to six weeks! If she wants to come home, she's coming home! Give me the list."

"What?"

"Give me the list. Go read your stuff, have a bath, eat something, and decide how you want to arrange the living space. Don't worry about anything else."

Jessica looked at her as if she had grown an extra head. She looked and sounded like a bubble-brain, and Jessica had pegged her as such. Now she sounded like an efficient and determined administrator.

"Give me the list, Jessica, and get moving. If we are to bring Lanni home tomorrow, we have to get on it right away."

"Tomorrow!?"

"No guarantees for the three weeks, so we can't afford to waste any time. The list, Jessica!"

With extreme reluctance, Jessica parted with it, and as she watched Reena race away, she panicked. How could she have trusted something so important to someone she didn't know, and who seemed to be a voluble flake?

She hurried inside and grabbed the phone.

"Alright. Let me see if I understand you," Brandon said, in the tone of one talking to a child who was not very bright. "You had a list of things to get for Lanni, and Reena took off with it. Why?"

"Well, she didn't exactly take off with it. I gave it to her. I mean, she insisted on taking it, and I gave it, but now I think I'd better get it back."

She listened to the silence and felt mildly foolish.

"Tell you what. Hang up and stay by the phone. I'll call you back in less than five," he said.

Three minutes and forty-one seconds later, Brandon called.

"Jessica? Don't worry about the list. Reena said she'll look after the things on it, and she will. I know she seems a bit scatter-brained, but trust me—she's good at this kind of thing. Give her until morning. You probably wouldn't be able to do anything before tomorrow anyway, so if you still want it back by morning, I'll personally bring it to you. Deal?"

She agreed, but only because he sounded so reasonable that to do otherwise would have been churlish. She still thought it was a mistake.

Morning proved her wrong. She had slept in patches, dreaming of hospital beds and bedpans wandering through the house, and had finally settled in for a few hours rest when the doorbell rang. The sound jangled in her tired, aching head, and she stared in confusion at the bedside clock. 6:15 AM. Mom! Something has happened. No. The hospital would have called, not sent someone to the door. She dragged on a robe and hurried down.

Pastor J.C. James leaned on the porch rail, talking to a young black man.

"Morning, Jessica. This is Mike. He's brought some stuff for you, but he has to get it off his truck so he can get to work for 7 o'clock."

Before she could get her bearings, she found herself moved aside. Mike murmured a quiet good morning, then moved to the tailgate of the big white truck taking up most of the driveway. She had not seen the truck.

Then she heard the doors. Mike had barely opened the back of the truck when six cars disgorged an assortment of bodies, both male and female. Reena and Brandon hurried up the steps.

"Did you decide how you want things arranged?" Reena asked.

"Um . . . not exactly. What are all these people doing?"

"They are helping me set up a room for Lanni. Don't worry, they all know her. Some of them go to JC's church; some are friends of ours. Most of them need to get to work, though, so we have to hurry. I'll take care of them. You go get dressed. Brandon will take you down to spring Lanni."

Jessica stared at the street signs flashing by as they sped down Bayview Avenue. She had left Reena directing people and giving orders in a tone that would have rivalled a boot-camp sergeant. Mike had unloaded quite a pile onto the driveway, and she had recognized a hospital bed, wheelchair, and bedpan. The rest meant nothing to her at first glance, and she didn't know where they would find room for everything.

It turned out that Reena's long arm extended all the way to the hospital. When they got there, Dr. Kent was waiting in her mom's room.

"Well, Miss Kaene, you made quite an impression on the charge nurse this morning. As per your instructions, your mom has been readied for immediate discharge."

Jessica noted the bemused expression her mom wore and hoped she didn't have an identical look on her face. She hadn't made any calls.

"Thank you, Dr. Kent. I know you don't agree, but this is the right thing to do. I have gotten everything on the list you gave me, and any instructions you give will be followed one hundred percent," she said, crossing her fingers behind her back and hoping she wasn't lying about the list.

"You must have had a very busy night. I've cleared you for a visiting nurse, and if Ms. Kaene has private insurance, it might pay for some in-home nursing. It would be best if she has a professional on-site as much as possible."

"It's been taken care of," said Brandon, who had been quiet up to that point. Now he grinned at them. "No worries. It's all covered."

When she walked back into the house, Jessica gaped in shock. The foyer was empty. The dining area to the left was also empty, and a giant folding screen was pushed up against the wall. She pulled on it, and it noiselessly unfolded to enclose the living/dining area completely.

Inside the living area, the couch and computer desk were gone. In their places were a hospital bed, a wheelchair, a walker and a shelf holding various items she couldn't name. There was even one of those wheeled hospital trays that hung over the bed for you to eat from. Beside the bed were two chairs that she didn't recall seeing before.

She walked to the kitchen and found the dining table and couch. They had replaced the table in the breakfast area. In the family room, the sectional sofa, which was her mom's pride and joy, had been angled to leave a wide-open space facing the TV, and a stand with her mother's favourite books was close by.

"The space is so we can wheel her bed out, and she can watch TV or look into the backyard. If she's up to it, she can sit on her sofa and read," Reena said as she quietly walked into the kitchen. Jessica surprised herself by dissolving into tears, and without breaking stride, Reena grabbed a handful of tissues and handed them to her.

"Did you sleep last night?" she asked Reena when she could control her voice.

"Sure, I did! You wouldn't believe how much of this fell into place when people heard Lanni's name. I called JC, and he called some folks. We know a lot of people, and Lanni is well-liked. She wants to come home, and we all think she deserves to get what she wants."

"I need to check if she has any private insurance. I don't know how much home care O.H.I.P. covers," Jessica said with anxiety, thinking of the nursing care that her mother would need. The Ontario Health Insurance Plan definitely didn't stretch to round-the-clock nursing.

"Don't sweat it. We have fourteen nurses lined up. They'll do twelve-hour shifts so that each one will do one shift each week. The insurance question is only about whether they get paid for the shift or not. They volunteered to do this and arranged the shifts around their regular jobs. Some of them are retired, so it's no problem. If the home care is not covered, they'll never know that payment was being considered, because they think it's free work anyway."

"Why would they do this?"

"Some because they know and like Lanni, some because JC asked, and the rest because Brandon or I asked."

"Where did all the stuff come from?"

"Friends, friends of friends, great aunts' cousins' friends. You know. Folks. People want to help, Jessica, so let them and don't worry about the little things. I had them fax me the menu that they would have used for your mom at the hospital, and I got enough groceries to last you the week, but you have to deal with the cooking. Not my area. If you can't manage it, let me know, and we'll find someone."

"No, no. I'll cook. How much do I owe you?"

"Later. I'll have to check. Here's the ambulance now. Let's get Lanni settled in."

And settled in, she was with a minimum of fuss. The look of satisfaction on her face removed any lingering doubts Jessica had harboured about the rightness of the move.

"Baby, I don't know how you managed all this, but it means everything to me," her mother said as she reclined on the newly assembled hospital bed.

"I didn't manage any of it, but that's a story for tomorrow. Today we're just going to relax and enjoy your homecoming," Jessica replied.

The next few days were a revelation to Jessica. There was a steady stream of visitors to the house. It turned out she didn't have to cook after all. Her mom's business partner, Gwen, took over the kitchen.

"I'm moving in," she said when Jessica opened the door to her the morning after her mom came home and walked in, hauling a huge bag that sort of rattled as she moved.

"You'll need to provide munchies for the visitors, meals for yourself and the nurse, and special meals for Lanni. You can't spend time with her if you are tied to the kitchen, so consider me your chef for the next few weeks."

With that, she started unloading pots and pans from the rattling bag, then went back to her car and started bringing in groceries. When given the hospital menu, she turned mutinous.

"Is she or is she not dying?" she demanded.

"She is dying," Jessica answered with a catch in her voice.

"Then why in the name of heaven does she need to watch her cholesterol and sugar intake? I'll feed her what she likes, as long as she can eat it, and if she wants triple cheese pizza and can't chew it, I'll blend it so she can suck it up with a straw!"

From then on, a routine evolved. Meal-times were Gwen's time with Lanni, and between visitors and nights were Jessica's time. Her mother got stronger over the first week and stayed that way for seven weeks. The visitors kept coming, and Lanni's laughter was a frequent and welcome sound. The nurses continued to rotate without a single complaint.

Eight weeks after she came home, Jessica looked up from the book she was reading and knew something was different. She couldn't tell what it was, but there was some kind of change.

"Mom?" The word was plaintive and urgent.

Lanni opened her eyes and looked at her daughter. For a moment, she gave no sign of recognition, then her eyes cleared. But before they did, she looked deep into Jessica's eyes.

"I've never forgotten those eyes. Two different colours. One blue, one green. They almost seemed to be changing from one to the other, so they both looked blue, then both green. Always wondered what caused it," she said fuzzily.

When her eyes focused, she looked at Jessica hanging over her with surprise.

"Are you alright, dear?" she asked.

"Yeah, mom. You were talking about my eyes. You're right. I should find out why they are like that. And you're right. When I'm excited or angry or feeling any strong emotion, it's hard to tell the difference. They're a total give away, these eyes. Can't hide anything."

She watched as her mother lowered the shield. Every time they talked about anything that would lead to questions about her father, her mother shut down. It had started in kindergarten when she first realized that most kids had a mother and a father.

She was twenty-six years old and might have been a product of a virgin birth for all she knew about her father. Not one picture. Not even his name. She was Jessica Kaene, daughter of Lanni Kaene. The spot on her birth certificate for her father was blank.

Her mother closed her eyes, and she felt a small knot of resentment. Even impending death could not bring her to break her silence on the subject. Jessica wondered if it was cowardice or compassion that kept her from pushing. Deciding that it was cowardice, she opened her mouth to broach the subject and saw her mother fumbling for the morphine pump. The pain had to be unbearable because her mom tried to use as little medication as possible. It was the third time in two hours that she had reached for it. She had enough physical pain, Jessica decided. There was no need to add emotional pain to it. She could live without knowing about her father.

That day marked the turning point. Lanni started drifting. She needed more and more morphine and spent less and less time awake. Sometimes she would moan while sleeping. When she was unresponsive for five hours one day, Jessica had her taken back to the hospital.

In the same room she'd had before, Jessica sat and watched her mother breathe. She was rarely conscious and Jessica refused to leave her side, terrified of missing any of her rare lucid moments.

Two sleepless days and nights, and her mother opened clear, pain-filled eyes and looked at her.

"Jessica. My beautiful baby. From the moment they put you in my arms, you have been my life. I've left some information for you, things you need to know. Just remember, I loved you from the first time I saw you. You have been the best part of my life. You're Mommy's very own special girl, and I love you."

Jessica leaned over so her mother could kiss her forehead. It was their night-time ritual from childhood.

"I love you, Mommy. You are the best mommy in the whole wide world." She kissed her mother on her nose, then laid her head on her chest. Ritual completed, she fell asleep listening to her mother's heartbeat, the wasted hand touching her hair.

She jerked awake when the heart hiccupped. She cradled her mother's head and held tight as the heart monitor flat-lined at 2:29 AM, November 19. Twenty-six years, six months, and fifteen days after she was born, Jessica Kaene was, for the first time in her life, completely alone. No mother, no father, no siblings, not even a distant cousin. Her mother was the only relative she could remember knowing. She was alone, with a heart too full for weeping.

CHAPTER THREE

Four months later, Jessica sat in the law offices of Bentley and Spade reading a letter.

Jess Darling,

If you are reading this, I am no longer with you. I have found out that my days here will be less than I would like, and perhaps I should have told you right away. I felt I should exhaust all the options before sounding the death knell . . .

She looked up at the man facing her. Seated behind the semi-circular desk, he wore such a blank expression she wondered how he maintained it.

"How long have you had this letter?" she asked.

"Your mother placed it in my keeping last June, with instructions to give it to you four months after her death."

29

"Why four months?"

"That, I do not know. I assume some of your questions will be answered in the letter."

She glanced down and saw that she was gripping it so tightly the letter was in danger of being mangled. With precise movements, she folded it back into its original creases and returned it to the envelope. She would read it in private.

When she stood and picked up her purse, he walked around the desk. Although it was long past the time most people usually left work, he still looked immaculate. His tan suit would have been insulted to see a wrinkle, and while she knew very little about fashion, it fit so well she doubted it had come off a rack anywhere. He was only about five-ten, so he didn't tower over her, but she would have preferred to feel dwarfed instead of shabby. Next to his pristine freshness, she felt like she had slept in her clothes.

Annoyed by her feeling of inferiority, she straightened to her full five feet seven inches and held out her hand. "I won't take up any more of your time. Thank you for waiting for me this evening. I know that it's outside of your normal hours, and I appreciate it."

He took her hand, brown eyes faintly amused. "The pleasure was mine," he said.

She had her hand on the door when he spoke again.

"I'm sorry for your loss, Miss Kaene. Your mother was a remarkable woman."

Her head whipped around. "You knew her?"

He took his time walking to her.

"Yes, I knew her," he replied and placed a card in her hand. The sympathy in his eyes made hers sting; she knew she had to leave, and quickly. "I was your mother's friend, and I'd like to be yours. Call me anytime," he told her.

She shoved the card into her purse and hurried out, thankful that the receptionist was gone and wouldn't see her tears. She stepped into the knifing wind of the mid-March evening. The day had started out mild, but now she was chilled through to the bones in a few minutes. She huddled in her inadequate jacket and looked around.

Yonge Street, just north of Sheppard, was a busy area, but not teeming with taxis the way downtown Toronto would be. It was the city of her birth, and she had missed it in the four years she had been away. Getting colder with each minute, she gave up on finding transportation and started walking. Her mother's townhouse was only a few blocks north-east of the lawyer's office. Not very distant, but in the icy chill, it might have been across town. She sped along, remembering the last time she was in the city.

She thought fondly of J.C. James. She had stepped out of her mother's hospital room almost an hour after she had died and found JC leaning on the wall facing the door. He'd opened his arms and simply folded her in without saying a word. He'd led her to the small lounge and held her hand as she gathered herself.

"I'm alone now. I've never been alone before. For as long as she was here, I was never alone. I always knew that if I needed her, she would drop everything and come, no matter when or where . . . I . . . I don't know how to be alone."

"It's good that you had that assurance of your mother's love. But you are wrong. You are not alone. Your mother spent her life collecting friends. Very good friends. That's her legacy to you. Do you know what that means? For as long as her friends live on, you cannot be alone. We cannot replace your mother, but we can be there for you. You'll never be alone unless you choose to be."

When she'd collected her thoughts enough to start thinking about funeral arrangements, she realized the depth of the friendships her mother had forged. The telephone rang early in the morning.

"I hate to keep doing this to you, but you must rise. None of us feel like shining but rise, we must. We have an appointment, Jessica. Half an hour to the door."

She'd shaken her head. There hadn't been enough time to pry information about this strange young man out of her mother, but Brandon Knight tended to be on time, so she'd gotten ready, wondering what kind of appointment they had.

It had turned out to be at a local funeral home. All the arrangements had been made. She just had to pick the day. She'd thought they would be using the chapel at the funeral home, but not so. A service was to be held at JC's church, which she thought strange since her mom wasn't a member.

Everything had been planned, down to the smallest detail, from the order of the service to the reception in the church hall after the burial. Jessica saw faces she'd recognized as visitors during her mom's illness. The nurses came—all fourteen of them. The only thing Jessica had had to do was write and deliver the eulogy. The people were so kind and friendly that she'd found herself agreeing that she would visit when she was next in town. The entire thing had been coordinated by Reena with military precision.

Now Jessica hurried to get back to her mother's house. By the time she fumbled her way through the front door, she was numb.

She sank down on the deacon's bench, thinking for the first time it might have some use.

Revived by a boiling shower and hot chocolate, she curled into the sofa and took out the letter.

. . . You are getting this now because I'm hoping that four months will be enough time for you to have gotten past the first surge of grief and be able to deal with additional information.

Don't think too badly of me for the way I'm going about this. I intended to tell you, but on finding that I couldn't, I accepted the cowardice I saw within myself and did the next best thing. You have asked me questions over the years, and I never gave you answers. I think you deserve to know, even if I couldn't tell you when I was with you.

Whatever you may feel over the next few days, please, please, please, remember that I love you. You should know that I loved you from the moment they placed you in my arms. You have been the best part of my life, and I wouldn't have changed that for anything . . .

It was almost exactly what she'd said before she died, and Jessica felt her stomach tighten. Some instructions followed that made very little sense, but they would have to wait for the next day. She re-read the letter, tears washing her face, and tried to shake the feeling of apprehension that was slowly enveloping her.

"Rise, oh long-unseen one. I might have to polish you up a bit but shine you will today. We have things to do. Half an hour. Be on your neglected doorstep."

She staggered into the bathroom, wondering if she'd ever spend a night in the house without being woken by one of Brandon's rise-and-shine phone calls. Since she didn't know where she was going, she dressed in navy slacks, a white turtleneck, and a navy and white striped pullover. The choice was simple. The layers provided warmth but could be shed if she got too warm or to change the outfit's look.

The letter had been vague. "I've asked a friend to take you to retrieve a package. JC, Brandon, and Reena all make good sounding boards if you need one. I have been tempted to talk to JC about things, but I resisted. I felt it would be unfair since I had not shared any of it with you."

She assumed Brandon was the friend taking her, so she tried to meet his half-hour deadline. When he pulled into the driveway, she was surprised to see JC with him. The minister hugged her, looked at her face that had not quite recovered from the previous night's crying, and gave her hand a squeeze.

"They say it will get better. I don't know if it's true, but I'm trying to believe it. You should, too," he said quietly.

"Time's a-wasting, short stuff. Gotta hustle."

Brandon's irreverence broke the sombre mood, and they climbed into the car.

"Where are we going?" she wanted to know.

"We are embarking on a long, five-minute drive to a bank on Yonge Street. May their coffers be full," Brandon answered.

"All of us are going to the bank?" she asked, puzzled.

"Yep. Lanni trusted me. Lanni trusted JC. So, she combined us and made us one super trustworthy unit. She had me take out a safety deposit box in my name, but it can only be opened in JC's presence. I'm supposed to turn the contents over to you."

"Suppose JC died?" she asked, curious.

"His death certificate and your presence would suffice," he answered.

"You're joking, right?"

It was JC who replied. "I don't believe he is, my dear. Your mother was very specific. She wanted the box's contents to be kept safe, but she only wanted one person to have access to it. That's you. Setting it up so Brandon can't open the box without me meant he couldn't take a peek—I wouldn't let him. She knew the reverse wasn't true. She knew that I wouldn't allow myself to give in to the temptation to look with Brandon's knowledge. He wouldn't stop crowing if I did."

"So, what did you deposit?"

"A box. And before you ask, no, I don't know what's in it. I was told you would be back four months after her death, and I should give the box to you then. So I, Brandon Knight in shining armour, have brought you to said bank to fetch the aforementioned box." With that, he screeched into a parking space on the street.

Jessica stared down at the small box on the table. She desperately wanted to open it, but knowing how much trouble her mother had taken to keep the contents private, she couldn't. She finally picked it up. Neither JC nor Brandon said a word, merely turned and led the way out. She waited with JC as Brandon cancelled the safety deposit box, then rode home in silence.

She dropped the box on the dining table and went upstairs to change into comfortable tracks. Forty-five minutes later, she admitted that she was stalling, went down, and quickly lifted the lid from the box.

She wasn't sure what she'd expected, maybe stacks of cash in twenties, or some kind of contraband, maybe even stock certificates. The sight of three books sitting in innocuous splendour in their cardboard castle startled her. Mom had had books locked up? She opened the top one. A diary. So were the other two. She started shaking. With fumbling hands, she fitted the lid back on the box.

She couldn't describe what she felt. Anxiety, elation, and underneath it all, fear. Finally, she was going to get some answers. She reluctantly left the box with its bounty and forced herself to eat some breakfast. She reasoned that she might not be able to eat after reading. The bowl of cereal could have been bits of cardboard for all she tasted it, but she virtuously forced it down, then picked up the box and curled up in her mother's favourite reading spot. The books were chronological, and she took the first one and began reading.

LANNI'S DIARY

August 26

I'm not much for writing, but the therapist said it might be good for me to write things down. I don't know why. It's not like I'm going to let anyone read it. I think she really wants me to tell her stuff, but I can't seem to. I don't know that writing will help, but if I'm careful to make sure no one reads it, I don't see how it can hurt, especially since I'm not doing so good right now.

It's hard to believe that it was only a month and a half ago that I came here. Not here, in the hospital, but here in Fraizers Gap. My sister lives here. She's a teacher at the high school. She'd usually come to Toronto to stay with us for the summer, but she was teaching summer school this year and couldn't come. I was majorly excited when she asked Dad if I could come visit her.

We couldn't afford it, but she said she'd pay the return fare if we could cover my fare from Toronto. Mom, who knows everybody and their grannies, knew someone from a church who had a trip going to St. Johns. That's in New Brunswick, but it is only a short drive across the border into Maine, and Fraizers Gap is in Maine. The church folks let me ride along on the children's fare. This was such a small amount that Mom slipped me fifty dollars when Dad wasn't looking.

"Emergency money," she whispered.

I wondered what kind of emergency I could run into travelling with a bunch of old church folks. We had already splurged and bought travel medical insurance. Of course, this was Mom's doing. Dad said it was a waste of money.

My sister's name is Lisanne, but we usually call her Anne, and she is eleven years older than me. We don't have all that much in common, but we get along well enough. She picked me up at the church where the bus went and brought me to her place. She has this neat apartment. It's built onto a huge house, a sort of servants' quarters or something. The people who own the house only use it sometimes in the summer, and this year they didn't come.

I went with Anne to school for three hours on weekdays during July, and then when she was finished, we did girly stuff. We went to the mall, cooked stuff that Mom would never dream of making, no meat and potatoes for us! We spent a lot of time in the pool. The owners pay to have it serviced whether they came or not, so it would have been a waste not to use it. We read books and argued about them. We went to the beach. I was having the absolute best summer of my life until August 23rd.

Anne had to go to her school to do something. School would be starting in two weeks, and she had to prepare. I was going to leave on the twenty-sixth, so we were going to shop for back to school stuff. I didn't want to hang around the school all day, so I told her I'd bike into town and meet her at the school at 2:30. It was only a fifteen-minute ride.

I left the house at 2 o'clock, just in case. It wasn't an especially lonely road, but traffic was light. I pedalled the borrowed bike past the pretty houses, thinking that if it was my bike, I'd let some of the air out of the tires to make the ride a bit more comfortable. I was riding on the sidewalk because that's what everyone did. There were these two empty lots, side by side, and I was about passing the middle of the first one when I went flying. No warning. One minute I was pedalling. The next, I was doing a summersault over the handlebar.

I didn't land on the sidewalk, but in the softer grass beside it. More surprised than hurt, I hauled myself over to the bike and bent down to look. A piece of wire was jammed into the back wheel, and the spokes were all bent around it. I was puzzled, trying to figure out how I could have picked it up when I realized I wasn't alone.

There was a Nike high-top cross-trainer on my right. I started to stand up, relieved that I'd have some help when I was grabbed from behind. One powerful arm wrapped around me, pinning my arms to my side, the other clamped over my mouth. My legs were free, and I kicked for all I was worth, but it's hard to kick behind you when your legs are dangling. And mine were.

I was being carried, without any apparent effort, into the vacant lot. The odd thing was, I wasn't really scared. Frightened, yes, but not scared. I mean, this is Fraizers Gap, where people go on vacation and leave their houses unlocked. Nothing bad ever happens here, plus this was daytime, by the road, with vehicles going by a wide-open lot that had no cover. Or so I thought until we seemed to fall into a narrow fissure. It was about three feet across, and deep enough that I could stand bent over in it and not see the road. I got scared in a hurry.

I woke up here, in the hospital, with only vague snatches of memory of what had happened. I could remember my shirt ripping. I could remember the pain, lots of pain. I could remember biting into the hand over my mouth.

I could remember two things about my attacker. He had huge hands with hair on them that was so blond they were almost white, and his eyes were blue and green. I know it sounds weird like I'm making it up, but they were. When I first saw them, one looked blue, and one looked green. Maybe the ski mask he was wearing made them seem brighter than they were, but they looked a very intense blue and green. Then this really weird thing happened. I blinked, and both his eyes seemed green. Then they seemed blue. I couldn't tell if they were actually changing colours or if I was focusing on one and then the other. But I'm sure they were both blue and green. Then I ended up here.

I've never been in a hospital before, and if I was here for any other reason, I might enjoy it. But being a rape victim sets you apart. Nurses, orderlies, doctors, other patients—they all look at me but never look at me. No one will meet my eyes; no one knows what to say. Some look with pity, some with revulsion, and strangely, some women especially, look at me as if fascinated. I'm a minor, so I was assigned a social worker and a therapist.

There is something called a Vittulo Kit. It's for collecting physical evidence in sexual assaults. They told me that Anne gave permission for them to collect stuff for one while I was still out of it. The stuff from it can be used for evidence if they ever find the perpetrator. I don't know why they all say "the perpetrator" as if it could be a female.

August 28

I've been here for five days. The doctor says I can be released tomorrow. My bruises are fading, my stitches are dissolving, and I can almost pee without having to grit my teeth to keep from screaming. My body is healing. The doctor says I'll be good as new in another week—what a load of crock. I'll never be the same, and my mind feels like it belongs to an old, old woman.

August 29

I'm back at Lisanne's. When I first woke up in the hospital, she was there, crying and holding my hand. She came every day and tried to cheer me up. Then this morning, she was there when the cops came. They wanted me to go over my statement, wondering if anything I'd said was induced by the drugs the doctors had given me. I didn't want to go over it, but since I didn't really remember talking to them before, the therapist said I should.

The room was pretty full. Lisanne, the doctor, the therapist and two cops. The cops asked the doctor and therapist to leave. I told them everything, from the wire in the spokes to the bitten hand with the white-blond hair and the weird eyes. Was I sure about the blond hair? What about the eyes? That's a very odd thing I was describing. Wasn't it possible that my fear caused me to see things that weren't quite so? I got mad.

"I don't know why you want to think so, but I didn't imagine any of this. The hair on his arm was blond—pale, white-blond. I bit a chunk out of the bottom of his thumb, and his eyes were blue and green. I didn't imagine it."

Maybe I should have yelled, but, even as mad as I was, I couldn't work up the energy for it. One of the cops, an older guy, looked really troubled. The younger one had been sympathetic; now, he looked speculative. They thanked me for my time and left. The doctor came and signed my release. Lisanne took me home.

She's acting real strange, walking around as if in a daze. I don't get it. I could understand if it was the first night. But this happened days ago. Why is she behaving like she just got a big shock?

August 30

I'm going home tomorrow. Lisanne just told me. "I've spoken with Mom," she said. "And we think it's best that you get away from here, where there are reminders. Plus, you need her, and she can't afford to come."

I wanted to know what would happen when they caught the guy, but she said I wouldn't be needed. She had spoken with Constable Downs, the younger cop from the hospital, and they would use the DNA sample from the kit. If I was needed at the trial, we'd worry about the money then. But then she said something odd. She said they weren't going to arrest anyone, anyway. I guess the whole thing must have weirded me out because I thought she was supposed to say they won't *catch* anyone, not that they won't *arrest* anyone. But I can't help wondering if what she said was what she meant to say, and I was too scared to ask.

The therapist gave me the name of someone at the rape crisis centre in Toronto. I don't know if I'm going to call. Maybe I can just leave this nightmare behind me when I go, and we'll all pretend I never came to Fraizers Gap, and nothing happened. I mean, why drag the whole sick mess to Toronto with me? No one there will know unless we tell, and I don't need the pity.

The book ended as abruptly as it had begun, and Jessica dropped it as if it was on fire. Only then did she realize that she was crying. Deep, racking sobs that couldn't relieve the pressure in her chest. She had spent years fantasizing about her mother's reasons for refusing to talk about her father.

Sometimes he'd died tragically, and she was too heartbroken to talk about it. Sometimes she'd fallen in love with someone who couldn't marry her for reasons Jessica had never worked out. A dozen scenarios she'd envisioned, but none of them involved her mother not knowing who he was. In her head, she'd always been the product of either a heart-wrenching love or a grand passion. Now she knew. She was the product of rape. The eyes couldn't lie. She looked at the second book and kept looking. She didn't have the strength to deal with finding out anything else. She closed the box and put it into the locked compartment of the sectional sofa. She needed company.

CHAPTER FOUR

She pulled into the empty parking lot of the church and hoped JC was there. The door was open, and she stepped cautiously in. Only one light was on, and the interior was dim. She hurried over to JC's office door and knocked. No answer and the door proved to be locked when she tried it. She could hear a vacuum cleaner running in the lower hall. It turned out to be the janitor, who informed her that the pastor would be there shortly. She decided to wait in the sanctuary.

She sat in the pew just inside the door, which was at the back of the room. She wasn't the praying kind but closed her eyes and let the silence pour over her. A sense of peace pervaded the place, and she absorbed it with acute hunger. Twenty minutes later, when JC arrived, she was calm.

"Did you come to see me, or were you just passing? Old Mrs. Jansen across the street says you've been here about half an hour. She kept watch, made sure you didn't make off with our vintage sound system!"

Jessica smiled at him, absently.

"I came to see you, but your church did such a good job of putting things into perspective that I'll defer the visit for another time."

He tilted his head at that familiar angle and gave her a look rife with speculation. Before he could speak, she asked him, "Are folks allowed to read anything inside the church that is not religious?"

"Is it sacrilegious?"

"I don't think so, but I can't be sure."

"Why don't you tell me what kind of material it is, and I'll decide from that."

"It's a diary, and I won't know the contents until I read it," she told him quietly.

"Was it written by a decent person?"

"Yes, very decent."

"Then, there should be no problem. *Mi iglesia es su iglesia!*"

"Shouldn't that be *mi casa es su casa?*"

"Yes, but you don't need my house, you need my church. Do you need me here while you read?"

"Not really, but it might help."

The trip back home to pick up the unread diaries was calm, with none of the frenzy that had driven her to seek JC earlier. She returned to the church and found a cushion on the bench she'd been sitting in. She sank onto it and took out diary number two.

November 17

Oh God! Oh God! Oh God! How can this be happening? What did I do? Am I being punished? Like being raped wasn't bad enough, now I must be reminded day after day for the rest of my life? Damn father and his puritanical, religious twaddle. How can this be God's will? How could it have been his will for me to have some base, vile excuse of a male force himself on me and violate me? I've never had a boyfriend, but I was looking forward to dating. Mom had said I could start dating next year. I guess she doesn't have to worry about that now. I don't want anyone near me.

I can't think. Every time I try to think it through, I come up blank. I didn't believe Dr. Lowen. I mean, I had barely noticed the missed periods. I just didn't notice with everything going on, but even if I had, it wouldn't have mattered. It's not that unusual for me to miss periods. I'd gone in for a follow-up check. The doctor in Fraizers Gap insisted that I had to see a doctor at the three-month mark. A clean bill of physical health would send me on my way, ready to heal my mind.

Well, the good news is that I am in good health, and while a bit young, I should have no problem carrying and delivering this child. I listened to her drone on about it being unfortunate that I was so young, as if it would have been better to be raped at twenty-five. Still, she claimed, I was young and resilient, and I'd recover from the traumas of the rape and the resulting pregnancy. I wanted to punch her teeth down her throat.

I've never given much thought to abortion, and I guess in the real world, I don't really believe in it. But this doesn't feel like the real world, and I know I don't want this baby. I don't care what Dad says. I'm fifteen years old, I'll be sixteen when the baby is born, and my life will be over before I have a chance to live it. Dad says it's selfish, and I should think about the unborn life that God has entrusted to me. Right. Like if God wanted me to have a child, he couldn't have found some other way of giving me one. I could have fooled around with Johnny O'Leary from school. He's always giving me the eye, and he's good looking. At least I would have known what kind of father the child was getting. I know I have to think about things, but I just can't. But I know I don't want to have a criminal's baby. And I know I don't want to have to give up my life to look after a baby planted in me by some lower life form.

Jessica hunched in misery and stared into space. Was she strong enough to get through the rest? She thought back to the year she'd turned sixteen. Mom had thrown her a big birthday bash. All her high school friends were there, and it had been a blast. She'd gone home and laughed with her mom about some of the quirkier gifts. Then mom had given her a set of Jane Austin books and hugged her tight. When she let go, there were tears in her eyes.

"Happy sixteenth birthday, my love," she'd said. "May your life go exactly as you want it to, and God bless you."

She'd thought her mom was just feeling sentimental, but now she realized she must have been thinking back to how different her sixteenth birthday had been. She continued reading.

November 25

Mom went with me to do the ultrasound. We didn't have to verify how far along the pregnancy was since the conception date was etched in my mind for all time. The doctor said it would be a good way to find out if there were any obvious birth defects. I didn't tell Mom, but I was hoping for a badly deformed fetus. Something that I could use as a bargaining chip to get them to support my getting rid of it. But the baby was perfectly formed, and I watched in fascination as the various parts came up on the screen.

When we got home, Mom told me that if I really wanted to, she'd help me get an abortion. But then she told me that she would raise the baby for me if I had it, that way I could go on and do the things I wanted. It's one thing to think about getting rid of some unknown baby, but now I'd seen it, it was real. I think she went to the ultrasound with me to make sure that I looked at the pictures.

She gave me a bunch of papers later in the day. It was for a change of name. She said it would be best if I'm keeping the child, to change my name legally to something other than our family name. I'm not sure why, but she is adamant. She even had one picked out. I can keep the Lanni, even though it's a short form of my name, but the last name must go. She said I could use Kaene. It was her mother's maiden name. I filled out the forms that turned Elaine Grange into Lanni Kaene.

November 30

Today I felt the baby move. I don't know if I've felt it before and not realized it. It was just a little flutter in my stomach, like butterflies. I went to the library and read a bunch of stuff about terminating pregnancies, and I don't think I can do it. It's not the baby's fault, so it shouldn't have to suffer. I mean, I still don't want a baby, but if Mom will take care of it, then I guess I can go ahead and have it. Plus, I found out so late about the pregnancy that it seems really cruel to do anything about it.

January 7

School reopened today, and I'm not there. I've only just started showing, but Mom agreed that it would be best if I didn't go and have to deal with other kids making fun of me. For once, she stood up to Dad. He felt that I should go to school. After all, he said, since I hadn't done anything wrong, why should I hide? But for people to know that the pregnancy wasn't my fault, I'd have to announce to the world, or at least the school, that I'd been raped. No, thank you! I'd much rather they think I'd been fooling around in the back seat of someone's car than have them staring at me in revulsion, or worse, pity.

March 4

I had a big fight with Dad. I've always gone to church with them, but I stopped going almost two months ago. The same reason I stopped school is why I stopped going to church. He pulled out the old "as long as you are under my roof" thing. I told him that if he was putting me out, he needed to say it clearly so I'd know exactly where I stood, but if going to church with him was the condition of my remaining at home, I was willing to go to a shelter.

I've never seen Mom so mad. "Not one more word, out of either of you," she said. It was said quietly, in the hoarse voice she uses when she is trying hard not to shout. She hauled Dad into their bedroom and blistered him. I couldn't hear what she was saying, but the tone was clear. She was majorly ticked off.

March 21

Today is my birthday. I'm sixteen years old, and I'm waddling. Until last week I was kind of discreetly pregnant. Then I sort of ballooned out. Dad bought me a book on child development. Mom got me a pair of maternity jeans. I thanked them politely and went to my room. I stared at them with tears rolling down my face. They gave me a baby book and maternity wear for my sixteenth birthday. I know they don't have much money, and every spare penny is going to buy things for the baby. Maybe if I had gone looking to have a baby, I wouldn't feel as if I no longer exist. But I'm sixteen. Couldn't they have gotten something for just me? Something that didn't have anything to do with this baby that has taken over my life?

March 22

I got a present today. Lisanne sent it. It's a cashmere sweater in a deep purple colour. The great thing is that it can't fit me! It's for me, and it's a size eight. So, when I've popped this baby out, I'll have one really nice new thing that's just for me. And I'm going to wear it, even if it's warm when the baby is born.

April 10

I just finished the eleventh grade course work. I'm really in tenth grade, but I was so out of it last semester, that I took on extra courses to keep myself from going insane. Normally I would do four courses for a semester. Last semester I did five in regular classes, then two by correspondence. In January, I started the eleventh grade courses through the correspondence school, and now I've finished them. After the baby is born, I'll think about twelfth grade. The plan was for me to go back to school in September, but I can't see myself doing that. I'll wait and see, but I don't think I'm going to. I feel like I'm about twenty years older than everyone else there.

May 3

Don't panic. Can't panic. I'm in labour. At least, I think I am. Mom and Dad went to church this evening, and I was sitting at the dining table reading when I wet my pants. I hurried to the bathroom, wondering if I was bleeding, but I wasn't. I was confused. I mean, I know all about my water breaking, but this didn't seem like it was enough to be that, and Mom wasn't home. I took a shower and changed my clothes, but I'd only just gotten dressed when it happened again.

I called Dr. Lowen, who told me to get my things together. Any pain? No pain. Well, she said, your water has broken, but since you don't have pain, you don't have to go to the hospital yet. Get everything together, and once the pains start, head for the hospital when they are five minutes apart. If you don't get any pain by midnight, then go to the hospital anyway.

So here I am, 2:30 AM, sitting in the maternity triage of Women's College Hospital. I'm alone. I'm scared. I still don't have any pain, and the nurse said they would have to induce labour before morning. I have everything I need, but I wish Mom had stayed. She is coming back. I'm to call her if they are ready for me before she gets back, but since the nurse told her it would be about five hours, she went to get stuff prepared for Dad to take to work tomorrow. They said I could go back home too, but I didn't want to. As soon as it's ready, they are going to give me a room.

May 5

It's over—thirteen gruelling hours of unbelievable pain. For the second time in less than a year, I have stitches that make going to the bathroom a unique torture. Mom stayed with me part of the time, but for the most part, it was just the nurse and I.

An amazing thing happened in that room. I finally managed to push out a screaming, seven-pound baby girl. They wrapped her in a little blanket and put her on my chest, and my heart just about rolled over. I clutched her to me and knew that if anyone hurt her, I would go to jail. I didn't want a baby. But she's mine. Only mine. My very own special baby girl and no one is going to hurt her without going through me. She has ten perfect little fingers that are almost transparent, and her head is covered with fuzz that is so pale it is almost white. Her eyes are a sort of pale, watery blue, but the nurse said that lots of babies have eyes that colour at first. She's perfect, and she's mine. I named her Jessica. Jessica Kaene. No middle name.

July 1

It's Canada Day, and we are supposed to be going on a picnic. I overheard Mom and Dad talking. After all his talk about God's will, he's embarrassed to have my illegitimate child at the church picnic. Of course, that's my fault. Had I simply told people what had happened, they wouldn't be looking down their noses at me. Since I didn't, they would now be looking down their noses at the entire family. Mom was livid. I pretended that I hadn't heard them and helped to pack the picnic hamper and load the car. I left out the things I would have taken for Jess and myself.

Mom didn't say anything when she realized I wasn't going, but she levelled a look laced with enough venom at my dad to cause him to scurry out the door and into the car. I smiled tightly at the thought of him trapped in that small, closed space with her for almost an hour. Mom doesn't get angry often, but when she does, you would be foolish not to be afraid.

August 9

I wonder if it is normal to put things into compartments in my mind the way I do. I found out today that Jessica truly has her father's eyes. I'd known before, since one is blue and the other green, but today, for the first time, they did that same weird thing his did. One minute, blue and green, then she started crying, and for a quick moment, I couldn't seem to tell the difference in colour. It gave me quite a jolt when it happened, but it didn't plunge me into bad memories like I would have expected. These are my baby's eyes, not those of the deviant who passed the genes on to her. She has taken over my life with my blessing. She is my life.

September 15

I didn't go back to school. I'm finishing up my credits through correspondence, and I plan to finish by December. I was supposed to go to George Brown College to do nursing, but I'm going to put that off until Jess starts school. In January, I'm going to do a six-week Health Care Aid course. It's six hours per day, and I can use it to work enough to look after Jess and myself. Mom is willing to look after her while I go to school so I could go to college, but I want to be with her, so I'll go to school when she starts school. Right now, I'll work nights so I can spend the days with her. Luckily, she's a good baby. She sleeps through the night, so when I put her to bed, Mom won't have to do much until I get home in the morning. That's the plan for now.

Diary number two ended, and Jessica put it down beside her. She looked around, pulling herself back to the present. She was in JC's church. She gathered her things and stood up. She was satisfied. She may have been forced on her mother, but her mother had loved her. She could live with that. She would have dinner before tackling number three. It could hardly have anything in it to rival the shock of number one.

CHAPTER FIVE

Diary number three almost caused her hair to turn grey. She had curled into the sofa with a mug of hot chocolate doctored with vanilla, almond extract and nutmeg, just like her mom used to make it, and settled down for a cozy read. She was four months old at the end of diary number two, and she expected more of her mother's description of her next few months. She couldn't have been more wrong.

July 6

Lisanne came home today. At almost three years, this is the first time my baby's seeing her only aunt. When Anne didn't come home the first summer I had Jess, we thought maybe she felt guilty because I'd been visiting her when it happened. Then she stopped writing every week. Mom was worried at first, thinking something

55

had happened to her, but then she got a letter saying she'd become vice-principal of the school and she was really busy and couldn't write as often. Right.

Dad was going to pick her up at the airport, but she said not to bother. She'd rent a car for the week, which is how long she planned to stay. Mom got this bewildered look on her face. We don't rent cars. Dad has been stitching our old wagon together with duct tape for so long, we've forgotten what it's like to drive something that doesn't shudder and shake.

She got to the apartment just before lunch, wearing an outfit that would have paid our rent for many months. I took one look at her and right away started noticing that my simple shorts and top had grubby little handprints on them, and Mom was wearing a house dress that I remembered from kindergarten.

Lisanne looked around the living room as if she couldn't remember having been there before. She was facing the kitchen door when she suddenly went paler than the cream suit she was wearing. A look of horror came over her face, and she stumbled. She would have fallen flat on her face if I hadn't grabbed her. She was still staring towards the kitchen, and I looked over to see Jess, face covered with strawberry juice and fingers dripping with the same, walking towards us.

"I done eating, Mommy," she announced and tilted her head back to better see Lisanne's face.

"Whosis, Mommy?"

"She's your Aunt Lisanne."

"Like in the picture?"

"Yes, Baby. Why don't you go clean up, and then you can give her a hug?"

Lisanne hobbled to a chair as Jess headed to the bathroom.

"Oh, God. This cannot be!" Lisanne moaned.

"What's the matter? What's wrong?" Mom asked with growing urgency. With the three of us looking on, she pulled herself together with visible effort.

"Never mind me," she said. "I was just surprised to see how big she is. I should have been here before."

Mom and Dad seemed to think this made sense, but I could tell that there was something else going on. For the entire week, she never picked Jess up once, never hugged her, never touched her. In fact, she avoided her so assiduously that Jess asked me why "Auntie San" didn't like her.

Before she left, she bought a card and wrote Jessica's name on it. Nothing inside, just her name on the envelope.

"For all the birthdays I missed," she told me. "Whatever you do, don't tell Mom and Dad."

I opened it after she left and found a money order for five thousand dollars. My eyes almost popped out of my head. The next day I used it to open a joint savings account in mine and Jess's names. I couldn't use it, but I'd save it in case Jess ever needed it. I might question the money, but if my baby needs something that I can't provide, I'm not going to let her go without. Lisanne and I were never close, but I am having a hard time understanding what's happened to our relationship. It's as if she took one look at Jess and decided to have nothing to do with either of us.

July 15

Mom dropped a bomb on me today. Her and Dad want to move. Not across town, but across the continent. Arizona, she says, has the right type of climate for Dad. He's starting to feel the winters, can't deal with the cold, which is news to me. He's going to be retiring in two years, and they'll move then. They are going to buy a small house there and go as soon as he retires.

"Don't look at me like that, child. You didn't think Dad was going to work forever, did you?"

"But how are you going to manage? What are you going to use to buy this house?"

"Actually, Lisanne is going to help us with that," she said, avoiding my eyes.

"I see," I said uncertainly.

"I'm not sure what you see, but what I would like you to see is that it would be best if you went to college now instead of waiting until next year. That way, you'll be close to finishing when we leave."

September 7

The day Mom told me they were planning to move, I went into overdrive. I sent off the application form for college in a hurry and prayed and prayed that I'd be accepted for the September term. I spent the rest of the summer agonizing about it, applying for student loans and regretting that I'd have to give up spending the next year with Jess.

God smiled on me, and here I am. First day of classes at George Brown College. I applied for the medical records program instead of nursing because it is shorter, and I need to finish quickly. I intend to do my third semester next summer, and hopefully finish the following summer. I don't want to be trying to go to school and work and look after Jess by myself all at the same time. So much for Mom's promise to raise her if I went through with the pregnancy. Good thing I hadn't depended on her to do it. Of course, I was relying on her to be there at night. The plan was to work nights so I could be home days, but that's not going to happen if Mom's not there. I don't really have anyone else that I'd trust to stay with my baby all night.

September 6

It's been almost exactly one year to the day since I last wrote in this. Today is a milestone in our lives. Jess started kindergarten. I dropped her off and didn't want to leave. She looked so small and alone in the class. Only the fact that all the other kids looked the same way convinced me to leave. I'm here, at school myself, at the start of my fourth semester. I managed to do one in the summer, and now I have just this one left before a practical segment. It's been a hellish year. I haven't heard from Lisanne. Mom hasn't mentioned her, so I don't know if they have heard anything. Mom not talking about her is strange in itself, so I've kept my own counsel.

June 4

Another shocker from Mom. They won't be going to Arizona after all. Dad has colon cancer. He's going to need health care that they can't afford in the U.S.A. He's due to retire at the end of July, and this is not welcome news. I'm in my final semester of college, doing what they call a pre-grad placement. I've been placed at Mount

Sinai Hospital, right in the middle of downtown. The supervisor says I'm doing really well, and it sounds like she might hire me full-time after I finish. All of which is great. I registered Jess in a camp down the street from here at a community centre. I'll drop her on my way to work and pick her up after. She'll be in school full day in September. If I get this job, I might find a place downtown and put her in school down there. I think the community centre has some good after school programs, so I'll go for some of them.

December 9

Dad is in the hospital. The doctors say he only has a few months. Mom is in shock, and I'm in a pickle. I can't stop working to be with her, since I have to support Jess. She can't leave Dad to watch Jess so I have to figure out how to fill the hours after school until I get home. At least he is downtown, at the Toronto General Hospital, so I can drop in on him when I have my break. One good thing about working full-time in one place is that you see the same people regularly so you can develop friendships. I have lunch with a nurse named Marilynn. She lives in a co-op across the street, less than a five-minute walk. She says if I ever want to find a place downtown, I should check her building. She brought me an application form for the building, saying I should apply, so I'm on the waiting list if I ever need a place.

February 16

Dad passed away last night. I've been trying to figure out how to tell Jess that Grandpa is gone forever. When I told her that he'd died, she said something interesting.

"You mean like old Mr. Jenks, Mom?"

"Yes, Baby."

"Grandma said Mr. Jenks will wake up when Jesus comes."

"That's true."

"So Grandpa will wake up too?"

"Yes," I said, relieved that the whole thing was taken care of. She seemed to be perfectly happy to go back to colouring. I had kept her home from school so we could both stay with Mom. A few minutes later, she came back.

"Mom, isn't Jesus everywhere? That's what they said at church."

"Ye . . . s."

"Then why doesn't he wake up Grandpa now? If he's here already, we don't have to wait for him to come," she said with perfect five-year-old logic. Luckily, Mom was right there and took her off to explain all about heaven and God's time and things being done only when God is ready. But I could see her hiding a smile, and I thanked God for anything that lightened the gloom around her.

February 25

We buried Dad today, and Mom is like a shadow. She drifted around. It was a simple service, just us and about twenty people from church. Lisanne came and looked with frightened eyes at Jess. She is only here for two days. She got three days of compassionate leave from work and is going right back. She asked Mom if she wanted to go back with her and seemed relieved when she said no.

May 4

My baby turned six today. I didn't have a party at home for her. Instead, I arranged with her teacher to let me bring a birthday cake and party hats to school. It saved me from having to find food and games for a party, but Jess still felt like she had one. I'm worried about Mom. I'm not sure she is even aware of Jess's birthday. These days I'm never sure where her mind is. She is only sixty-three, but she's behaving like someone twenty years older. She doesn't eat enough to keep anyone alive. It's almost as if she is trying to die.

May 5

Got a birthday card for Jess from Lisanne, sent to Mom. There was a note that Jess's birthday present was in Mom's stationary box. I hunted through it and found another card with a money order for five thousand dollars. I've given up trying to understand. I'll put it in the account that the first five thousand went into. I've managed to put another two thousand aside in that account over the past couple of years, so these five will bring it up to twelve thousand. I'll call it an emergency fund or college fund, whichever comes first.

July 10

Mom's in some kind of coma. I don't quite get it. She went to church and collapsed. They called me, and I met the ambulance at the hospital, Jess in tow. I had to take a chance and ask Marilynn to keep Jess for a few hours while I did the hospital stuff. Mom was unconscious by the time I got there, and in a coma by the time she was admitted. I spent the night waiting while they did multiple tests, most of which showed nothing conclusive.

It's been three days, and they say she's going deeper, not coming out of the coma. And all they have determined is that she seems to have some kind of infection. I've been juggling Jess and camp and work. Even if Mom recovers, I'll have to make some major adjustments to our lives. This can't happen again. Marilynn has been a rock. When she's not working, she watches Jess so I can go to the hospital. Luckily, I had registered her for camp. If she was supposed to be home with Mom during the day, I'd be in a real bind.

July 19

Mom is fading. The doctor says they are doing what they can, but they don't really know what they are dealing with. Her body has gone septic. Being associated with medical professionals is a double-edged sword. If I wasn't familiar with medical terminology, they would have told me some gibberish in medical speech designed to make me think they have the treatment worked out and all will be well soon. Out of courtesy, the doctor told me the truth. They don't know what's going on, don't understand the nature of the infection and are relying on massive doses of antibiotics to try reversing it. Sometimes it works, most times it doesn't.

I couldn't find a home number for Lisanne, so I got one for the school and called there. I knew they did summer school, so I figured someone should be there. She seemed more distressed about my having called her at school than about Mom's condition. She would call me back at home. That was yesterday, and she hasn't called yet.

July 25

Mom's kidneys have failed, her liver is compromised, and they are afraid she will develop pneumonia. Lisanne hasn't called, and I'm not going to stress myself over it. I think I'll go through Mom's paper drawer tonight and see if there's anything important I should know.

July 26

Last night I went through Mom's stuff and found a funeral package. When she got the package for Dad, she got one for herself as well, complete with the purchase of the plot next to his. The whole thing ticks me off. If she was planning to die, at least she could have told me.

July 28

Lisanne was at the hospital when I got there today. She looks good but thinner than I remember. She's still wearing the drop-dead clothes, and she looks every inch the successful career woman. Luckily, it's summer, so she has a bit more time. She'll stay for a while. She had me go to the bank with her and add my name to Mom's account and a safety deposit box registered to Mom. I didn't even know that Mom had one. I also had not known Lisanne had the power of attorney for Mom.

August 10

Mom's system shut down today, and they took her off life support. Lisanne signed the form. I'm glad I wasn't called on to do that. She died a few hours later. Lisanne wants the service as soon as possible. No problem since there are no real arrangements to make.

August 15

Lisanne is leaving in the morning. She has been staring pensively at Jess on and off for the last hour but has not addressed her in any way. Just before bed, she handed me an envelope.

"Mom gave me the power of attorney when Dad died, and my name was on her account. When I added your name to the account, I transferred most of the money to your account. This way you don't have to wait for any of the legal stuff to access her money. The rest of her papers are in here as well. Go over them when you have time."

August 16

I'm sitting here on the old, faded, sag-down-the-middle couch my mother has had in this run-down apartment for longer than I can remember. We've always lived here. The building is old. The furniture could not be given away, and we have always been scrimping and saving and trying to stretch every penny in ten different directions. So how is it that there is a receipt for the transfer of three hundred and eighty thousand dollars in the envelope?

Lisanne is already gone, and I bet she knew that the last thing I would do on the night of Mom's funeral is go through her banking information. If Mom and Dad had this kind of money, why were they living the way they were? I didn't know what else to do, so I went to the bank and made an appointment with the same client representative I'd spoken to when I opened the savings account for Jess and me.

When I showed her the receipt, she checked the records. Yes, she could see where the money was transferred, and she'd make an appointment with an investment advisor for me if I wanted, and someone to help me figure out the taxes. Investment? I told her I'd get back to her and hurried out. I couldn't shake the feeling that there was more to the money than Lisanne had said. That she didn't find it an unusual sum was enough cause for suspicion.

The rest of the things in the envelope were innocuous in comparison. A hand-written will leaving everything to me, and if I predeceased her, then to Jess. The details for the place they had planned on getting in Arizona, and her wedding band. I slipped the band on my right middle finger and threw out the Arizona dream stuff. I looked around the apartment. I need to move. Jess deserves better.

May 4

Ten years old. My baby is ten years old. I'm twenty-six years old, have a ten-year-old daughter, and I haven't heard from my only sister in four years. She went back to Fraizers Gap after Mom's funeral, and she has never been in touch since. My daughter is all I have, and I'm pouring everything I have into her. She's accomplished for her age. I've made sure that she can do things: swimming, music, tennis, reading club, French, Spanish, ballet, karate. If the lesson was available and could fit into the schedule, I put her in. Karate was the only one I would have insisted on if she had demurred. She has to know how to protect herself. But she's such a sweet kid. She goes to every lesson, never complains and still does alright in school. She's kind of artsy, which is odd for me, 'cause I'm all for the sciences, but I'll let her choose her own path.

March 11

I don't know why I only write in here during crises. It's been almost six years since I last opened this. Lisanne is dead. I didn't think her passing would hurt this much. I mean, I haven't heard from her for over nine years. Every now and then, I'd check to see if the school still employed her. She moved from vice-principal to principal about four years ago. I had respected her unspoken wish to have nothing to do with us. I checked to be sure I knew where she was, but I had never tried to make contact.

I got a call today from the funeral home that we'd used for Mom and Dad. I actually remembered the sombre little man who ran it, Mr. Boswell. Anyway, he called me today and asked if I could drop by his office. I was more than a little surprised. I've never heard of anyone having to meet with a funeral director unless planning a funeral, but I was curious enough to go.

He handed me a newspaper clipping. It was an obituary.

Lisanne Grange, age 43, was killed in a hit and run accident on Main Street, Fraizers Gap on March 7. She has no known relatives. Her body will be cremated as per her instructions at the Fraizers Funeral Parlour. Miss Grange was the principal of the high school and will be missed by students, staff and parents.

I sat frozen in my seat. No known relatives? She had asked to be cremated? She wanted nothing to do with us, even in death? My heart clenched, and I held onto my control with vice-grip strength. Then I thought of the strangeness of the situation.

"Why do you have this, and why did you ask me to come to see it?" I asked.

"Your sister came to see me when your mom died and asked me to do a small service for her. She requested that we put a marker by her parents' grave with her death information if she passed away before returning to this city.

"She paid us to secure the spot and the marker and said that if she passed away, I would receive a death notice from the funeral parlour in her town. The notice came by courier last evening, and I'm giving it to you, as per the agreement your sister and I had."

With that, he fetched an envelope and inserted the obituary. Then he gave me a larger envelope.

"The funeral director in Fraizers Gap sent this along and asked that it be given to you along with the obituary. I'm very sorry for your loss," he said.

I thanked him and stumbled out. What next? I went home and opened the envelope. A tiny key and a single sheet of paper fell out.

This key opens P.O. Box 1739. Remove the contents immediately.

An address in Mississauga was included. Mississauga? A city less than half an hour west of Toronto, but why have a P.O. Box outside of Toronto?

March 12

I took the day off work and went just after Jess left for school. I didn't tell her about her aunt's death because I don't think she remembers that she had an aunt. She'd only seen her the two times, and there had been almost no interaction between them. Since Jess never mentioned her, I assumed she'd forgotten her.

There was no problem getting into the box. I took the simple cardboard box to the car, then saw the scrawled note on one side. *ME FIRST!* I smiled. Lisanne had made up a game when I was young, which involved putting packages inside other packages. I would have to figure out how to open the first without wrecking the ones inside. *ME FIRST*, meant I was to open that part of the package right away. I carefully pulled the side of the box away. Inside, there was a package with a piece of paper taped on top. The tape was so old it no longer had any glue, but the paper was still in place. It simply stated, *Cancel the box and take this package home.*

I hurried back inside and did as instructed, then broke all kinds of speed limits getting home. I guess I could have opened it in the car, but I felt the need for real privacy. I ripped open the brown paper packaging and watched a pile of paper spill out on my dining table.

There were some old newspaper clippings, and I read those first. Two of them gave sketchy details of the rape, no names and no real information, just stating that it had happened and the police would be investigating. Anyone with information that could lead to apprehending the offender was encouraged to come forward.

The next one, about a year later, talked about the appointment of Constable Bribank as Chief of Police, an appointment that surprised many. The favourite contender for the position was a Constable Gray, and no one could understand why Bribank was favoured over Gray. Neither Gray nor Bribank had any comment.

The next one spoke of a former Constable Downs, who had bought a racing yacht and managed to capsize and drown in Somes Sound. There had been some speculation about the source of Downs' new-found wealth, and while some suspected drugs, there had never been any proof. Bribank and Downs were the policemen who had taken my statement at the hospital.

The last one was the announcement of the results of the mayoral election. By a large majority vote, Barrington Justin Welch III was elected mayor of Fraizers Gap. He was the youngest person to have held that office and was well respected in the community. For a young man, he had an unsullied reputation. He and his young wife had a three-year-old daughter and a one-year-old son. There was a grainy picture of the family in the paper.

I collected the clippings and put them back into the envelope and turned my attention to the pictures. There were a bunch of glossy prints, and at first, I was confused. Where did she get a picture of Jess? She looked to be about three or so, but I couldn't remember seeing that one before. Then my world tilted. The next picture showed the same little girl with a smiling couple. The woman held a little boy who seemed to be trying to squirm out of her arms. I stared at the little girl. She was a clone of Jessica. I slowly focused on the man, and those piercing blue eyes jumped right out of my nightmares. I sat down abruptly. The little girl could be Jess's twin, and they were both the image of the man in the picture. With shaking hands, I reached for the last thing on the table, an envelope with my name.

Dear Lanni,

I don't know what's going to happen, but I have only one thing to say.

Be careful, be very, very careful. I'm not going to keep in touch with you, and that will hurt in ways you wouldn't believe. We don't have much family, but if I keep in contact with you, they'll find out about your daughter. I've watched you with her, and I don't believe you want her endangered. These people are dangerous. The two policemen who took your statement knew who attacked you. So did I. They made Bribank Chief of Police, even though he can't do the job, and I'm sure there is some money involved there, too. Downs took straight cash and bought himself some expensive toys. He was foolishly obvious, and they had him removed. I found out that his boat was sabotaged.

So, what about me? Sister of the victim? They don't know for sure that I know who did it. I only know because I overheard a member of his family talking about his eyes one day when I first arrived. I've never met him, and I understand that he usually wears blue contacts, so his eyes are one colour in public.

They offered me the vice-principal's job, with a salary so high that it makes no sense unless they are trying to buy something from me without saying so. I accepted because to do otherwise would have made even less sense than the offer and might have given rise to some uncomfortable questions. I've been sending Mom and Dad

71

money because, with that ridiculous salary, I don't know what to do with it, and I don't want to keep it here.

I didn't come home for a couple of years after you left here, to give the impression that we weren't all that close a family. When I did come home and saw Jess, I almost lost it. No one who sees her could doubt her parentage. I can't come back to see you. If they get even the slightest hint that she exists, that will be the end of her.

You and I have never been really close, too big an age difference, I guess, but I love you, and I'm going to miss you. Believe me. This is for the best. I understand that Mr. Welch has his eye on the senate. I don't know what to do with this information, so I'm putting it away. I'll continue to collect things, and I'll try to keep them safe for you. If anything happens to me, I hope I'll have gotten them to you in time.

If, for any reason, you end up going back to Fraizers Gap, trust no one. Everyone in that town is either related to or owned by the Welches, except for the funeral director, Gene Foster.

Love always

Lisanne

I sat and hugged myself, crying for all the unkind thoughts I'd had about her and her decision to ignore us. I cried for her, myself and my child, who never got to know her only aunt. I cried for the lost years, and I cried for the sacrifice she'd made for us. And I mourned the death of my only sibling, my only relative, and knew that somehow they had finally decided that she was too big a threat. Someone had killed my sister. I cried because I knew that I would never do anything about it, not as long as it would mean endangering my child.

April 21

Mr. Boswell, the funeral director, called today. He wanted me to stop in and check the marker for Lisanne. I told him it wasn't necessary, but he was insistent, so I went in. It was a simple marker, and I agreed that the information was correct, and he could go ahead and have it placed. Then he pushed a package towards me. There was no name on it, but he clearly wanted me to take it, and with Lisanne's words in my ears about the funeral director in Fraizers Gap being the only one not in bed with the Welches, I opened my bag and let him slip it inside. He didn't say a word about it.

At home, I again attacked a brown paper package; this one clearly newer than the last. Out tumbled more recent pictures of the same family, accompanied by the newspaper announcement of his intention to run for a senate seat. Jessica's sixteenth birthday is coming up, and I intend for her to have it and many more. He could run for president for all I care, as long as he stays away from my child.

I don't know how she got them, but there were copies of the police report and the hospital records from that fateful summer. Finally, there was another envelope.

Lanni

I think the Welches are getting nervous with him planning to run for the senate. I've fielded a few leading comments in the past weeks, and I don't like where they seem to be going. I have been careful over the years not to accumulate anything here that I can't leave behind. All my money is in bonds. I'm asking a friend to get them to you if anything happens to me. Use what you need and give the rest to my niece when she turns thirty. I have a feeling that my days in this town are numbered. If I can, I'll get out before they dispatch me, one way or another.

    Love,

    Lisanne

There was a simple will in the envelope, leaving everything to me, and a stack of Canada Savings Bonds, totaling eight hundred and fifty thousand dollars. I stared at them in shock. I bundled everything, added the stuff from the P.O. Box, and hurried out. I didn't want them lying around. I opened a safety deposit box, with instructions that Jess could open it with proof of my death. Unless I write otherwise in this book, the box is still there and still in my name.

July 10

Jessica darling, it's been ten years since I opened that box. I just found out that I'm sick and not likely to be here on your thirtieth birthday. I went to the bank and amended the records for the box. Everything is the same, except I added your name. That way, it is yours as well, and you don't have to present proof of my death. I love you, my very own special girl. Please, I'm begging you, be careful. I won't ask that you leave this alone, because you may not be able to. It would be safer for you if you did, but if you can't, please, please, please be careful. Remember, always, I love you and have always loved you.

Jessica put the diary down with trembling hands. She didn't know what to do, so she decided to do nothing, at least not yet. That something needed to be done was not the question. It was more a matter of what and how. It would require some thinking, and maybe some input from others. Jessica read and reread the three diaries, then rubbed her grainy eyes and reached for the phone.

CHAPTER SIX

When Jessica pulled into the driveway, JC, Reena and Brandon were sitting on her mother's house steps. She lifted her tote bag over Brandon's head and motioned them in.

"Alright," she said when they were all seated. "I've spent all night thinking about this, and I don't know how to proceed. I don't have any friends here that I would be willing to share this with, so I'm turning to you because Mom trusted you all. The easiest way to approach this is for you to do some reading. It's not a lot to read, but it's a lot of information to assimilate."

She moved to the table and picked up the diaries. "There are three of them, but you need to read them in order. Who goes first?"

"I do, by virtue of my advanced years," JC said. He took the first book and settled in. Reena and Brandon started a low-grade argument about who would be next, and, ignoring them, Jessica moved to the table and opened the package she had picked up at the bank.

She read the newspaper clippings her mother had described and stared in shock at her own image in clothing her mother would never have bought. The older pictures showed a teenage Jessica in different poses, some with the man who'd given her face to her. Except it wasn't Jessica. It was the eeriest thing, seeing her face on someone else. The body was a bit different than hers as a teenager, but had they been identical twins, they could not have looked more alike. She didn't know how long she'd been sitting there when JC put a hand on her shoulder.

"May I?" he asked and reached for the pictures. She handed them over and watched his eyes widen in shock. Next to them, she put some of her own pictures, childhood and teenaged ones.

Reena and Brandon finished reading and approached the table together. When they had viewed the pictures, everyone returned to the comfort of the sofa. No one spoke.

"So. What do I do?" Jessica asked in the lengthening silence.

"I don't know what you should do, but I can tell you what *I* would do," said Reena in a deceptively soft voice. "I'd squish him, like the creeping insect that he is."

"That's our Reena," scoffed Brandon. "No subtlety. You don't want to just squish that type of bug. You want to bottle it up. Let it have just enough air to live, cut off the air now and then so it knows what it feels like to look at death. You want to prod it now and then, with a sharp, pain-inflicting instrument. You want to tease and torment. You want to let it almost escape, keep hope alive. THEN you squish it."

JC sighed loudly. "So callous, these young people. Jessica, before we talk about what should be done, you'd better tell us what you want to accomplish. Do you want him dead, jailed, sitting on a street corner begging? What?"

"I don't know JC, I don't want him dead. I wish it was because I'd object to his death, but it's not as altruistic as that. I think death would be too easy on him, but I also don't want to do anything that will cause his wife and children to suffer. What he did, started before their time, so they shouldn't have to pay, but he does."

"What part do you want him to pay for?" demanded Reena. "The rape, the death of that dumb policeman, the years Lanni and her sister had to spend apart, or killing your aunt?"

Jessica gave a grim smile. "All of it," she replied. "I don't know yet what form the payment should take, but he will pay for all of it."

"Just remember, my dear, that you will have to live with whatever decision you make. Don't allow him to ruin your life by causing you to do something you'll regret," JC cautioned gently.

"That's why you're here, JC. To keep us from planning a hit!" said Reena, bouncing to her feet. "I need writing stuff," she announced. "Nothing should be recorded electronically."

Armed with paper and pen, she perched on the arm of the sofa.

"Alright. Let's see what we know about this man. Barrington Justin Welch III. Do we know anything about him? No? Then we'll list the things we need to find out. Age. Current marital status. Number of children. Income. Hobbies. Obsessions. Is he still politically active? Where does he live? Number of houses. Close friends. Does he have a lackey?"

"A lackey?" Brandon interrupted.

"Yes. A lackey. Someone who gets sent to do everything from picking up the dry-cleaning to running down a woman in the street. Someone he'd trust with a dirty little secret," she said with more relish than was decorous.

"Since you don't want him in jail, perhaps you should stay away from the alleged murders. It would be a lot safer for you," JC interjected.

"You might want to add the statute of limitations on rape to that list," he said to Reena.

"Jessica's biggest problem is that she doesn't want to humiliate the family. Why don't we check out his family before we start to think about how to get him inside our bottle. Let's see what his family situation is like. Maybe they deserve to be humiliated, or maybe we can use them in some way when planning our strategy," said Brandon.

"I do not at all like the sound of this bottling, Brandon. I really hope you never did it to an insect. As inhumane as it sounds in talking about an insect, when applied to a human, it is quite frightening," JC said worriedly.

"Go home and pray, JC. Pray that we don't give in to the temptation to put him in a bottle too small for his size. Sort of squeeze him in, you know? Don't worry, we aren't going to squish him, just let him see the shoe poised over his head," said Reena with deadly calm.

JC looked at Brandon for a moment, then turned to Jessica. "Bring me a Bible," he said quietly.

He took the book and turned the pages almost absently, keeping his eyes on Brandon. Finally, he looked down.

"Here we go," he said. "Romans chapter 12, verse 19: '. . . avenge not yourselves . . . for it is written, vengeance is mine, I will repay, says the Lord . . .' I understand the desire for revenge, but you can trust God to fulfill his promise. The senator will pay for his sins," JC reminded them in quiet tones. In equally hushed tones, Brandon replied.

"We are not going to take revenge JC, I promise you. Bottle him up, yes. Poke and prod him a bit, yes. Maybe even partially squish him, yes. But avenge ourselves? No. Vengeance would be to castrate and put him on display someplace on Capitol Hill, tied to a placard with a synopsis of how he violated a young girl. That would be vengeance. We aren't looking for revenge JC. Just a small amount of justice."

Jessica stared wide-eyed at him. Could he be serious? His eyes were hooded and gave nothing away. JC looked even more worried. Only Reena seemed to think it was normal to hear this from the mild-mannered Brandon.

Before they left, Brandon pulled her aside.

"I know we haven't made a decision about what we are going to do, but I think it would be best if you got some legal advice. Just to know where we stand. We should know how far we can go without getting ourselves in a bind," he told her.

She glared at him.

"I do not need a lawyer. I am not going to allow anything illegal to be done."

"Illegal, no. But you don't want him sent to jail. I don't think there is a statute of limitations on rape. How do you stop him from going to jail if the information gets into the wrong hands? Get some advice. You don't have to let the lawyer know who you are talking about. Just book a consultation on a hypothetical case and see what is said. Alright? But use someone you know. If you don't know any lawyers, I have a couple of friends."

She reluctantly agreed, and they took their leave. Alone in the house, she locked up the material and looked around. Her mother's things needed to be packed away. All those trendy, beautiful clothes. She took her mother's favourite sweater as a keepsake, and in a burst of energy, lugged boxes from the basement and packed everything away.

She decided to keep the many rows of shoes with matching bags. She couldn't wear the clothes, but the shoes were a perfect fit. She'd never have bought twenty-two pairs of footwear, but since they were already there, she might as well enjoy them.

There were fifteen neatly labelled boxes packed in the two smaller bedrooms when she was done. She took another walkthrough and fetched two more boxes.

Her mother liked knick-knacks and the house was full of them. She picked out two to keep and packed the rest in the two boxes. She didn't wrap them, just layered newspaper around them to keep them from banging into each other.

Her mom's precious crystal collection she left on its display glass. That she would never part with. Many of them she had bought herself as gifts for Mother's Days, birthdays and holidays. Her mom had started the collection when Jessica was ten, and with sixteen years of collecting, there were over thirty of the little crystal things. They ranged from musical instruments to animals and even a model ship that Jessica had found in a little out of the way store while vacationing in Florida.

She walked from room to room, noticing how bare they looked without the things her mother had surrounded herself with. She called JC.

"I have boxes full of clothes, coats, knick-knacks and other miscellaneous things. It's all good stuff. Do you have a program that could use them, or should I just call the Salvation Army?"

"Indeed, I have a program that could use them. When would you like them picked up, and what kind of vehicle will I need?"

"I want them gone yesterday. If they sit here, I'll lose my nerve and not be able to give them away. Mom would hate for her things to sit here and gather dust if they could benefit someone. As for a vehicle, there are almost twenty boxes, and they are fairly big. A car will not do."

"Alright. Give me ten minutes," he said and rang off.

In less than five, he called back. "Remember Mike? He delivered the stuff when we were bringing Lanni home. He is about forty-five minutes from you. He'll stop by and get them if that's okay with you."

"Wonderful," she told him. She carted the boxes to the foyer and helped Mike load up when he arrived. She watched him drive away and turned back to a house that felt empty. Never mind that she would never have had most of those things; they seemed to belong to the house. She could almost hear her mother telling her not to be idiotic.

Unable to settle down, she remembered Brandon's admonition to get legal advice and grabbed the phone.

"Bentley and Spades, how may I help you?" the efficient receptionist enquired.

"I'd like to make an appointment to see Mr. Bentley, please. Tomorrow if possible. It's Jessica Kaene calling."

"One moment Ms. Kaene." She listened to the music and was amused to hear Beethoven instead of modern rock.

"Ms. Kaene." The smooth baritone vibrated down the line, and she jumped.

"I'm sorry to interrupt your day, Mr. Bentley. As I told your receptionist, I was merely trying to make an appointment."

"So, she informed me. Don't blame her. I insisted on speaking with you myself. My day is quite full, but if lunchtime would suit, you can join me for lunch at Cartiers."

"Ah, actually, that won't do. I mean, I don't object to lunch, but I need to speak with you about something, and I don't think I can do it in a public place. If possible, I'd like to do this in your office."

"Alright. Come at noon. I'm holding you to lunch, so we'll meet first, eat after."

She hung up, feeling just a bit steamrolled and trying to deny the frisson of excitement that had coursed through her. There was no doubt about it. Denile Bentley had a voice that could give a nun the shivers.

She walked into the law office wearing a forest green pantsuit that she usually reserved for meeting with magazine editors. She'd teamed it with a cream blouse and a tiny cream and green scarf that softened the suit's severe lines. Her hair was a glistening blond curtain hanging down to the middle of her back. When the receptionist showed her in, she was gratified by the hastily concealed pure male appreciation.

"Ms. Kaene. A pleasure to see you again," he said as he stood and walked around the desk. He took her hand and led her to the same chair she'd occupied the last time she was in his office.

"You're very punctual," he smiled at her.

"You said noon, and I hate to wait myself, so I make sure I don't keep anyone waiting. Besides, you promised me food, and I'm starving," she said with a grin.

He leaned his head to one side and looked at her intently before laughing out loud. "You are a very pleasant surprise, Ms. Kaene. Let's take care of business so you can be fed."

Jessica had worried about how much to tell him and had finally typed up a summary of the events. On a single sheet, she had covered the rape, pregnancy, corrupt cops and her aunt's death. All hypothetical and without names. She handed it over and watched him read. He slowly lowered it to his desk.

"Would you be planning to try to identify some of these parties? Hypothetically, of course?"

"No. I guess what I'm curious about is whether or not one could get into any legal difficulties if the parties were identified and this information was made public."

"That would depend on the lifestyle and level of influence these people have, and who the information was given to. It would also depend on where they live and whether there is a statute of limitations on rape there. Of course, that is assuming that the information is one hundred percent accurate and provable, or a hefty libel suit could follow. Since there is no statute of limitations on murder, there might also be the tangle of a homicide investigation."

She stared in silence at the paper on the desk.

"Give me a dollar," he said softly.

"What?"

"Give me a dollar," he repeated, with a hint of impatience.

Looking as confused as she felt, she dug a five-dollar bill out of her purse.

"Even better," he said, as he took it from her. "You have just retained me as your legal counsel. Anything you say to me is confidential. Now would you like to tell me what's going on?"

She looked at him as thoughts raced through her head and stood up.

"Why don't we go to lunch, and you can tell me how you came to be friends with Mom?"

"Lanni mentored my little sister in a community program that she volunteered with. After listening to Monique sing her praises, I decided I'd better meet this person who was wielding such influence over our family baby.

When I finally met Lanni, she convinced me to volunteer with the program too. We spent some memorable times together, usually arguing about the best way to get some teenager to give school another try. She was a good woman, and a very nice friend to have," he told her, leaning back in his chair and sipping his Perrier.

Cartiers was hidden away on a side street and had a nondescript front that did not invite entry. This was an illusion immediately dispelled as you entered the door. Warm mahogany panelling lined the walls that led to a desk tucked in at the side of an arched entryway. Inside was all beiges and varying shades of brown and glittering silverware. The table they occupied was in a corner, and far enough away from any other, you could speak comfortably without being overheard. The waitress had quickly removed four additional place settings from the table.

"Why are we eating at a table for six?" Jessica asked.

"Because I always use this table. I often conduct business over lunch or dinner, and it's easier to have a table that is too big than try to get a bigger one when needed. If there are more than six of us, I use the board room."

"They keep this table reserved for you?"

"Unless I call and tell them I will not be using it, yes."

Jessica stared at him in amazement, then looked slowly around the rapidly filling room.

"Have you decided to tell me about your hypothetical situation yet?"

"I need to talk to someone first."

"Lanni used to do that. Usually, she meant she would bounce something off JC, and if he thought it wasn't too incendiary, then she would tell."

"You know JC?" she asked in surprise.

"I know most of Lanni's friends. She was a social being and had a very interesting mix of friends. I enjoyed going to her gatherings. She always said it wasn't a party, just a gathering of friends. She liked to share her friends with other friends. You were the only person in her life she didn't share with everyone. Whenever you came home, she cancelled everything so she could maximize her time with you."

Jessica's eyes stung. "I wish I'd known. I was always so worried about her being lonely without me. She'd just laugh and tell me not to be silly. I feel like I've been living in a fog for the last four months. Every morning I get up and remember that she is gone, and it feels like she's taken with her all my energy, my drive and my will to live. I didn't know anything could hurt this much."

He reached across the table and took her hands in his. He didn't say anything, just held them.

CHAPTER SEVEN

In East Washington, Marrion Welch stared at her reflection and wondered what people saw when they looked at her. Maybe they saw what her husband saw, a nice-looking ornament, to be taken out and shown when necessary, otherwise to be neglected, ignored or denigrated.

The senator called her spineless, a sentiment she gladly embraced, having spent years cultivating it. She'd foolishly married Barrington Justin Welch III shortly after her twenty-first birthday. Called himself *Barry J*. Starry-eyed and romantic, she'd thought he could walk on water. Then, she'd met Larson French, called Lars by all who knew him.

Even a naive twenty-one-year-old could recognize that there was something unusual about the friendship. They were rarely seen together in public, but wherever Barry J was, Lars was nearby. He lived at the house and seemed to wear a number of hats. Lars was meant to see all, hear all, know all and do all, and he fulfilled these expectations with no apparent effort.

Whatever information Barry J wanted, Lars could procure. When she stopped at the pharmacy, Barry J knew before she arrived home and requested an account of her purchases. When she had a brief and casual conversation with a young man by the photocopier in the library, he demanded an explanation of how they'd met and how often they had spoken.

She'd learned early to guard herself well. It was Lars' job to flush out all weaknesses—it was Barry J's pleasure to exploit them. It pleased him to think her a beautiful milksop, and it suited her purpose to keep him believing it.

She looked closely at her mirrored image. Forty-three years old, and she'd been married for twenty-two of those years to a hyena dressed as a house cat. By the time she was pregnant with her first child, less than a year after the wedding, she'd already begun wondering if her marriage was a mistake. Four years later, she knew it was a mistake and one that would be close to impossible to correct. She closed her eyes and went back to the day she found out the kind of family she had married into.

"Don't cross him. He'll have you killed if you do."

Marrion stared at her mother-in-law in shock. Jullienne Welch was a svelte forty-nine-year-old who looked thirty-five. She and her fifty-six-year-old husband were known in Washington as the best looking and most well-suited couple. They never quarrelled, never had a disagreement and always arrived together at any well-publicized function, often holding hands.

"The man is a sadist, and he's raised our son in his image. I'm just saying that you need to watch yourself. Lars has one main function, and that is to watch you. For years I had Benny. He lived with us, just like Lars lives with you. Now that Benny has moved on, I'm hoping I can too. It's a chance I'm willing to take, but in case it doesn't work out, I'm warning you. Watch yourself. My son is almost as bad as his father, and that is pretty darn nasty.

You've heard him boast that we never argue? He's right. A mouse doesn't argue with a tiger. I can't do this anymore, and I'd rather not live if this is the life I have to live." She blew a ring of smoke and playfully poked her head through it.

"Don't look so terrified, child. I'm not going to do myself in, but I'm telling you that I am going to do something. I have to before he finds someone to replace Benny, and he will. This is the first opportunity I've had in more than twenty-five years, and I'm not about to pass it up. If you hear that I've had a sudden demise, then the tiger has sprung, and the mouse wasn't fast enough to get away," she said, pushing her chair back.

"Come, you must be getting back to the house, and I have an appointment at Reggie's. Don't forget, when they ask why you left me behind, tell them I've gone to Reggie's." She started putting things into her purse.

"Take good care of my grandchildren. And do whatever you must to keep them from turning your children into little monsters like themselves. And keep your daughter away from Lars. He likes them young, and neither my son nor my husband would think it of any consequence if he decides to dishonour your child. Women mean very little to them, except as convenient showpieces." She stood and grabbed her purse.

"For your information, if you ever want to know what they are plotting, go to the library. If you stand by the vent, you can hear what they are saying in the study."

Kissing the air beside Marrion's cheek, she whispered. "Goodbye, dear. I have enjoyed having a daughter. You are a good woman. Don't let Barry J change that. Check the New York Times Personals on Thursdays. If I manage to get away, I'll send something to them periodically. You'll recognize it." Marrion watched her walk away as she gathered her few things together.

She'd barely made it into the house when her father-in-law appeared.

"Marrion!" his round, friendly voice echoed in the foyer. "Did my wife treat you to a nice lunch?"

"Yes, Sir," she answered, trying to see him without the fog of the conversation she had just had with his wife.

"Where is she?"

"She said she had an appointment at Reggie's, and I didn't have to wait for her," she replied.

"Did you walk her to Reggie's?" he wanted to know.

"No, Sir. The car was parked in the other direction. She said she'd call when she was ready to come home."

"I see. What's your plan for the rest of the afternoon?"

"I haven't made any. I thought I'd catch up on correspondence and spend some time in the nursery. Barry J said he'd be back today, so I left the time open in case he comes in and needs me for anything."

"Smart girl. You'll be a good wife for him to have now that he's about to enter public service."

With that, he went back to his study, and as she turned to go up the stairs, she could see Lars just disappearing around the corner. She hadn't even known he was in the house.

Barry J had moved into what they called the North Wing of his parent's home in Fraizers Gap when they got married. She'd been hesitant about living with his parents, but he pointed out that the house was massive, and they would have no need to see them if they didn't want to.

In the end, she realized that she didn't have any choice, and he was right. The house was huge. Unfortunately, they had no choice about when to see the elder Welches. They were required to show up for breakfast and dinner whenever his father was in residence. Luckily, he kept a house in Washington and spent much of his time there. As the senior senator for the state of Maine, he was required to be in the capital regularly. Of course, there was still Lars.

"Where's Mom?" Barry J asked over dinner.

"Gone on a quick visit," the senator responded with a careless wave. He looked at Barry J then gave a significant glance at Marrion, and Barry J dropped the subject.

After dinner, the men retired to the study, and Marrion took herself off to the library. Lars poked his head in and watched her settle with a book by the fireplace, then joined the Welch men in the study. Marrion inched her chair closer to the vent.

Her mother-in-law was right. If she listened closely and the men spoke loudly enough, she could just hear them.

"Well, where did she go? Marrion said she was going to Reggie's," was her father-in-law's opening question.

"She did and had her hair done very nicely too. But she didn't linger when she was done. She timed it well and walked down to the bus station just as the Greyhound was getting ready to leave. She bought a ticket to Bangor, but the bus stops in many places before it gets there, so she might not be going all the way."

"And what are you doing about the stops?"

"I had someone get on the bus at the first stop after it left here. We'll know where she gets off. What do you want me to do when we know where she's going?"

"Oh, let her get wherever she is trying to get to. I want to know if anyone is helping her. When you take her out, I want anyone who encouraged her in this behaviour removed as well. I can go back to Washington without her a couple of times, but after that, there will be too many questions. I need her publicly removed so that there'll be no speculation," the senator said in conversational tones.

Smash! The sound of a glass hitting the wall made Marrion jump.

"Damn her!" he exploded. "I will not be humiliated like this. The entire town must have watched her taking that bus. Welches don't take buses, so what are they to think but that she's leaving? She wanted that. Make sure you find her, Lars, and get rid of her. A nice accident will do, but I'm not averse to some suffering. By all means, pass her around to some of your less savoury friends before you do her in. With her puritanical ideas, that's probably the worst

93

thing she can imagine happening to her. Let a few of them have a go at her, teach her a good lesson."

"Do you want me to let you know when I find her?"

"Yes. Just in case I change my mind and want to haul her home. I don't expect to, but you never know. And Barry J, you'd best find out if your woman knows anything about this. I doubt if she does, but you'd best sound her out just the same. Can't have this happening in two generations."

Marrion quickly brought her chair back to the fireplace and feigned sleep when she heard them getting ready to separate. The fear that lodged in her heart was to stay with her for years. She haunted the library the next day and was finally rewarded.

"She's holed up at a Ramada Inn in Bangor under the name Marlise Hunt," Lars reported.

"Who is Marlise Hunt?" the senator asked.

"Don't know, but that's the name she's using. Do you want her brought home, or should I take care of her?" was Lars' monotone question.

"Let her stew for today. But don't lose her. Just send two of your worse men to visit her tonight, two more in the morning, two more at noon and two more in the evening. Save the worst one for last and let him have her for the night. Then she can have an accident on the way home early the next morning. Just make sure that each new set arrives before the others leave. You don't want her to have time to make any unwelcome phone calls."

He might have been talking about the menu for dinner. Marrion shuddered as she listened to Lars leaving the house and crept up to the room she shared with Barry J. She dared not use the house phone, so she grabbed her purse and headed for the door.

"And where are you going, my dear?"

She jolted at the sound of her father-in-law's loving tone.

"Just into town to pick up a few things at the pharmacy. Can I get you anything?"

"No, no. Be careful on the road."

She thanked him for his concern and hurried away, sickened at the hypocrisy of the man. At the pharmacy she bought a bunch of feminine products that she didn't need, a best-selling paperback, a newspaper, a notebook, some pens, a chocolate bar and a prepaid phone chip. She hoped that if Lars bothered to check with the pharmacy, he'd lose interest when they mentioned the feminine products.

In her car, she quickly removed the chip from her cell phone and inserted the new one. Directory assistance connected her to the Ramada Inn.

She didn't identify herself when her mother-in-law answered.

"Lars knows where you are. He is supposed to pass you around to his friends for twenty-four hours. Then you'll have an accident. The first two are to show up tonight, but I don't know what time."

There was silence at the other end, then a quiet, "Thank you, my dear," and Marrion hung up the phone. She replaced her phone chip and, keeping the phone on her lap, dialled the number of an old friend who she knew wouldn't be home. She let the answering machine pick up and record silence for the length of time she thought she'd been on the phone. She stopped in at the public library and went to the bathroom after browsing a few minutes. She flushed the chip and the paper it had come attached to and went home.

"Who were you calling today?" Barry J asked as they were getting ready for dinner.

"What?" Fear was a liquid heat running through her veins.

"You heard me. Who were you calling after you left the pharmacy?"

She stared at him for a minute. His eyes were icy, one blue and one green.

"Raina. I was calling Raina."

"Give me your phone."

"What?"

"I said, give me your phone. I want to see the number you called today. If you wanted to call Raina, there was no reason not to call her from the house phone."

"I see. So now I'm lying." She stalked to her purse and grabbed the phone. "Well, here you go and feel free to keep it since I'm to be allowed no privacy in using it," she told him with open irritation, even while she locked her knees to keep them from shaking.

Without answering, he scrolled through the numbers and handed it back to her. She continued dressing and took a chance as they were leaving the room.

"When will your mom be back? We'd talked about setting up a book drive at the library, and I want to get started on it. I just want to know if she's coming back here before they head to Washington.

If she isn't, maybe I can ask Mrs. Barns to help?" She made it a very haughty question, in keeping with her obvious anger over the phone incident.

He swung around and treated her to a piercing look.

"You'd better get someone else to help. I believe my parents plan to meet in Washington," he said with studied nonchalance.

"Funny she didn't mention that she was going on a visit when we had lunch. But then, there's no reason she should have, is there? It's not like she would normally tell me ahead of time when they are leaving. I usually find out as they say goodbye at the door . . ."

She let the statement trail off vaguely as they continued down the stairs and hoped she had allayed any lingering suspicions. Dinner was a curious affair. She said very little and listened as the senator told ribald stories of fellow senators and other colleagues. No one mentioned his wife, and except for an occasional glance at his watch, he could have been unaware of the fate he had planned for her.

In the library, she pulled a book hastily from the shelf and hurried to the vent.

"Where is Lars?" the senator barked.

"Probably out checking on his pals," Barry J said absently. Did his mother mean so little to him?

"Get him in here. Now!" There was a brief murmur, and she assumed Barry J was calling Lars on his cell phone. She huddled in the chair by the fireplace, knowing that Lars would never pass the library without looking inside.

"Well?" demanded the senator when Lars entered the study.

"We have a small problem, Sir. I was trying to get to the bottom of it when Barry J called," Lars said.

"What kind of problem? It's not terribly important if they killed her quicker than I intended. An accident can still be arranged. But I do not want a body found in that room. I refuse to deal with that kind of lurid publicity." The senator's voice was very quiet.

"There's no body, Sir. In fact, there's nobody in the room," Lars said.

"What do you mean?" Barry J asked.

"When my men showed up, there was no one in the room. She didn't check out, her purse and a small case are still there, with the credit card and driver's license registered to Marlise Hunt. No one even remotely resembling her left the hotel, and we had a watch on every exit."

"So, she is still there. Check the other rooms," he was told.

"That's what we are doing right now, but it's going to take a while. She got a phone call today. The girl at the switchboard thinks it was a man that called. She wouldn't swear to it, but she said the voice was gruff and sounded male. She didn't come down the elevator, didn't come down the stairs. We had people inside watching those. She didn't exit the hotel, but we haven't found her inside anywhere yet."

"Did she order dinner?" the irate husband wanted to know.

"Yes, but a bit early. She had a meal sent up at 3:30," Lars answered.

"A lot of people leaving the hotel after that?"

"A few, but none that could have been her."

"She left, and your men missed her. Find her. Tonight. And forget playing. I want her gone. I expect to be planning her funeral tomorrow night, or I'll know the reason why!"

Three weeks later, there was a small notice in the New York Times Personals. "Thanks to the mole, the tiger failed, the mouse prevailed. The mouse knew the tiger was watching, had planned for that, but had to scamper away faster than expected on speaking to the mole."

Marrion breathed easy for the first time since that phone call, though she wasn't sure she appreciated being called a mole. Her father-in-law had a much-publicized funeral with a closed casket two months later. His wife was on her way back from an extended visit to a sick relative and had met a fatal accident. Marrion almost believed it was true, but two weeks afterwards, there was another ad in the personals.

Poor mouse. RIP. Hope the tiger is satisfied. How the mole must have laughed!

She never knew where Jullienne Welch ended up, but over the years, the personals kept coming. Not often, but enough to let her know that she was well. Once there was an ad telling the mole about a P.O. Box, and eventually, a key and the location found their way to her.

When Marrion finally got a chance to open the box, there were forms for opening a bank account in the name Marie Warrick and some change of name forms. She had never formally changed her name when she got married, and the forms were changing her maiden name to her mother's maiden name. She was used to being called Marie. Only the Welches refused to use the name she'd grown up with, saying it sounded common. The forms were already filled out. All she had to do was sign everything and send them to another P.O. Box.

Six months later, another ad mentioned that the mole could access documents in a certain safety deposit box, and funds were available from the bank account when needed. Eventually, the key for the box arrived at the P.O. Box, and Marrion sewed it into the underwire of a sturdy sports bra. She had yet to access the safety deposit box but took comfort in knowing it was there.

If you are reading this, then you can now say 'Mouse, RIP.' This time it is real, and this is being sent two weeks after the departure date as per instructions. The last year has been difficult as the mouse battled illness. Won some battles but lost the war. Still, it was a good fight. Be well, mole, and stay alert around tigers and their young.

Marrion read the ad and wept. Jullienne was sixty-seven years old.

She opened her eyes and sighed. Eighteen years. She had lived with the knowledge of her husband's unwholesome character for eighteen years. She had a twenty-one-year-old daughter about to finish university and an eighteen-year-old son about to enter his first year. It was time to shed the woman in the mirror, but first, she had to make sure her children were secure. She'd been biding her time for eighteen years, knowing she wouldn't be allowed to live if she tried to leave with her children, knowing she couldn't leave without them. She would continue to bide her time. Mistakes would be fatal.

CHAPTER EIGHT

She joined her son and husband in the elegant dining room for breakfast. Although he rarely spoke to them, Senator Barrington J. Welch III had decreed that his family should meet for a formal breakfast whenever he was in residence. Just one more small habit learned at the knees of his father, Barrington J. Welch II.

He lowered his newspaper and glared at his son with distaste. And well, he might. Barrington J. Welch IV was a most unattractive young man. His long blond hair hung about his shoulders in greasy strings, complementing the equally greasy beard and moustache. What could be seen of his face was pimply and covered with red blotches.

Senator Welch averted his eyes. He was once heard to comment that he could hardly believe he'd fathered such an aberration. He'd ordered a haircut and beard and moustache removed. They had dealt with the face first, and when he saw the

102

uncovered, pimply, blotchy and pock-marked face, he had quickly recanted. He'd managed over the years to keep his son out of the public eye as much as possible and avoided looking at him whenever he could. He spoke to him now from behind the shield of his newspaper.

"You don't have to like Georgetown University, but you will go there. It's the alma mater of all the males in our family, and you will continue the tradition. We are a political family, and you will do your duty."

"Father, I do not have any interest in politics. I want to study science. They have a good science program at Howard," the boy whined.

"Science. Of course," the senator sneered. "You can barely stand the sight of your own spittle. You'd make a pitiful scientist. Not that you'll make a better politician, but at least you'll have the family name behind you in that."

He lowered his paper for a moment.

"It's going to take every favour your grandfather and I can call in to get you started as it is. We are hoping that in a few years you won't be quite as unsightly as you are now. It's a pity you inherited your mother's weak mind. It's going to be your downfall. You don't even know what you're capable of. Science! As for Howard, I've already withdrawn your application there. The head of the political science department at Georgetown will meet with you after you arrive on campus. Lars will tell you when."

The young man looked worriedly at his mother. She gave an imperceptible shake of her head.

"I was wondering if it would be alright for me to go with him, get him settled in somewhat?" The timid question caused the senator to turn a disgusted eye on his wife.

"Marrion, let the boy grow up. He doesn't need you to wipe his nose on campus. He will arrive like every other Welch before him, unaccompanied by his mama. You can console yourself that he is only going across town instead of across the country. If he wasn't such a sniveller, he could have lived at home. As it is, I need to get him away from here, or he'll never become a man. And be warned. You will not visit him. You'll see him on major holidays, just as if he was across the country."

A uniformed maid stepped into the room.

"Sir. The car is here, Sir," she announced in reverent tones. Without a word, he tossed down the paper, picked up his briefcase and walked out. He paid no attention to the light blue Toyota that drove past as he stepped into the waiting car, or the dark green Nissan that arrived at the four-way stop at the next block, just in time to pull out behind him.

Barrington Justin Welch IV, usually called plain Justin, kissed the air beside his mother's cheek and resisted the urge to give her a hug. Hugging would irritate the senator, and an irritated senator meant misery for the senator's wife.

She didn't say goodbye. Without moving her lips, she murmured as his ear passed her mouth.

"The handle of your gym bag."

"Check the cubby," was his equally quiet response. He glanced at his father, unsure if any leave-taking was expected. It was mid-August, and he was officially leaving home for university.

"What are you waiting for then?" was his father's terse question. He hurried into the back of the car, hauling the gym bag beside him. Lars climbed into the front passenger seat and looked over his shoulder.

"So, what do you need a gym bag for? Stocking extra acne medication?" His grin was malicious, and Justin ignored him. The years had taught him that Lars was best dealt with by feigning deafness. The trip was mercifully short and provided Lars with little opportunity to needle him. Even so, it was with difficulty that he managed to present a calm facade throughout.

The campus was crowded and loud, and he looked around with an air of complete disinterest as he went through the process of getting the keys for his dorm room. His gaze lingered briefly on a rather scruffy young man milling about with the rest of the throng. Lars followed him to his room, hefting the two bags effortlessly. He dumped them on the floor inside the door and backed out. Justin set about unpacking, unable to shed the habit of having everything in the appropriate place in case his father should look in.

Lars returned when he was finishing up. "You need to go to the cafeteria for dinner," he announced.

"I'm not hungry. Think I'll just skip tonight."

"No, you won't. The senator paid for your meals, and I expect to tell him that he's getting his money's worth. I want to see the food, so let's go," he said, expecting no argument. He got none.

105

It was with relief that Justin watched his back disappear as he left to return home.

Back in his room, he looked around and quickly spotted the copy of Hemmingway's "The Old Man and the Sea." He grabbed it and gave the pages a spin. A single sheet of paper was taped to page 24.

Your companion met with a character of Mexican descent. Long hair, ponytail. Was talking to girl on desk duty when you returned from dinner. While you were out, Mex spent 15 minutes in your room. Phone bugged. Left in place, use with discretion. Bug on back of mirror. Disabled. If need to give info, carry this book in your hand when you leave your room. I'll make contact.

He reread the note, then turned it into confetti and flushed it. He thought he remembered the young man in question and would recognize him if seen. Of course, he wouldn't see him if he was any good at his job, but just as he and his mother had surmised, Lars had hired someone to watch him.

It amused him to think of the writer of his note watching the person Lars had hired. He had a simple plan, weakened only by the fact that it depended on someone else to be perfectly successful. He had done everything he could to lessen the impact of a break in that weak link and would not waste time worrying about what he couldn't change. He turned his attention to the gym bag.

His mother had told him, many years ago, that Lars was a simple man with simple ideas, and the easiest way to thwart him was to use his simplicity. She wanted to give him something Lars wouldn't find, so she hid it in plain sight. He had followed her lead and emptied his gym bag but left it carelessly lying in the middle of the floor. He doubted it had been given more than a cursory glance. He picked it up and went to work on the handle.

She had taken the entire thing apart, widened it and then re-sewn it. It would have taken her a few hours because she would have had to do it by hand, and most likely at night. He undid one corner and withdrew a piece of black heavyweight construction paper. Chuckling, he held it up to the light. He could just make out the gold writing.

Don't remove until find safer place. Don't worry. I got it safely.

He carefully worked a flattened tube free of the long strap of the bag and unzipped it. Inside, wrapped in plastic, was $15,000.00 in travellers cheques. He sat down abruptly. He didn't know how she had managed to get the money, but if she said it was safe, he knew it was. She had been surviving since before he was born. He pulled a small road atlas from his shelf and, after poring over it, adjusted his plans. He would avoid using electronics for the time being.

For three days, he went through the motions of campus life. It was orientation week, and classes had not yet begun. He visited the booths set up by various clubs. He wandered around looking lost. He spoke to no one and mumbled if addressed directly. He met with the head of the political science department and strove to leave an impression of stultifying dullness. The poor man could barely disguise his surprise when he met the son of Senator Barry J. Welch III and failed completely to hide his disappointment when faced with Justin's apathy and muttered responses. Each day he would get on the local bus and go for a ride. He went to the mall, the Greyhound bus station, the train station and once he got off and walked two miles in a residential neighbourhood. He never looked behind him.

By Friday evening Justin was established as an awkward, not too bright young man who had nothing to say and was happiest when nothing was said to him. He was careful to avoid being unpleasant and made sure no one knew his connection to Senator Welch. He was shy, uninteresting and unattractive. Totally anonymous. A very satisfying few days.

On Saturday morning, he began walking early. He had nothing with him and looked much the same as he had the previous day. He roamed the campus and watched it slowly come alive. He paused by a bus stop and looked at the bus, then made an apparently snap decision to get on. He went to Union Station and settled on a bench to watch the trains. With his head tipped back, he could see both the clock and the door of the closest men's restroom in his peripheral vision.

To the people carefully avoiding him, he seemed to be asleep. At twenty minutes to nine, he unfolded himself and walked listlessly to the restroom. At ten minutes to nine, he emerged and took himself back to the bus stop. At 9:30 AM, he was sitting down to a late breakfast in the cafeteria.

CHAPTER NINE

The group gathered in Lanni's living room were eagerly passing around photographs and sheets of paper. Reena, Brandon, and JC had been surprised to arrive and find Denile Bentley.

"I told him about the situation, and he's managed to come up with some information for us," she explained. It was almost six months since she'd had lunch with him and decided to trust him with her history. He'd come back to the house with her, read the diaries, looked at the pictures and hadn't said a word, but she could almost see the waves of anger coming off him.

"JC would tell me that it was all part of God's plan, and maybe it was, since you meant so much to Lanni, but senator or not, he isn't going to get away with this," he'd said in a soft, hoarse voice. He'd asked her permission to have a friend check out the senator and his family. None of them wanted any kind of electronic trail showing interest in the family. They had decided not even to look him up online.

She went to Atlanta to empty out her apartment and wrap up all her writing assignments and, on her return, he'd offered her the information his friend had gathered. She invited him to share it with the others.

"Here we go. Before we touch the family, my instructions are that special attention should be given to this man. His name is Larson French, a.k.a 'Lars'. He lives with the Welches and seems to have a hand in everything that the senator gets involved in but is never publicly acknowledged. Word is, he's been around since the teen years, and is usually the one to deal with any um … unpleasantness that the senator doesn't want to be bothered with."

"Aha!" Reena grabbed for his picture. "I knew he had a lackey somewhere." She gazed at the picture. "Definitely not someone you'd want to meet in a deserted area," she decided.

"Here we are then. Recent photos of the daughter who turned 21 three months ago. Jordana Welch. She's in her final year at Cornell, an English major," Denile said, handing the pictures to Brandon. Her hair was a bit darker than Jessica's, and she wore it in a short pageboy cut, but her face was almost identical.

"And here we have pictures of Mrs. Welch. She spends a lot of time at the local library," he grinned, as he gave the pictures to Reena. They showed a poised woman who could have been about 30 years old, sitting at a table surrounded by books, walking down the steps of the library and another in a parking lot with the library in the background. All the pictures were taken at different times, but in each one the same elemental grace could be seen.

"She's scared," Reena announced.

"Scared of what?" demanded Brandon, peeking over her shoulder.

"Of something, someone, everything, life . . . I don't know. But there is fear in her eyes, and it doesn't look new. I think she's been afraid for a long time," she said softly.

Denile looked at Reena with open curiosity before moving on.

"Can't forget dear old Dad. This is the senator, as of four days ago, and here we have his most recent publicity shot." He gave this set to Jessica, who managed to look without reaction on the man who had fathered her and charted the course of Lanni's life.

"He may be rotten at the core, but you must admit that he is an extremely handsome man," she said calmly. No one disagreed.

"And now, here is brother dearest," Denile said with a ring of admiration. He gestured JC forward and gave him six pictures. The first four showed an unhealthy-looking young man with long, greasy blond hair and an unsightly moustache and beard. His shoulders had the permanent hunch of someone used to being abused and trying to disappear. He had chosen the un-kept look adopted by many teenagers, and it served to make him even more unattractive.

The last two pictures were of a young man with a neat brown beard and brown hair that was just getting to the stage of needing a trim.

"Who's he?" asked JC, pointing to one of the last two pictures.

"That is Barrington Justin Welch IV, after a visit to the men's room of the local train station," he said with obvious satisfaction. JC looked closer at the pictures.

"How do you know it's the same person?" he wanted to know.

"I know because the person who took the pictures says it is, and he's never wrong about things like that. Read the last page of his report. You can see the life of the young fellow during his first few days on campus if you read the entire thing but read the last page for now."

JC slowly picked up his copy of the report and read out loud.

Saturday

BJW1V rode bus to Union Station. Sat on bench and appeared to sleep. Young man of Mexican descent followed from campus and watched. Young man with brown beard and slightly shaggy brown hair followed Mex. At 25 minutes to nine, brown hair entered rest room. At 20 minutes to nine, BJW1V entered rest room. At 10 minutes to nine, brown hair exited rest room wearing BJW1V's clothing, and sporting long greasy blond hair and acne troubled skin. Brown hair returned to bus stop, Mex followed. Brown hair went back to campus, changed clothes in BJW1V's room and went to cafeteria for breakfast. Mex followed. At 5 minutes to nine, BJW1V emerged from rest room, with neat brown beard, brown hair and acne free face. He bought a return ticket to Baltimore.

"So, what did he do in Baltimore?" asked Brandon. "It must have been something big for him to set up such an elaborate ruse to get there without his watchdog knowing."

"We'll have to wait for the next report to find out," he was told.

"I'm more curious about the acne free face. Since the young man who went back to school in his place had a sudden outbreak of acne, it's obvious that young Mr. Welch has been making himself pimply and ugly on purpose. I want to know why," Reena said musingly.

"Wonder how long he's been doing it and who knew," JC wondered.

"I think it is safe to assume that neither the senator nor Lars knew, but I would be willing to bet that mommy helped him create that face. The staging is feminine," suggested Jessica.

Denile Bentley tipped his chair back and looked at their faces, alive with interest.

"You might want to give some thought to a timeline. How long you want to be gathering information, and how you plan to deal with the senator," he said.

"What we do about the senator will depend on what kind of information comes in. As for time, there's no big hurry, is there? This is a twenty-eight-year-old offense. I doubt another few months will make a difference," Jessica answered.

"It might, if you consider the last bit of information I have. It's not in the report because it's only a rumour at this point, but the source says it's a given. The presidential election is two years away, and the senator plans to be his party's candidate for the presidency.

Unless someone else pops up, he has a good chance of winning the primaries. He is currently the favourite in all the polls."

He smiled at their shocked faces. "I don't know about you all, but I don't want the senator in the White House."

Brandon gave a shout of laughter. "JC, you can stop worrying. I have found the perfect bottle for our senator. And it is just the right size," he said, grinning at them. "Think about it. His political career is the most important thing to him, so we hit him there. Let him win the primaries. Let him start his campaign. Let him get high in the polls, and then we let loose our information. It will demolish him."

"Yes, it would," agreed Jessica. "But it would also demolish his family, and I don't want to do that. They don't deserve it."

Denile looked at Brandon. "Tell me about the bottle," he said.

"You're right—it is perfect," he said, when they told him of Brandon's bottling theory. "And it can be done so his family doesn't suffer. In fact, it would hurt even more if we force him to withdraw himself from the campaign. Then he'll have to come up with a plausible reason himself. Not only will he have to give up the presidency, he'll have to give up public life. And the public will not know why, so his family will be safe."

"We might be able to use the wife and son, if they are in cahoots to fool the senator," said Reena. "Jessica is right. There's no way the son could carry off this masquerade without his mother's help. I think if we can approach them without the senator finding out, they might prove useful."

"Alright. Let's find out what the son is up to, check on the wife and get as much as we can on the senator. We have more than a year before the first primary. I want him to almost win the primaries, then withdraw. It isn't fair to the public to let him win and then force a withdrawal," Jessica said, as they started packing up. She turned to Denile as the others went through the door.

"We need to talk about this friend of yours. Is he a private investigator?"

"Yes, he is. He has a well-established company, but he is the sole owner, so he has a lot of flexibility."

"How do we pay him?"

"So far we haven't. He owes me a few favours, so he did this on the house. If we want to keep him on, he'll send us a bill every two weeks with a detailed report of what he's done and how many hours he logged. I would recommend that we continue to use him. I know him, so I can guarantee his discretion, and that of anyone he allows to work with him."

He picked up his briefcase and turned to the door.

"I have tickets for the TSO tomorrow evening. If you wouldn't find it a complete bore, would you consider accompanying me?" he asked rather abruptly.

"The TSO?"

"The Toronto Symphony Orchestra," he said with amusement. "You have definitely been away too long, Jessica. Come with me tomorrow, and we'll try to reintroduce you to the finer points of your birth city."

"You're on, but only if you let me buy you dinner either before or after the performance."

"After. After will give me more time in your company," he said lightly, and went through the door, leaving her with an unfamiliar but nice little tingle. Anticipation of the evening drove the senator from her mind.

CHAPTER TEN

Barrington Justin Welch IV kept his head down as he climbed aboard the 9:45 AM train to Baltimore. From his briefcase, he extracted a sheaf of papers and pretended intense concentration on their contents. He gripped them tightly to prevent rubbing his hands over his face. He felt exposed, almost naked.

It was the first time in two years that he was appearing in public without a certain number of pustules and pimples. Even though he'd chosen to wear them, he still reacted to the way people looked at him or, rather, didn't look at him. He hunched himself behind the papers, sure that everyone was eying his face until he remembered that his face was now that of an average person.

Baltimore was busy, and he found a motel in a rundown part of town and paid cash for a room for the night. He took off his belt and unzipped the insert from the handle of his gym bag. It was the perfect size for most pants loops, something he was sure his mother had worked out. He piled the travellers cheques into the briefcase with his passport and driver's license and went car hunting.

He'd originally intended to take the train, but he now had twenty-one thousand dollars, counting the travellers cheques and what he'd managed to save, which gave him the freedom to change plans a bit. He started looking for used car lots.

It had to be the right one. Busy enough that he wouldn't be remembered easily and have enough low-end vehicles so he could get one for under a thousand dollars. On the fourth lot, he found the perfect one. For eight hundred and sixty dollars, he got an inconspicuous little Toyota Tercel. Licensing and insurance were quickly taken care of, and he thanked whichever wise person had instructed some of these places to open their doors on a Saturday. He filled his tank with gas and went back to the motel and straight to bed.

Morning found him behind the wheel on the I-95. Traffic was nonexistent, and only two things kept him from Indy speed. The first was that he couldn't risk getting a speeding ticket, the second was that he wasn't sure how far he could trust the car. Pressuring it wouldn't be wise because he had a major distance to cover. He intended to be in Philadelphia before nightfall.

A hurried dinner let him check into a slightly seedy motel on the outskirts of Philadelphia just before dark. He guzzled a bottle of water and stood for ten minutes under the shower's tepid dribble. He was in bed and asleep before the streetlights were fully on. He had a full day planned for the morrow.

He rolled out of bed and made sure he left no evidence of himself in the room, right down to wiping off everything he'd touched. He checked out with the night desk clerk, who was still mostly asleep and walked away. He drove to a public lot and left the car there. At 8:30 he was standing across the street from his first chosen bank, waiting for the doors to open, and by 10:30 he had cashed all the travellers cheques. He'd gone to six different banks and cashed five checks at each one. He retrieved the car and drove to a self-serve storage unit. It was big enough to house the contents of a small apartment, and the two large duffle bags looked incongruous sitting in the middle of the floor.

The bags contained about the same amount of clothing that he'd taken with him to Georgetown U. He was pleased to see that his counterpart had not failed him, and all his things were intact. He lugged them to the car and settled himself for the long drive. By Tuesday evening, he was installed in his room in a dorm at Brown University. Providence, Rhode Island, was a beautiful place in September. He shed the beard and shaggy brown hair and prepared to face the world with a naked visage and the dark blond crew cut that was his natural hair.

Marrion Welch walked down the steps of the library. She clutched her purse nervously, wondering who Lars had spying on her. That there was no one was not considered. The ride home was short, and she left her purse on the side table in the foyer. Someone may check it, or not, but leaving it there lowered the level of scrutiny.

She tamped down the urge to bolt for her room and strolled into the kitchen to check on the progress of the dinner her husband had demanded for his guests. Then she looked in on the dining room, verifying the place settings. She detoured to the library and picked out a book. Only then did she head to her room. She had given Lars enough time to inspect her and decide that she had nothing to hide. She didn't retrieve her purse.

She didn't know what she had to hide, but instinct told her that if Justin had gone to the trouble of hiding something in the cubby at the library, then she needed to keep it hidden. It was tucked securely into the lycra teddy that she had put on for just that purpose. She still needed to wait a while before removing it.

When enough time had passed for it to seem reasonable, she ran water for a bath and locked herself in the bathroom. Peeling off the skinsuit was harder than cramming herself into it, but she managed to extricate herself and the packet from it.

It was a five by seven envelope, and she glanced with amusement at the inscription. It simply said, "bean count." It was a silly game they'd made up when he was small to detail Lars' involvement in their lives.

She sat on the toilet lid and upended the envelope on her lap. A birth certificate, a driver's license and a passport tumbled out. The driver's license and passport had a picture of her with short blond hair. She had worn the wig and allowed Justin to take pictures of her in it at his insistence. She smiled at the name, Marie Warrick. He would have gotten documents for himself as well, using the same last name. They had decided on Jason Warrick.

There was no picture of Jason Warrick, but she knew exactly what he looked like. She hoped he was enjoying wearing his own face in public again. He was a handsome young man, whom neither his father nor Lars had ever met. If the double at Georgetown U did his part, then no one would suspect anything for some time. If he didn't, she'd plead ignorance. Partly true, of course, since she didn't know which university he was enrolled in. With knowledge of his name, she could find out easily enough, but she wouldn't. What she didn't know, she couldn't tell.

She did what she always did when she needed to hide something. She hid it in plain sight. Years of observation had shown her that Lars was uncomfortable around overtly female things, a fact she shamelessly exploited when she needed to. She covered everything in plastic, then dumped tampons from a box and taped the birth certificates and driver's license to the sides, and the passport to the bottom. Cardboard from another box was glued over these, and tampons were stuffed back inside. She didn't close the box. If Lars opened the cabinet under the sink, which he would surely do at some point, he might glance at the box, but wouldn't touch it.

After a quick wash in the rapidly cooling water, she was ready for a rest. She'd lie down for an hour before getting dressed to meet her husband's guests at 6:45 PM. It promised to be a long and excessively boring evening.

"Marrion, you get better looking every time we meet. You ought to tell my wife how you do it!" boomed the loud and brash senator from Arkansas. She murmured an acceptance of the

121

distasteful compliment and tried not to notice him leering at her bosom. As was typical, her husband had chosen the dress. It draped her figure, hugging more closely than anything she would have chosen herself.

"You have only one asset, my dear, and I intend to capitalize on it," he had informed her when she'd dared to question one of his choices. As was also typical, he had neglected to let her know that there would only be male guests. He'd simply said there would be thirteen for dinner. So far, none of the senators and governors had shown up with a wife.

Barrington Justin Welch II showed up last. She looked at her father-in-law and saw a still robust man at seventy-seven years. He had given up his senate seat only when it became clear that his son would succeed him. Something big had to be up for him to have made the trip to Washington. He still had a lot of clout on the Hill.

She spoke briefly with each guest as they gathered in the library for cocktails, keeping her eyes on her husband to read his signals.

"If you gentlemen will excuse me, I'll go check on dinner," she murmured to no one in particular and started edging towards the door.

"You're excused from dinner, my dear," her husband followed her to the door. "We have business to discuss while we eat. Perhaps an early night will help repair your complexion? You are looking a bit peaked," he said with obvious malice.

She kept all expression from her face as she checked with the cook and sent the server to announce dinner. In her room, she slipped off the clingy dress and pulled on a long flannel nightgown. When the maid came in with a dinner tray, she was propped up in bed with a book and headphones in her ears. She pretended not to see Lars peeking in and hid her glee at not having to suffer through an interminable evening. Lars wasn't to know that the headphones weren't plugged into anything. At least, not yet. She may not be welcome at the dinner table, but she would still hear everything they talked about.

CHAPTER ELEVEN

Jessica dressed carefully for her first evening at the symphony. It was a variation of the "little black dress," only this was a deep wine-colour, with what could be a lightning bolt in sharp black across the front. Strappy black high heels from her mom's closet and a lightweight, calf-length black coat completed the ensemble. She stepped from Denile's car with confidence, knowing she looked her best. It was a bright, crisp evening, and Toronto's theatre district on King Street was hopping.

She didn't try to hide her awe as she gazed at the Princess of Wales Theatre with its hundreds of little round lights.

"Another day. I understand *Cats* will be coming back there soon. We could go see it when it starts," he said, watching her with amusement. He took her elbow and gently led her down the street, away from the glittering theatre.

"Here we are, then. Roy Thompson Hall, home of the Toronto Symphony Orchestra," he said, tugging her forward. She turned her attention to the building in front of her and simply stared. On the corner of King Street and Simcoe Street, the building seemed to squat in a circle of blue sky and fluffy clouds. It was a circular concave, with a glass canopy that invited you to stare. The building reflected the evening sky, and Jessica was mesmerized.

"Why don't I remember this building?" she asked.

"Maybe it looked different when you saw it last," he answered. "We are a bit early. I wanted you to see the lights come on." She waited for an explanation, but he gave none—just led her to one of the many benches scattered in the small parkette beside the building.

Although she had her eyes on the building, she couldn't tell when the slowly darkening sky reflected on its surface disappeared. She only realized that she was now looking at the interior of the structure. The glass was transparent in the night lights, and she gave a contented sigh as Denile took her hand and led her towards the entrance.

Later, over a dinner of braised salmon and angel hair pasta, she questioned his choice of entertainment.

"Is the symphony a normal evening pastime for you? I don't think I know too many people who would go out of their way to hear this music."

"You didn't care for the music?" he asked as he tipped his chair back and reached for his glass.

"Come on. Beethoven's Symphony 8. What's not to care for? I'm just saying that it's not the typical pastime among my acquaintances."

"My roommate in college was a music major. He often had tickets to concerts, but he was usually too shy to get a date, so I often ended up with the second ticket. He'd even give me both tickets sometimes so I could take a date myself. Eventually, I introduced him to a friend. She decided he'd make a good husband, and my free tickets dried up. By then, I was hooked, so I started buying my own. If I look at the line up for a few months and like what I see, I sometimes buy a season pass."

He took a sip of Perrier, and she gave the glass a pointed look.

"I don't drink much," he told her. "Once or twice per year, I'll have a glass of wine, but I tend to avoid alcohol. I like to know exactly what I'm doing when I'm doing it, and more importantly, why I'm doing it. I don't handle alcohol well, so I stay away from it."

"Smart. I'm the opposite. I can drink most people under the table. Don't know why—it can't be my size! I wanted to experiment when I was about eighteen, so Mom bought some stuff. We started with beer, moved on to vodka, brandy, rum, wine and ended with shooters. B52s. After about ten shots, we called it quits.

"She'd matched me drink for drink, and neither of us was even tipsy and no hangover the next day either! I don't know why we didn't get alcohol poisoning. Mom told me that she'd tried it once when she was seventeen and realized that she couldn't seem to get drunk. She never drank again until she joined me that night.

"I've never bothered to drink since then either. Plus, I don't like the taste of most alcoholic drinks—it would be a double waste. Unpleasant taste and no buzz. Pointless. Then again, I don't like Perrier either," she grinned, toasting him with her glass of cranberry juice. Then she sobered.

"What am I going to do about the senator?" she asked.

"Make that, 'what are we all going to do about the senator.' You aren't in this alone, Jessica. We'll have to decide fairly soon, though. My source says the senator will announce his candidacy and start campaigning at the end of December. You want to hit him before or after the primaries?"

"After the early ones. He needs 1,191 delegates to win the Republican nomination. I want him to win enough to be confident that he has a decent shot at the nomination. Then we'll hit him. I want him to know precisely what this is going to cost him."

"We'll have to wait a bit to see what the son is up to, but unless something extreme happens, I have an idea how to off-load this on the senator."

When he finished outlining his plan, Jessica looked troubled.

"What don't you like about it? Remember, it's just an idea, and you don't have to do it," he said gently.

"It's not that," she told him. "It's quite brilliant and will accomplish exactly what we want. It just seems so cold."

"As cold as killing your aunt? Every time I think about him hurting Lanni, I want to slowly strangle the little cretin. Since I can't do that, this seems like the next best alternative." His voice was mild and completely at odds with the rage smouldering in his eyes.

127

"Alright, let's run it by the others. If they agree, we'll do it," Jessica said with a resigned sigh.

Jessica had never been to Providence, or anywhere else in Rhode Island for that matter, and would have welcomed the chance to look around, but that was not to be. She needed to hold on to that element of surprise and get out as quickly as possible. She stared at the picture the investigator had sent. Young Mister Welch had changed yet again. He now sported a dark blond crew cut, and his face was clean-shaven and quite attractive.

The girl at the desk popped gum loudly while giving her the once over.

"I need to see Jason Warrick," Jessica told her in business-like tones.

The gum popped in a rapid little burst while she made the call. Jason stepped uncertainly into the hall and stopped abruptly.

"Dana? What are you doing here?" he asked, his shock obvious. Even the gum-chewing receptionist could see the resemblance between the two. Jessica, though better prepared, was still amazed at how similar they looked.

"Come on," she said. "Let's go outside." Luckily it was warm enough, and they walked quickly to a bench in the courtyard.

"You've let your hair grow," he said absently. She nodded, keeping the speaking to a minimum. He might notice her voice wasn't right, and she wanted no complications.

"I didn't think Mom would tell you about the name right away, but I guess she had her reasons. Not that I mind you knowing.

It's not like you're going to run to Lars or the senator with the info. Still, it might have been easier for you not to know just yet. At least until after he finds out that I'm not at Georgetown U."

"Don't worry about any of that right now. I can't stay long. I was visiting this way and thought I'd best see you when I have the chance. It's been almost two years, hasn't it?"

"At least. Mom misses you," he told her with a slight note of reproach.

"I know. But Mom and I will work it out soon. She knows why I haven't been back. I'm not sure when you and I will be home at the same time, so it seemed a shame to come this far and not see you."

They sat in silence for a few minutes, then she got up.

"I have to go. Here. This is for you."

She handed him a sealed envelope, squeezed his shoulder and walked away quickly. She had a brother. A handsome, intelligent baby brother who was trying to break ties with their monster father. If he gave her a chance, she'd help him as much as he allowed.

Justin watched his sister walk away and wondered what was different about her. It wasn't just the hair, although she'd always worn it short before. She seemed older, more confident. Of course, he hadn't seen her for over two years, so it made sense for her to have changed somewhat. Still, it was strange that she hadn't given him a hug, something she'd always done. Maybe she'd outgrown that in the two years as well.

He was happy that she'd come to see him, but the visit left him feeling sad and very lonely. He sat on the bench, idly stroking the bulky envelope, then went back to his room.

He eased the flap open and dumped the contents of the envelope onto the bed, gaping at the shower of hundred-dollar bills that fell out. He looked around nervously, almost expecting Lars to appear and demand an explanation. He counted them. Fifty. There were fifty bills in the envelope. Where did Dana get that kind of money to give away? He stacked the bills and picked up a smaller envelope that had also fallen out. This, too, was sealed and had a short note.

Dear Justin,

By now, you may have noted a few things that you don't recall about your sister. That's because I'm not your sister Jordana. Forgive me for misleading you, but I needed to see you. You may not be aware that your father has his eye on the White House. I object to that, for reasons that I won't disclose at this time. When the campaign for the primaries begins, I suggest you avoid him as much as possible. Use the money to finance the effort to stay away from him and Lars. They are not a good influence on a young man.

Justin stared at the letter and forced himself to breathe. He read it again. He wished he could talk to Mom. He couldn't call Dana—Lars no doubt had her phone tapped. He shoved everything back into the envelope.

He wasn't sure what to do about the money. For the time being, he'd just hide it. Of course, if it came down to using it or going back to the senator, he'd happily use it. He'd just hold on to it and consider it extreme emergency funds since he had no way of returning it.

He hadn't known his dad intended to run for president, but it made sense. He was a big name in Washington, and Granddad Welch still had the ear of most people there. If he wanted to be the presidential candidate for his party, he would get his desire. Granddad would see to it. He wondered how his mom would cope. He was confident the senator would not be calling on his pimply, pustule-ridden son to make any public appearances. His double should be safe.

Jessica sat in the car and took a deep breath. She either looked more like the senator's daughter than she initially thought, or the young man and his sister were not close at all. Two years is a long time when you are a teenager.

It was a quick drive over to the North Central State Airport, where she had a flight booked to Boston. Her final destination was the Bangor International Airport in Maine, but she didn't want to arrive there from Providence and cause anyone to look at the city and university too closely. When she got to Boston, she pulled her hair back into a tidy ponytail, to look more like the twenty-one-year-old her newly acquired passport claimed. Before checking in, she nervously put a bag with all her real identification in the trunk of the car and parked it in the long-term parking, hoping it would all be there when she returned.

"Welcome home, Miss Welch," the customs officer said as he handed back her passport in Bangor. A hurried thank you was all Jessica could manage as she hustled out. She didn't want to meet anyone she was supposed to know. They had banked on Jordana not having been back to the area in a while and wouldn't be immediately recognized.

The rented car was waiting, and she drove to the far end of the lot and pulled over. She needed to review the notes from the private investigator one more time before she hit Fraizers Gap.

Housekeeper, Mrs. Landers—Marrion Welch always brings her Dark Belgian chocolate when she visits. Gardener is known as Sir Sam. Ask after Denny, his grandson. Go to kitchen and ask cook (known simply as Cook) for seed cookies. Must stop at local library and put five dollars in book drive box. (Should do this before going to house.) If in trouble, go to funeral parlour, side door, but try not to be followed there. If no trouble, return to airport.

When she was sure she'd committed it to memory, she tore it up and drove away. She opened her hands on the highway and let the little pieces flutter away in the breeze. Fraizers Gap had a main street, with all the businesses lining it. Main Street, where her aunt was run down. She saw the library and hurried inside. There had been no information on the Librarian, and she tensed as she opened the door. Suppose someone greeted her by name? She needn't have worried. The book drive box was on an unmanned desk, and she stuffed the five-dollar bill in. She pretended not to hear Jordana's name being called as she scurried back out.

She drove the length of the street, looking down the few side streets that branched off. Down one street, she glimpsed the school and doubled back to get another quick look. She didn't drive down to it, although she wanted to. Instead, she located the funeral parlour and checked the different approaches, noting where she could ditch the car and sneak up to the building. Then she headed out of the town.

Welch Manor rose tall and majestic at the bottom of a cul-de-sac five minutes from the town, but it could have been an hour away. There were no houses close by, and the land on both sides of the small street was fenced in. Welch Manor was on Welch Manor Street and was its sole occupant. She pulled up and keyed in the code she'd been given and watched the massive gates slowly open.

"Mrs. Landers," she greeted the tall, thin woman who opened the door.

"Goodness, Miss Dana. Nobody told us you'd be coming in. I'll have to air your room a bit. Nothing wrong with your mama, is there? Not that we could help, mind you, seeing as the senator is away. Won't be back till tomorrow, neither," she said as she bustled away.

"Oh, don't bother about the room, Mrs. Landers. I'm not staying. I just wanted to drop something off for Granddad since I was already in the area," she said, halting the woman's forward rush.

"That's alright then. Come on down to the kitchen when you're done. Cook will be right glad to see you."

Jessica waited until she was out of sight before pulling on a pair of latex gloves. The key fitted the study door perfectly, and she slipped inside and locked it behind her. She hadn't asked how the key was obtained but was told to leave it in the desk's top left-hand

133

drawer. She reached into her bag and withdrew the brown envelope. B. J. Welch II was written across it in a bold, masculine hand. She placed the envelope on the desk, wiped the key and put it where she'd been instructed, then took out the box of chocolates for the housekeeper. She wiped it carefully and put it in the crook of her arm, nestled against the long sleeves of her sweater. She opened the door and slipped off her gloves before stepping out. The door locked behind her, and she stuffed the gloves into her purse. She didn't plan to touch anything else before she left.

"Mrs. Landers, I have to go. Here, take these for me," she said, leaning her arm with the chocolate towards the housekeeper. "Mom would be upset if she heard that I came here and didn't bring them."

Chuckling, Mrs. Landers took the box. "Was always a kind lass, was your mom."

"Hey, Cook. Got any seed cookies?" she called out as she entered the kitchen. Cook turned with hands on her hips.

"Told you a thousand times, Miss Dana. I don't make seed cookies. Seeds are things birds eat. I don't put them in my food," she grumbled, even as she stepped forward to open an overflowing cookie jar. She reached for a plate.

"No, no plate. I have to leave, so just throw them into a bag. I'll munch them while a drive," Jessica told her and snatched the bag as it was filled. She didn't start breathing normally again until the car was on Route 1 on the way back to the Bangor Airport.

Barrington Justin Welch II heaved his bulk out of the car and started up the steps as his chauffeur drove away. He stopped and gazed in satisfaction at the house he'd built on land passed down through his family for over two hundred years. A mansion by anyone's standard, it was isolated from the town started by his family, two-thirds of which he still owned.

He was in a good mood. If the circumstances had been right, he would have had a stint in the White House himself. Having his son there was the next best thing, and he wasn't averse to calling in every marker to make it happen. The past week had been spent greasing all the right wheels in Washington, and he had swelled with pride as he stood beside his son when he announced his intention to run for president.

He wasn't worried about the primaries. The campaign was going well, and money was not an issue. He'd known enough about most of the potential contenders for the candidacy to keep the competition to a minimum. Barry J was a popular favourite. He would be the next Republican presidential candidate. He had a thick file on the Democratic candidates, and at the right time in the presidential campaign, he'd leak enough damaging information to sink him, whichever one it turned out to be.

As expected, the front doors opened before he got to them, and he walked through, tossing a careless hello to his housekeeper. He didn't bound up the stairs—he was almost eighty-years-old, after all, but he did ascend at a brisk pace that might have taxed someone twenty years younger. A quick shower and a sensible dinner increased his sense of wellbeing. He allowed himself one glass of after-dinner wine each day and held it carelessly as he unlocked the door to his study.

He entered and sat, savouring the wine, and glanced idly at the envelope sitting in the middle of his desk. He didn't recall leaving it there, but no one had a key to the room except Barry J and himself. He opened the drawer where he kept the only spare and found it exactly where it was supposed to be. Since Barry J hadn't been to the house in over four months, he had to have brought it in himself and forgotten about it in the rush to leave.

He sipped his wine, wondering if he was going to start forgetting things. He'd been lucky to escape the maladies affecting most people his age, and the thought of any kind of diminished mental capacity was troubling. He drained his glass and reached for the envelope.

Shock leached the colour from his skin. He went cold and clammy. His heart started pounding hard enough to scare him. He closed his eyes and took deep breaths. No panicking. He would not panic.

The sins of the fathers will be visited on the children unto the third and fourth generation..." Exodus 20:5. Do you believe in the Bible, Senator? This quote doesn't quite apply to you, but I'm sure you'll understand that I am more interested in the reverse. The sins of the son will be visited on the errant father, who condoned his child's wickedness. The Bible also says, "Vengeance is mine, says the Lord, I will repay." God doesn't lie, Senator. The time has come for Barry J to pay for his misdeeds, and you will have to pay as well, for your complicity.

He read it again, and the fist around his heart eased its grip. It was a very vague note, after all, and could mean anything. It didn't have to refer to that unfortunate time. He had paid dearly to have it all taken care of. He struggled to his feet and opened the safe. Yes, it was all still there. The police report, the hospital records. This note could not be about a twenty-eight-year-old incident. Everyone connected had been quietly eliminated over the years. The social worker was alive, but all her records had been destroyed. The sister and both cops were dead, and he didn't have to worry about the doctors. With the hospital records removed, there was nothing to substantiate any claim. Still, it would help to know what they were all up to now. He reached for the phone.

When he was finished, he hung up and tapped his fingers on the desk. Where did the envelope come from? He grabbed the house phone and summoned Mrs. Landers. The housekeeper hurried in, having been interrupted in the middle of her evening meal.

"Did you leave this envelope on the desk, Mrs. Landers?"

"Well, no, Sir. The door is always kept locked, and I don't have a key. When we want to leave something for you, we always leave it on the secretaire in the hallway outside your bedroom," she answered, baffled.

"Did anyone come to the house while I was away?"

"Just Miss Dana, Sir. She came yesterday but didn't stay. Said she wanted to drop by since she was already over this side and didn't know when she'd be back. Was right sorry to miss you, she was," she told him with an uncertain smile.

137

"Thank you, Mrs. Landers," he said, dismissing her. Why would Jordana be in Fraizers Gap? She must have left the cryptic note, but what was her purpose, and more to the point, how did she get into the study? This time, when he picked up the phone, he gave very specific instructions.

CHAPTER TWELVE

"Where's my wife?" Barry J snarled as he slammed through the door.

"Sh-sh-she's in her room, Sir," the startled maid stuttered, then blinked with terror when she saw Marrion edging back from the top of the stairs. Charging to his study, the senator didn't notice.

"Lars!" he bellowed, dragging the door open with such force it almost caught him in the face. Swearing under his breath, he threw the briefcase on the desk.

"Lars!" he yelled again and dropped into an armchair.

Upstairs, Marrion quietly closed her bedroom door. Something was very wrong. Senator Barrington Justin Welch III prided himself on spending a full day on the job, and it was only a few minutes after one o'clock. He obviously hadn't come for lunch. Even through the closed door, she could hear him yelling for Lars. She sat on the bed and waited. Before long, the door opened a crack,

139

and Lars peeked in. She feigned great interest in the magazine on her lap and purposely didn't see him. Satisfied, he closed the door and made his way down the stairs. Marrion picked up her headphones and plugged them into a little box built into the headboard of her bed. One turn of a knob and she could hear as clearly as if she was sitting in the study.

"So? Report!" the senator commanded.

"There's little to add to what we already know. It wasn't her. She was on campus all day on the day in question. She gave an oral presentation at the same time she was supposedly boarding the plane in Boston. Her passport has not been used, and both it and her driver's license are where they are supposed to be. She hasn't drawn any money from her account. She hasn't used any credit cards. My man says she never left the campus, and I see no reason to doubt him."

"You'll need to go to Fraizers Gap. Find out who breached my father's home. I'm running for president in the next election," he said hoarsely. "And I'll be very displeased if something you were supposed to take care of twenty-eight years ago rears up to bite me on the ass."

"Don't see how it could. I personally took care of the dumb cop, the sister and all the records. The other cop is dead. The doctor has Alzheimer's disease, and the social worker is a drunk. With no records to back them up, it would be impossible to mount any kind of smear campaign using those two. I wouldn't worry if I were you," was Lars' laconic reply.

"You're not me. I want you in Fraizers Gap tomorrow. Find out who this woman is and find out how she got into my father's study. I have my key. He has his, and he says the spare was locked in the room. I want an explanation, and I want to know who she is."

"Could be a prank, couldn't it?" Lars suggested.

"A prankster who travelled from Boston, impersonating my daughter? I don't think that's a likely explanation. Are you sure my wife didn't leave the house?" he asked in agitation.

"Quite sure, plus she's a mite dark to impersonate your daughter, isn't she? Jordana looks like you, not your wife," Lars reminded him. After a moment's silence, he continued.

"Have you considered the possibility of a child?"

"A child? From where?" Barry J asked, startled.

"Either the same incident or a later liaison?" Lars asked with some uncertainty.

"You've been with me for years, Lars. You would have known if I'd fathered a child away from home," was the mild reply. "As for that naive, country child, if a baby had entered the scene, and the sister knew who I was, they would not have been able to resist pumping my family for money. The sister didn't give any indication that there were any new additions to her family, did she?" he asked.

"No. Fact is, she didn't even bother to keep in touch with her family. She went home three times between then and her demise. Twice she asked for compassionate leave to go to her parents' funerals, and we had the school board ask for copies of the death certificates. I doubt she would have been able to keep away from a niece."

"What became of the girl?" the senator asked absently.

"We searched the sister's place a few times after the incident. According to the letters the mother sent, the girl was moody and uncommunicative. Then the mother sent a tearful letter about the girl's death. Something about a combination of alcohol and other drugs. They weren't sure if it was an accident or suicide. That was about a year after she left the Gap."

"Why wasn't I told about that?" asked the startled senator.

"Why would I tell you about it? You've never wanted to know about unpleasant things that have no direct effect on you. Hearing about the girl's death would not have helped you and may have hampered your plans. Your dad knew," Lars said with a shrug.

"I see. Well, at least we can cross her off the list. As far as I know, it was just the two girls and the parents. No inconvenient aunts and uncles to produce equally inconvenient little cousins. What about friends?"

"I had someone check around at the school, and the girl didn't tell anyone what happened. We spoke to a few of the kids she used to hang out with. They said she'd changed over the holidays. They thought that because she had gone away on vacation, she felt she was better than them, and that was the reason she'd stopped talking to them. She sat alone at lunch and went to the library when she had free time. It is possible she might have called the crisis centre, but if she did, she never identified herself. She's gone, her family is gone, and her little adventure in the Gap is gone with them," Lars said with evident satisfaction.

"Well, now you know where not to waste time looking. Since you mentioned a child, do a quick search and see if her name pops up on any birth certificates. I want you in the Gap by morning. Find this woman. I want to know what she's up to and why. I'll skewer her and roast her slowly if I have to. No one will come between me and the White House. No one," he finished in a raspy whisper.

"What about your wife? Should I put someone on her while I'm gone?" Lars asked.

"Do you think it's necessary?" her husband countered.

"I would say not. For such a pretty woman, she is excessively boring. I've been watching her for over twenty years. If she was going to do something worth reporting, I'm sure she would have done it by now. I only plan to stay in the Gap for a week. She can't get into too much mischief in that time. And she won't know I'm gone, will she? I make sure she doesn't usually know where I am," he chuckled.

In her bedroom, Marrion Welch listened as Lars shut the door on his way out.

"If Jordana is involved in this, I will personally disembowel her." She shivered as her husband's quiet words floated up to her.

She disconnected the headphones and covered the box. She wasn't entirely sure how it worked, but four-year-old Justin had found the box up in the attic and asked her what it was for. When she couldn't tell him, he had taken it apart and found a small rolled-up diagram inside. Before he could shred it, she'd looked it over and found the schematic of an old intercom system. She had cut the recess in the headboard for it herself, and over the years, had fine-tuned the system to almost perfect clarity.

Many of her hours in the library were spent looking at schematics and diagrams of other intercom systems and the components they used. Of course, she always had fashion magazines around her as well for the quick Lars pass-bys. Contrary to Lars' belief, she had a very well-developed Lars radar. Even without the intercom, she would have known that he wasn't in the house.

She could plug in and listen to the dining room, the study, the library and the kitchen. She rarely tuned in to the kitchen. She thought it would be a gross invasion of privacy, plus, she preferred not knowing what the staff were saying about her. The rest she used often. Knowing what her husband and Lars were cooking up helped her manage her life and that of the kids. They always managed to do just the right thing to avoid bringing Lars' or the senator's unwanted attention down on themselves.

She pondered the new information. She didn't know what had happened in Fraizers Gap, but she really hoped Jordana wasn't foolish enough to have gotten involved in something that would anger the three worst men she knew. Her husband and Lars were monsters, but they had been taught by a master. Her father-in-law was the king of monsters.

Twenty-eight years ago. Barry J would have been twenty-two years old. What incident were they talking about? A rape? Could Barry J have raped someone? She wished she could say it was impossible but knew her husband was more than capable of raping a young girl. That Lars and her father-in-law knew about it was no surprise either.

With Lars gone, she would go to the library and search the newspaper archives for anything in Fraizers Gap for that year. With Lars gone, she maybe could try to make contact with the kids. With Lars gone, she could do a thousand little things that always had to be put off because of prying eyes. With Lars gone, it would be like living in a whole new world.

"Hello?"

Jessica was only half aware of having picked up the phone. She was looking over an article proposal, frowning as she tried to figure out what she didn't like about it.

"Go to sleep, Jessica. You have a very early flight to Baltimore tomorrow. You will be going dark," said Denile.

"Tomorrow? I didn't make any plans to go anywhere tomorrow. What are you talking about?"

"Open the door. I'm outside."

"Well?" she demanded as she hauled him inside. "What's this about a flight? I'm sure I haven't booked anything."

"You didn't. I did. You are going to Baltimore by plane and to Washington by car. You will be travelling as Signorina Celeste Marcioni. Your hair will be dark, so figure out how to fit that black wig, and do something about your eyebrows. Your eyes will be dark brown."

"I see. Actually, that's not true. I don't see. Why am I going to Washington? Who is Signorina Macaroni, and why am I using her name?"

"Marcioni, and you are using her name because her passport is readily available. She is in no state to mind, and her bone structure is vaguely similar to yours. With the right colour, you will look enough like the five-year-old picture to pass," he answered.

"She is in no state to mind? What state would that be?" she demanded.

"Deceased," was the succinct reply.

"Okay," she said slowly. "And why will I be impersonating the dead in Baltimore?"

"Lars French has gone to Fraizers Gap. His return ticket says he'll be there for a week. This will be your best chance to get to the senator's wife. You need to do it while the watchdog is gone, so you are going to Baltimore tomorrow."

"Why can't I fly directly into Washington?" she asked in curiosity.

"Because you'll be scrutinized less in Baltimore."

With this, he gave her a quick hug and left. She looked around, dazed, and saw the bag. It contained a shoulder-length, curly black wig, black mascara, brown contact lenses, a passport, driver's license and credit card and her flight information. She sighed when she realized he hadn't been joking about the early part. The flight left at 5:45 AM, which meant getting to the airport by the latest at four o'clock. She picked up the small scrap of flesh-coloured material, wondering what it was. It crackled, and when she unfolded it, there was a small piece of paper declaring it to be a wig cap. She pulled it on and struggled to get all her hair stuffed into it. It looked ridiculous when she was done, but with the wig on, you couldn't tell she had hair under it. It would work.

Marrion almost skipped down the steps of the library. The morning had been fruitless, but she didn't mind. There were no archival mentions of Fraizers Gap, but it had been a long shot. She was still euphoric. Just being able to search without having to worry about Lars watching was a unique experience. Not since her pre-married days had she felt so free.

She unlocked the car and climbed in before she noticed the paper on the passenger seat. She stared at it, skin prickling with fear. The car had been locked. How did the paper get there? Slowly, she picked it up.

Mrs. Welch. Please believe that I mean you no harm. With Lars gone, this seemed like a good time to give you some information about your husband. We know that you helped your son get away from them. We even know where he is. We know why Lars is in Fraizers Gap, and we know that you are afraid of them. We are willing to help you. We won't ask anything of you that will endanger either yourself of your children.

If you want to know why Lars is in Fraizers Gap, put this paper on the seat again and drive over to the Washington Monument.

If you don't want to know and want nothing to do with getting more information about the senator, simply get out of the car and walk back into the library. When you return, this paper and all potential information will be gone.

Her hands were shaking so badly the paper fluttered to the floor. She retrieved it and read it again. *All potential information will be gone.* She'd built her life around gathering pertinent information without her husband's knowledge. If she could risk having a hidden intercom in her bedroom, she could drive to the Washington Monument.

She eased out of the parking lot, looking around to see if anyone would follow. No one drove out behind her, and though she took a circuitous route, she could spot no one following her. When she pulled up in front of the monument and looked around, there was only one person there.

An old woman in a wheelchair sat almost in front of the spot where her great uncle's name was. Coincidence? Maybe. She walked over to stand directly in front of his name. The woman in the wheelchair made the sign of the cross.

"There's a luncheon booking at the Four Seasons Hotel. Ask for the Marcioni party."

The words were quiet, and before Marrion could ask any questions, the chair whirred away. She spent a few minutes staring at the names, then slowly returned to her car. At the Four Seasons, she was led to a private dining room, trepidation dogging her steps as she cautiously entered. A door at the far-left corner opened, and she gaped at the woman who stepped out.

"Who are you, and why are you dressed up to look like my daughter?" she asked.

"Good afternoon Mrs. Welch. My name is not important right now. What you need to know is that I'm here to help you."

Marrion stumbled to a chair and collapsed, not taking her eyes off the young woman who could be her daughter's twin.

"Were you in Fraizers Gap recently?" she asked, nerves shaking her voice.

"I was, but only briefly," the young woman replied.

"Brief or not, your visit has put my daughter in danger," Marrion replied in a stronger voice.

"No, it hasn't. I very carefully chose a day when she could prove she hadn't left school. It doesn't matter how much the senator or Lars wants to pin it on her, they won't be able to," came the firm reply.

"My husband swears he'll personally disembowel her if she's involved in this, whatever this turns out to be," she told her daughter's double.

"He's lying. He wouldn't do it himself—he'd have Lars do it."

"What did you do in Fraizers Gap?"

"I reminded your father-in-law that, sometimes, old sins won't stay buried."

"What old sins?"

"What were you looking for in the library?" Jessica asked, ignoring the question. "I know the good senator didn't tell you about Lars' little trip, or his intention to disembowel your daughter. How did you find out?"

"What makes you think I knew that Lars was away before your note informed me?" she asked.

"Because you've been floating on air all morning. You almost danced to your car when you left home, and on the steps of the library, you looked like you felt that if you jumped off, you would grow wings and fly away. You sat down in the library and didn't bother to surround yourself with camouflage reading material. You might as well have worn a sign in big, bold letters proclaiming, 'I'M

FREE!!' Oh yes, you knew before you left home, and I really don't believe that Lars would have told you," was the amused reply.

Marrion looked at her for a long time, weighing her answer. If they were watching her this closely, did that mean they were giving Lars and her husband equal attention?

"I have a listening device," she finally said quietly.

Jessica stared at her, face filled with amazement.

"Aren't you afraid that Lars will find out?"

"I'm terrified. But I'm more afraid of not knowing what they are plotting," Marrion said, giving a fatalistic shrug.

"How long have you had it?"

"Thirteen years."

Jessica looked at her with growing respect.

"The senator doesn't know you at all, does he?" she asked.

"He knows as much as I want him to know," was the calm reply.

"If you could have anything right now, what would it be?"

"A quiet, uncontested divorce, with the assurance that the senator and Lars would leave my children and me in peace," she said without hesitation.

"Do you think that will ever happen?"

"No. Since I can't have that, I'll have to look at alternatives," she said.

"How do you feel about going to the White House?" Jessica asked.

"I don't plan to go, but if going is what it will take to get away from him, what's four more years?"

"Well," said Jessica, "I'm not letting him get to the White House. I have the means to stop him, and I will. I could do it a lot easier with a bit of help from you, but I can manage without you if I have to. If you help, I promise to get you your quiet, uncontested divorce, and the assurance that neither Lars nor the senator will come anywhere near you."

"That's a weighty promise, but I don't know you. I will not endanger myself or my children because of an unsubstantiated promise by a stranger," she answered with forced calm. What if this woman could actually deliver on the promise?

"There would be no danger involved. If I ask you to do something you deem unsafe, just don't do it. You have total control over what you do or don't do. Our plan requires that the senator believe you to be ignorant of certain things, so it would not suit our purpose to endanger you in any way," Jessica told her gently, putting a folder on the table in front of her.

"Here, read through this, then we'll have some lunch. I'm willing to give you this information whether you decide to help me or not."

Jessica left her to read a carefully edited version of events in the Gap twenty-eight years before and went back through the far door. She hadn't given Marrion any information that would cause her to identify her husband as the perpetrator positively, but she would understand that he knew about the attack and could have been involved in some way. Whatever deductions she made would be her own.

Moments later, Signorina Marcioni emerged. Marrion peered closely at her and gave a faint smile. The two had a quiet lunch, punctuated by suggestions and comments as the seeds of the senator's downfall were carefully planted.

CHAPTER THIRTEEN

" . . . successful nuclear families, traditional families, are the building blocks of a successful and moral nation. It is in the home that we teach the values that underpin our society. And how do we tell our children not to kill when we sanction the killing of innocent babies? How do we . . . "

The group gathered in Lanni's living room watched in silence as Senator Barrington J. Welch III performed in front of a packed audience in New Hampshire. He'd been there before, and he was sure of his support there. He expounded on family values and the importance of traditional morality in society.

He was anti-abortion, anti-same-sex unions. He was eloquent, forceful, believable, likeable and eminently electable. If all you knew of him was his TV image, you would have no reason not to vote for him.

"The man is a marvel. Just the type to sell you acres of sludge with the promise of paradise being built on it. Even knowing he is full of horse manure, you're still tempted to fall for his charm. If that isn't a marvel, I don't know what is," Denile said in amusement.

"The more votes he gets, the more it will hurt when he has to withdraw from the campaign," Jessica replied, switching off the television.

"So how did the Marcioni babe get on?" asked Brandon, twirling the black wig around on his finger.

"Busy woman, Signorina Marcioni," commented Denile. "Much busier than anticipated, wasn't she?"

"Yeah. She had to make a few unscheduled stops," answered Jessica. "But you'll be happy to know that she managed to convince the lovely Mrs. Welch to help us, and the unscheduled stops have placed her firmly in our debt."

"Tell us about these stops," JC requested.

The group of chattering co-eds burst into the lobby of the Holiday Inn and swarmed around the reception desk. They were all there for the writing workshop being presented by a well-known author, and as delegates from Cornell University, they were pre-registered.

Jordana Welch grabbed the key to her room, hiding her irritation at having to share the double room with "Simpering Sydney." If she managed to get through two whole days without braining her, it would be a miracle. She hurried to the room, glad to be there a few minutes ahead of the annoying roommate.

She'd barely entered when she heard the rustle of paper being pushed under the door. Irritation mounting, she turned to pick it up, ready to toss it into the garbage. Her strides towards the dustbin slowed and then stopped.

Signorina Marcioni would be honoured to take afternoon tea with you in the hotel's private dining room at 1:45 PM today.

Afternoon tea? In New York City? She didn't know a Signorina Marcioni and had no desire to "take tea" at 1:45 or at any other time. Just as she started to crumple the note, the signature jumped out at her. It was signed J. Bean La Count. Could it be possible? She checked her watch. 1:37 PM. If she was going to make it to tea, she'd have to move quickly, and if the signature meant what she suspected, she couldn't afford to miss it.

She looked at the two women who turned towards her when she entered the room. One had curly black hair that seemed a bit too dark for her very fair skin. The other had a chic blond bob and a slightly rounded face. She looked closely at her but couldn't be sure.

"Mom?" she asked in a very hesitant voice. The blond wig was snatched off and tossed onto a table, and her mother enfolded her in her arms, sobbing uncontrollably. They hung onto each other, and Signorina Marcioni quietly left the room to stand guard by the door.

Three hours later, Marrion stood in a courtyard at Brown University and smiled at her son, tears dripping down her face. A handsome young man with his mother's eyes. His hair was much darker than his father's, but still blond, but the brown eyes were hers.

She went over the list of questions she'd been given in her mind even as they clung together. She eased back and gave him a quick kiss on the cheek.

"Mom, how did you manage this? Are you sure it's—"

"Don't worry," she interrupted. "I would not have come if there was even a slight chance that I'd lead them to you. Lars is away for a few days," she told him. Before he could give voice to the questions reflected on his face, she rushed on.

"I don't have much time, and I need to find out a few things. First, who is the young man in your room at Georgetown U?"

"Some guy I met at the library. I think he's homeless. At least he was sleeping at the bus depot or sometimes at the train station when I met him. He used to haunt the library, and I got to talking to him one day. I often took extra lunch so I could give him some after school. If it hadn't been for Lars, I would have sneaked him home sometimes. Instead, I used my allowance to help him when he would let me. He wouldn't always accept things from me. I helped him get a GED, and he agreed to cover for me at the university. It gave him a place to sleep and three meals per day for as long as we can maintain the charade," he said with a shrug.

"What happens if your father finds out?" she asked.

"I'm supposed to warn him as soon as I suspect something— give him a chance to get away before Lars gets to him," he replied.

"And if he doesn't get away?" she asked softly.

"He doesn't know where I am. I just paid him to stay in the room. That's the story, and he's willing to take his chances with it. He likes the idea of going to college, and it's not likely to happen.

He says he'll soak up as much knowledge as he can while he's there, and run for it if father finds out," he told her.

"How long do you plan to keep this up?" she wanted to know.

"As long as it takes," was the bald answer.

From across the courtyard, Signorina Marcioni watched as mother and son said a tearful goodbye. At 8 PM, Marrion Welch stepped through her front door, secure in the knowledge that Lars was unaware that she had not attended an evening exhibit at the Smithsonian, her proposed story if anyone questioned her late return. Since the senator had indicated that he would be late himself, she didn't expect to be questioned. Just to be safe, however, she studied a copy of the information pamphlet about the exhibit.

Jessica looked around at her companions.

"So, there you have it. Madam Welch got a chance to see her daughter for the first time in over two years. Turns out the daughter is avoiding home because she thinks Lars is taking an unhealthy interest in her and doesn't think her father would put up too much objection if Lars decided that she would make a tasty holiday tidbit," she ended with disgust.

"Of course. Just one big, happy family. Mind you, with all Lars knows, the senator might not be able to object, even if he wanted to," observed Brandon.

"That may be so, but neither mother nor daughter thinks dear old dad would choose to object, hence Jordana hasn't been home in over two years," she responded.

"And did Jordana meet Jessica?" asked JC.

"No. I didn't think we should put her in the position of having too many things to hide. Remember, Lars is having her watched. It's best if she doesn't know too much. She thinks Signorina Marcioni is someone her mom hired to help get her out of Washington undetected," Jessica replied.

"And how did you get Mrs. Welch out of Washington?" Reena asked.

"Wouldn't you know! Her son, the disguise guru, managed to procure a passport and driver's license for his mother in another name. She already had a disguise hidden away. It was an easy one. A simple blond wig and some padding to round out her cheeks. Later, she can "lose weight" and have her cheeks thin back down to their original patrician cast. Oh! And she says the name is legally hers," she told them.

"What did we find out about the son's double at Georgetown U?" Brandon asked.

Jessica relayed what the mother had told her.

"If Lars catches up with him, it will be like shooting fish in a barrel. I think we'd best do something about that situation. No point in leaving the poor kid there for Lars to terrorize," Denile said.

"Pity we can't work out some way for that boy to stay on at school. He sounds like he would understand the value of an education," JC murmured with a sigh.

"Well, what about the senator? We have him nicely bottled. When do we start tormenting him?" asked Reena, her face filled with unholy glee.

"Patience, love. Torment can't be rushed. If I understand Denile's plan, we have a few months to go on with life and ignore the good senator. Let him and Lars chase their tails trying to figure out the message left for Granddaddy Welch. We'll leave him alone for a while. The New Hampshire primary is what? Almost a year away, isn't it?" Brandon responded.

"But what do we do in the meantime? We can't just leave him alone!" Reena exclaimed.

"Sure we can! But we won't leave him entirely alone. We have a nice little campaign guaranteed to give both him and his dear old dad ulcers. Subtlety is what we are aiming for throughout the next few months. The gears of politics grind slowly, but they grind at prescribed times. We'll put a loose bolt in his gears at just the right time," said Denile with quiet intensity.

A few days after his mother's visit, Justin received a letter. He read and reread it, but it made little sense to him.

At Georgetown U, your double will be given the following instructions spread over a few weeks. Number one has already been delivered.

1. *Remove half your pimples and spots immediately.*
2. *One week later, cut your hair. Do it yourself, so it isn't too neat.*
3. *One week later, openly buy some hair dye and colour your hair and beard brown.*
4. *One week later, remove half the pimples left on your face.*

5. *On the same day, start wearing clothes in brown suitcase under your bed. Outfits are labelled for each day for two weeks.*

6. *At the end of the two weeks, go to a barber and get a proper haircut. Don't recolour hair. Let natural colour grow in.*

7. *One week later, start wearing clothes in black suitcase under bed. Outfits labelled for one week.*

8. *At the end of the week, start wearing new wardrobe in closet and drawers. At same time, remove beard and remaining pimples.*

9. *Go to Registrar's Office and request a transfer into the program of your choice. All documents are in order, and the student number you are currently using is yours, registered under your real name. All school records will reflect this.*

Justin, if he should contact you, please encourage the young man at Georgetown U to follow the instructions as they are delivered. If he does, it will sever all connection to you. There will be no record of your having been at that school, and he will get a full college education in his own name.

Justin folded the letter and put it away. The Bean La Count signature told him that his mother was involved, and he trusted her. If she said it was best, it likely was.

CHAPTER FOURTEEN

Jessica tucked her legs under her and cradled the giant mug. She closed her eyes and savoured the aroma of cinnamon and chocolate.

"You make absolutely the best hot chocolate," she told Denile, taking another deep breath.

"That's because you haven't tasted my mother's. Now that's a brew that will make you think you're in heaven," he said, dropping down beside her on the couch.

"You can have some when you come to the surprise birthday party she's having for me next Saturday night," he told her.

"How come you know about it if it's a surprise?" she asked, sidestepping the invitation. She had managed to avoid meeting his family thus far, and it looked like she was about to run out of excuses.

"Let's see. She told me to come to dinner. It's the day after my birthday. Every year since I left home, she has had a surprise party on the Saturday night closest to my birthday. It's elementary, my dear Jessica," he said with a grin. Then he turned serious eyes on her.

"I haven't pushed, but I think it's time you told me. Why don't you want to meet my family? We've been seeing each other for months, and you always have a reason to avoid being with me when I go to see them. We've never really talked about the boundaries of our relationship, and I think it's time for some clarification." He stretched his legs out and stared up at the ceiling.

"I haven't asked if you've been seeing anyone else because I didn't think I had the right to. I'd like to change that. I haven't been seeing anyone else. Would you consider an exclusive relationship with me?" The question was abrupt, with none of his well-known finesse. She smiled at him.

"I *have* been in an exclusive relationship with you, despite us keeping it on the level of friendship. I wouldn't have had the energy to see anyone else, with you hauling me from one end of the city to the next. But that's alright since I didn't want to. So no, I won't consider an exclusive relationship with you, but I'll be happy to have you join me in the one I've been having with you," she told him and watched his eyes lighten with laughter.

"As for your family, I just needed some time. Families reminded me too much of Mom. I know I've been avoiding them, and as long as we were supposed to be just friends, I could justify it. But you're right. It's time. I'd be honoured to come and act surprised at your birthday party," she said, smiling as he reached for her. Sometime later, he returned the mug he had taken from her hands.

"Perhaps you'd like to hear a few details of our campaign to give the good senator an anxiety attack on *his* campaign trail?" he said, pulling a folder towards him. She curled her legs under her again and prepared to listen. When he was finished, she shook her head. The man was brilliant.

"Assuming we succeed, what exactly are we going to ask him to do?" she asked.

"Isn't that your department?" he questioned mildly.

"Not really. I want him to lose out on the chance to be president. I think that is a fitting punishment. What I'm asking for is the specifics."

"Alright. He has to voluntarily remove himself from the race and provide a plausible enough reason, so his family is not subjected to any ridicule. He has to promise to have Lars leave his wife and children alone, and he has to agree to the quiet, uncontested divorce his wife wants. Oh, and he has to agree to resign from and never take another public office."

"That's taking it a bit far, isn't it?"

"Your call, but I don't think so. Had it not been for his desire for public office, your aunt would still be alive. She lost her life. I don't think it is too much for him to lose his chosen career. At least he'll be alive to try something else." He got up to take the mugs to the kitchen.

"That's all a while away, though, so if you want to revise it, feel free. As I said, this is your campaign. If you want to go easy on him, you'd better not let Reena and Brandon know. Sometimes I think they might be enjoying this whole sting just a bit more than is decorous, as JC would say."

Senator Barry J. Welch III picked up the Washington Post and leaned back in his chair. There was little of interest in the news, but he had to be sure. You never know when a reporter will find out something that would affect the campaign. He threw the paper down on the table, just missing the breakfast dishes, and picked up the mail. He glanced at his wife, who was quietly nibbling on toast while staring off into nothingness. *Pity, she'd never lived up to her potential*, he thought, ripping open the first envelope. You could not find the vivacious twenty-one-year-old he'd dated in the mousy dowager sitting at the table. The twenty-one-year-old would have made a better First Lady.

He unfolded the single sheet of paper and frowned in confusion. A list of events? Was there a news conference that he needed to prepare for?

Floods in Bangladesh kill hundreds
Earthquake in China kills thousands
Lunar Probe Ranger 1 reaches 190 km from earth and falls back
600 German Luftwaffe bombs Stalingrad, killing 40,000

He stared at the paper. There was nothing else on it. He turned it over.

If you check through history, some very bad things have happened on August 23rd

"Are you alright, dear?"

He must have made some sound because his wife was looking at him with concern. He barely managed a strangled reply, then grabbed the envelope and rushed to his office. His hands were shaking as he dialed his father's number.

In the dining room, Marrion checked to make sure the door was closed and reached for her husband's briefcase. Though she'd never done it before, she didn't fumble as she set the combination she'd committed to memory and snapped it open. She picked up the bunch of keys he kept in it and pressed one into the little box she had been carrying around for days. She quickly cleaned off the keys and wiped her prints from the case. When Lars came in to retrieve the briefcase a few minutes later, she gave him a disinterested glance and calmly sipped her tea.

Despite his father's reassurances, Senator Barry J. Welch III was not at his best when he entered the auditorium of The University of Maine. He tightened his grip on his briefcase and looked at his campaign manager. Everything was in place, and this appearance was just for publicity. It was his home state and he was far ahead of the competition in the polls. With those numbers he could hardly lose—a Welch had never lost an election in Maine. He would have gladly cancelled it, but there was too much time for things to sway the public. He couldn't afford to offend anyone, even people he was sure of.

Where had the letter come from? The postmark was so smudged it couldn't be deciphered. Except for Lars and his father, who else could know about the significance of the date? He ruthlessly buried the worry and turned to greet the young man hosting the rally.

Years of practice rescued him, and he delivered an eloquent speech, filled with engaging witticisms that charmed his audience. He wound down, feeling much better than he had on arrival, and the obvious approval of the crowd calmed him. He took a few sips of water and turned back for the question period. An eager young girl jumped to her feet, blond ponytail bouncing.

"Senator, if we look back through history . . . " He couldn't hear over the buzzing in his ears. For a moment, he was back at the dining table, and the morning's shock slammed into him again. He had to clench his fists to stop the trembling in his hands. He stared at the girl, who looked innocently back at him and continued with her question. He couldn't tell how much of it he had missed.

" . . . so what I'd like to know is, do you think the American people put too much emphasis on the past sins of those running for office? I mean, you always talk about morality and standards, but people make mistakes, don't they?"

He swallowed hard, tempted to swing his platform around and talk about forgiveness, but he had just spent half an hour talking about the need for morality, past, present and future—so how could he?

"Yes, people do make mistakes, but your mistakes are usually the result of an underlying character trait. Should you be considered a thief because you once got caught shoplifting in your youth? Maybe not, but the character defect that caused you to try to get away with shoplifting is likely still there. In what other ways will it be manifested? It is best when putting someone in public office that we choose someone who has not shown any obvious character flaws, and past sins are perhaps the most reliable meter on which to measure character," he answered.

"So you don't think we should forgive them and let them move on?" asked the young co-ed, almost bouncing on her feet.

"By all means, forgive them, and certainly let them move on, but not move on with the wellbeing of the nation in their hands. Immorality will not remain hidden when placed in a position of ultimate power," the senator admonished.

A young man in the back left corner stood up, tiny dreadlocks falling neatly around his dark face.

"Do you really believe that how a man runs his home is an indication of how he'll run the country? You said something to that effect in New Hampshire two weeks ago," he said.

"Yes, I firmly believe that. What is a country but a combination of families? A well-run country is made of well-run families, and a man who can create and maintain a stable family is one who has had practice in running a country, at least on a micro level."

"So, your wife and children would be the best people to talk to if we want an opinion on the type of leader you would be?" asked the same young woman from before.

He gifted her with the smile that had been charming viewers all over the country, even as his stomach clenched.

"I'll leave that one for you to think about. Just remember when you ask, that father's sometimes do have to say no, for the good of the family!" he told her with a grin.

The young man stood again.

"Senator, it is understood that your daughter has returned home only once since her first year at university. That does not bode well for a country if its citizens leave to visit another country and choose not to return. It would seem to indicate some lack in the leadership, some element of discord, or some need is not being met for those citizens who leave." The undertone of mockery in the young man's voice could not be missed.

"Many of the people who populate this great country of ours came here from other lands. We have met their needs. Our country also produces many different types of people, and their needs and desires are diverse. When they find that these needs and desires can be more adequately met on other shores, it would be very unsporting of us to try to keep them here. You should know, though, that most Americans who live abroad eventually return home, and even if they don't, they still consider this land their home," Senator Welch responded.

The burning in his stomach increased as he made his way from the podium. Lars would have a chat with the impudent young man, he thought, as he prepared to shake hands with the crowd. He expected the voluble young woman to be among the first greeters, but when it was time to leave, he realized that she had slipped away without meeting him.

"The man is a troll, but he is a charming one. And I can tell you this. He is even more charismatic in person than he is on the screen," Reena reported, as she paced around Lanni's living room.

"Denile, I don't know where you find these people, but the young man didn't even blink when I told him what I wanted him to ask the senator. Simply took the paper, read it and shredded it. He was perfect," she told him. "And he very neatly eluded the security types who were obviously planning to have a chat with him. Someone somewhere is going to start to wonder why the senator's daughter never goes home."

"It sounds like he handles himself well under pressure, though," said Brandon thoughtfully. "Pity. We could have had him cracking if he was weaker."

"He had a bad moment at the beginning. I don't think there is any doubt that he received our little early morning memo. My opening statement nearly sent him into orbit, but he recovered really quickly. If I wasn't watching for it, I wouldn't have noticed the reaction. If there was a crack, I promise you no one saw it," Reena observed.

"He isn't the cracking type. He might fumble the ball, but he won't drop it. By the way, we now have a key to his study. The lovely Mrs. Welch came through for us with a beautiful wax impression," Denile responded.

"Good. Full speed ahead then. With caution, of course!" said the irrepressible Reena.

"What's next?" asked Brandon.

"A Straw Poll dinner. You and Reena will be attending," Denile answered.

"What is that, and why are we going?" Reena wanted to know.

Surprisingly enough, it was JC who answered.

"A Straw Poll is an unofficial vote that can indicate the political candidates' standing in the popular opinion of members of a State. They used to have one at a fundraising dinner for the Iowa Republican Party in Ames, Iowa before each election, and the poll was taken among the attendees who would come from all over the state. It was a pretty big deal. They may be having them in different places now, but wherever it is, I think you do have to be a legal resident of the State so just showing up is not an option, and last I checked, neither Brandon nor Reena are legal residents of any State," he said, looking at Denile with obvious disapproval."

"How important is this poll?" Jessica asked.

"It doesn't have any official standing in terms of its effect on the actual presidential primaries, but it is a good showing for the winning candidate. It serves as a good indication that he has support in the state. I strongly object to your involving yourselves in this fraudulent activity," he said, still glaring at Denile.

"JC, I would never ask them to do anything as wrong as going there to vote. They will pay $35.00 each for a dinner ticket, get close to the senator and goose him a bit, that's all," Denile responded.

"No, that is not all. They will have to provide proof of status in the State, and I refuse to be a party to that type of blatant fraud," JC said adamantly.

"Alright. Nix the Straw Poll. We'll let the good senator rest for a bit," Denile gave a good-natured shrug.

"Spoilsport," Reena said, sticking her tongue out at JC.

CHAPTER FIFTEEN

"Let me see the note," the Welch patriarch demanded. His son obediently handed it over. The older man read it slowly, then smoothed it out on the desk. They were in Barry J's study, his father having flown out following his distress call the previous morning.

"Get me some brandy," he said calmly.

He sipped in silence, then looked at his son.

"Not the best situation, but not the worst either. We know that someone somewhere knows something. I think she's baiting you, trying to see how you react. I can tell you that there is no proof out there, so they can taunt and bait all they want. What did Lars say?"

"I haven't told him. I've been wondering. Only three of us know for sure about this, and he's the third. Do you think he might have told someone?" asked the senator with fear in his voice.

"Tell them what? That he killed two people to help you out of a bit of a scrape? How would it help him to be named a murderer? He has no proof of any wrongdoing on your part, but I have him on tape reporting on the murders. He doesn't know, of course, but he wouldn't be that foolish. I'd like to know what he thinks of this situation. Call him," his father insisted.

Both men watched Lars closely as he walked into the study.

"Senator," he greeted the elder Welch, as he had addressed him from youth.

"It's good to see you, Sir. Barry J always does better with you around," he told him with a sincere smile.

"And so he should. I've forgotten more about the workings of this game than he'll ever have time to learn," the older man answered in jovial tones. He genuinely liked Lars, a man of his word who didn't balk at carrying out difficult tasks.

"We have a bit of a problem, and I'd like your views on it," he said, handing the sheet of paper to Lars. Lars read it and looked up without concern.

"It is public knowledge, and anyone who wanted to badly enough could dig it up. Lots of people know that something happened on August 23, and any number of them might choose to throw it at you. But I can tell you that there is not a single shred of proof anywhere that they could lay hands on. Only two people knew for sure, and they are both dead. The only other person of concern we disposed of as a precaution. She left nothing behind to indicate she knew anything. I spent two days going over her house. There wasn't a book I didn't look in. I emptied out her flour container. I myself shredded every scrap of paper in that house. There was no evidence that she knew anything damaging. I agree that she had to be removed, but I don't think she knew."

"So, you think this is a prank?" Barry J asked.

"No, I think it is serious. Someone suspects something and wants to shake you up. It's probably that woman. She can't openly accuse you, and no paper will print a suspicion of that nature without proof. *Barry J, there is no proof*," he reiterated.

"Thank you, Lars," the elder Welch said, waving him to the door.

"Well?" he asked his son.

"He seems very sure. I wish I could borrow his certainty," he replied, prying open a bottle of antacid tablets.

"Alright," said the father. "We'll proceed as if exposure is imminent. We know there is no proof but assume someone knows something and is willing to talk. We don't know what this person wants, and we'll not bow to blackmail. To do so would be to admit guilt, and that we'll never do." He paced the study in measured steps.

"Rumours can sometimes be as harmful as an open accusation. If this woman starts one, you will go on national TV with the current chief of police and the hospital administrator, and address the lack of evidence to support such a damaging accusation. If you are open about it, people will think there can't be any truth to it," he said with authority.

"Suppose the chief of police and the hospital guy refuse?" his son asked.

"Refuse? What do you mean *refuse*? And continue to live and work in Fraizers Gap? Don't be idiotic," he said with a dismissive wave.

"We'll have to change our strategy a bit," he continued. I was going to let everyone get in on the New Hampshire primary and pull out the two holding third and fourth places right after, but we need to narrow the field a bit if this thing is going to be nipping at our heels. We'd best take them out early. There's a good chance that most of the people who would have voted for them will vote for you. We'll remove the number two contender before Super Tuesday and clean the slate," he told his son.

Barry J was pensive. "Do we know enough about the three of them to force the withdrawals?" he asked.

"Oh, we know more than enough. I've been planning for this day since you were sworn in as mayor. I have something on every breathing soul on this hill. The few who have nothing to hide aren't likely to ever become potential adversaries. Don't worry. When the time comes, they'll withdraw," he answered with quiet confidence.

"Do we ask them to withdraw or expose them?" he asked with only mild curiosity.

"The first two we expose. We don't need them, and a couple of provable scandals will set up the public to expect proof if someone does start a rumour. We'll have something to hold up in contrast. Here is a proven misdeed, and here is an unfounded rumour. The former Governor of California is number two in the polls. We'll ask him to withdraw and instruct him to endorse you. With his endorsement, you'll have his share of the votes, and you won't need to campaign beyond Super Tuesday."

"That will win me the primaries, but I'll still have this woman hanging around during the presidential election. I don't know if I could stand that," Barry J said petulantly.

"You won't have to. I've launched a full investigation since Lars found out nothing in the Gap. The housekeeper and cook don't see how it could not have been Jordana. The librarian didn't see her up close but is willing to swear it was her. Various people saw her driving around, and all swear it was her, although a few wondered why she hadn't waved to them. Of course, the woman wouldn't have, not knowing that these were people she should acknowledge," he said, reaching for a glass.

"How did she come to know enough about your house to be able to fool the housekeeper and cook? She even brought the chocolates that Marrion always brings for Mrs. Landers. How did she know about them?" Barry J wondered.

"That's what we are going to find out. I launched a full investigation and fingerprinted the entire house. She left none. I even checked the box of chocolates. It had only Mrs. Landers' print on it. She'd wiped it before handing it over. Had it in the crook of her arm, Mrs. Landers said," he told Barry J with a hint of admiration.

"She sounds like a professional. I mean, she broke into your study—"

"She didn't break in," his father interrupted. "She had a key. I haven't figured out how, but the lock wasn't tampered with, and I know it was locked when I left. Are you sure your key never left your possession?" he demanded.

"Quite sure. Remember, I have a vested interest in making sure that your study is secure. When are you going to get rid of those documents? I get nervous with them sitting around," he said, sounding just a bit grouchy.

"You can have them when I'm done with them," his father smiled.

"When will you be done with them? What do you need them for?" he asked.

"I'll be done with them when I'm dead, and I no longer need a bargaining chip with you. You have a tendency to be rebellious and not follow the rules. That's what got you into this in the first place. Had you followed my advice, you wouldn't be sitting here sweating over what some unknown woman could be up to, because you wouldn't have done something so stupid in the first place," the older man said with callous calm.

"I'm helping you get to the White House, and you will very well listen to me when you are there. Your juvenile stupidity cost me my chance at the presidency. Oh yes, you did," he said when his son tried to interrupt.

"I didn't enter the race because just at the time I was poised to run, you decided that you couldn't wait to find a willing partner to bed. I had to spend valuable time and resources buying off people. I couldn't afford to have the entire world focusing on the Gap at that point. I could contain the story there, but had I been in the presidential race, it would have been impossible to keep nosy reporters from digging around. Someone would have gotten to the girl, and someone other than the cops would have heard her description of her attacker.

"It wasn't just keeping you out of jail. It would have ended my political career in disgrace if it had been found out, so I covered it up for myself as much as for you, but it cost me the presidency. I had an open run at the primaries. I would have been the default candidate, and believe me, even then, I had enough material that the democratic candidate would have become a household name for scandal.

"Yes, you cost me the presidency. Well, I'll get you the chance to sit in the White House, but I'll hold on to the material to ensure that your chance is also my chance," he finished.

Barrington Justin Welch III could almost feel his facial muscles going slack. He stared at his father with incredulity spreading slowly over his face.

"You are planning to blackmail me? When I'm president?" His shock was complete.

"Don't be an ass, Barry J. Why would I need to blackmail you? I'll simply remind you sometimes that advice from your father should not be ignored," the older man told him with a benign smile.

"When I first asked why you didn't destroy the documents, you said it was too early, and they might be needed if there were any questions.

"You told me that the reports on their own were no proof of guilt, but as long as there were people around who remembered the incident, we should have the reports. That way, if anyone asked, they could see the reports and see the police did everything they could to investigate but found nothing. You told me that the reports on their own were not harmful, so it was alright to keep them," Barry J mused.

He poured himself a small glass of brandy.

"I might not be comfortable having them out there, but you were right. On their own, they don't implicate me in any way, so why should I be worried about you having them?" He sipped his drink, watching his father.

"What can you do with them? Announce to the world that you've had them for over twenty years and suspect the perpetrator might be your son, who just happens to be running for president?" His smile was grim.

"There are those out there who might think it has something to do with dementia. You are quite old, after all. Then some might think it has to do with jealousy. You didn't get a chance at the presidency, so you don't want your son to do what you couldn't," he finished, toasting the older man with his glass.

"Very good," his father replied. "I'm proud of you. That is very logical thinking and would be effective if you hadn't ignored one very salient fact."

"What's that?" his son asked.

"Have you forgotten the rape kit?" he asked, belatedly returning the toast his son had given him. The colour leached from Barry J's face, and he stumbled back a step.

"You told me you'd had it retrieved and destroyed!" he said in a hoarse shout.

"Barry J, Barry J. We are politicians. When have you ever known one of us to throw out evidence of someone else's culpability? Sure, I had it removed from the station. I could hardly leave it there in the evidence box, could I? But you used the right words. I TOLD you I'd had it destroyed," he said with a malicious smile.

"As I said, your chance in the White House will be my chance there, even if it will be almost thirty years later than I intended." He walked over and slapped his waxy, pale son on the back.

"But you have nothing to worry about. I've never steered you wrong, and I never will. Don't concern yourself overmuch about the evidence. I've kept it safe for twenty-eight years. I'm not about to let it get into enemy hands now." He picked up the brandy bottle.

"Here, have another drink and go to bed. You look like you could do with a bit of rest. I'll turn in myself in another hour or two. I'll just sit here and nurse this excellent brandy you've thoughtfully provided for your old man," he said in a jocular tone.

His smile was evil and terrible to see.

Marrion's hands shook as she unplugged the headphones. She almost felt sorry for her husband, but only almost. He should have known by now his father was a total bastard. He had sat at his feet and soaked up enough of his nasty ways that he really shouldn't have been surprised to have some of it directed at him. She hoped the newest addition to her store of gadgets had worked.

CHAPTER SIXTEEN

They didn't even use his name. They didn't have to. It was a genuine case of a picture telling more than a thousand words. There he was, the independent contender from North Carolina. He held third place in the polls and was gaining popularity. Barrington J. Welch II, in Fraizers Gap, held the Washington Post on his knees and gazed in satisfaction at the picture he had sent anonymously to a hungry reporter. There was no mistake. The worthy candidate from North Carolina was smoking cocaine.

We have all seen this visage many times over the past two and a half months. Without having spoken to the person pictured here, who, strangely, was unavailable for comment, it is unwise to say with certainty that this is who the picture would claim it to be.

This reporter can say, however, that this was not a picture from a digital camera. It was not doctored on a computer. It was taken with a camera that uses 35mm film, as the negative will prove. Who took the picture? We must admit we don't know.

Where was it taken? By comparing the background to many well publicized photographs, it would appear to be on the back porch of the home in North Carolina owned by the person who looks to be the one in the picture. A very private back porch, I must say, but, well, is the person in the picture who we think it is? You be the judge.

While making up your minds, here is a bit of very, very deeply buried information. A certain person, bearing the visage of the person in the picture, has checked into an exclusive little hostel in Switzerland five times in the past four years.

The visits are on record as being "short holidays." Since the hostel is a very expensive drug rehab facility, one might wonder at the reason for taking a short vacation in that particular place.

This person must be commended for taking the initiative to attempt rehab on his own, but the recurring attempts seem to indicate a recurring difficulty. It would appear that a cocaine problem plagues the good man in the picture.

It is said that he only smokes freebase cocaine. Freebase cocaine is the base form of cocaine and is not soluble in water. This means that the user can't inject it, drink it or snort it. But smoking? Perfect. It is absorbed directly into the blood by way of the lungs and gets to the brain in only a few seconds. The rush is almost immediate, in other words, and more intense than sniffing.

Freebase cocaine is fairly pure, and producing it involves a very dangerous procedure involving ether. Ether can combine with oxygen to form peroxide which may spontaneously combust and KABOOM!!

What does this mean? Freebase cocaine is murderously expensive.

Our good friend in the picture doesn't have to worry about track marks from intravenous injections, nor the nasal problems that seem to plague those who sniff. So his only worries are high powered lenses that can reach into his private porch; the bottomless chemical hole his money is disappearing into and the number of times he'll go to rehab before it gets the better of him and he ends up on the overdose statistics.

Oh, and of course, if he's who we think he is, whether or not the American public would be interested in a president with a drug habit. But then, who knows. Maybe it isn't our good friend who was doing so well in the polls.

The by-line read Janelle Christy.

Barrington J. Welch II carefully cut the article out and put it in an envelope. By tomorrow other papers would have picked it up and the senator would be forced to withdraw, increasing his son's chances. Number four in the polls was next. He pulled another envelope towards him and wrote Janelle Christy's name on it. By morning it would be on her desk and by the next day another campaigner would be running for cover.

"Well, there you have it," Brandon announced, as he walked into Lanni's living room. The others turned to glare at him. He'd interrupted a spirited argument between Reena and JC about the role of the man in the family.

"Whatever it is, I'm not getting involved. I've seen that look before, and I want no part of whatever caused it," he said, advancing on Reena.

"Here, read at your leisure." He tossed a copy of the Washington Post on Jessica's lap.

"Your sainted father now has only one serious opponent and who knows how long that will last. His fellow campaigners seem to be dropping out at the starting block," he said, sliding into a chair.

Denile snagged the paper from Jessica, and quickly glanced through the article. The junior senator from Massachusetts had once accepted a substantial bribe. In return for a hefty campaign donation, he'd agreed to award a government contract to a certain construction company. There were tapes of phone calls and pictures of the parties meeting at a restaurant. The senator could not be reached for comment, but there was no doubt that his next public statement would be to announce his withdrawal from the presidential race.

"There's only a little over a month before the Iowa Caucus. That's going to be the first of the primary elections. After that I believe it will be Wyoming. Our latest intelligence is that Daddy Welch means to remove the only other serious contender right after the New Hampshire primaries. Daddy Dear is proving to be even worse than we suspected. I have a recording I want you to hear," he told them.

They listened in shocked silence to the conversation between father and son, and JC shook his head in amazement when it was done.

"What's bred in the bone. His poor son would have needed an iron backbone to end up a better person than he is, having been raised by such a reprehensible personality. Where did we get this tape, Denile?" he asked.

"We added a new feature to Lady Welch's listening device. Worked like a charm. The lady is turning out to be quite a find. She's gutsy, that's for sure," he answered.

"I wonder if she has any concerns about betraying her husband," JC wondered.

"She probably would, if she considered him her husband. But I suspect that he lost that status soon after she met Lars," was Reena's dry response.

"We've left the senator alone since August. I'm sure he's recovered by now. Isn't it time to increase his blood pressure a bit? Or do we have to wait until JC is gone to plan something?" Brandon asked with a grin.

"Nope. JC gets to veto anything that is too far off the charts. He's our moral meter here, and we'll accept when he says something shouldn't be done. None of us wants to have a guilty conscience later, so I'm glad he's here to hold us back," Denile answered.

"Even JC won't be able to object to our next little adventure," Jessica put in. "Reena, you and Brandon get to go to dinner after all. It will no doubt bore you senseless, but it will serve our purpose. There will be an awards dinner at the Ritz-Carlton in Georgetown, and you will be seated at the senator's table. The conversation will likely focus on these two recent scandals in the Republican campaign, and your duty will be to lead the senator to air his views. Shouldn't be too difficult. He's a politician—they love to talk."

Jessica stood in front of the mirror and gazed at her reflection. The short-sleeved t-shirt and matching cardigan were cream, with large alternating squares of deep blue and green. She had teamed them with blue slacks, left her hair loose and wore no jewelry. Her make-up consisted of a light dusting of powder, a colourless lip-gloss and mascara to darken her light lashes. She looked wholesome, she decided.

"You O.K?" Denile asked as they drove up Madison Avenue. "You're very quiet."

"They may not like me," she said, and immediately regretted it. She sounded like a nervous teenager.

"Doesn't matter if they do or not. You're with me, and I like you. That's all you need to be concerned about." He reached for her hand and brought it to his lips.

"I've never paid much attention to what my family says about my friends, but even if they hate you, they would not be impolite enough to let you know. At least most of them," he said with a grin, as he pulled into the driveway. Before they were finished parking, the house door flew open.

"Denny, Lue says he's going to beat you to a pulp if you don't return his baseball card collection," a gangly young girl yelled, jumping down the steps.

"Baseball cards? Why would I have his baseball cards, brat?" he asked, pulling on the single braid hanging down the girl's back.

"I never said you have them. But Lue thinks you do, and he wants them back," she said, mischief written all over her face.

"And why does Lue think I have his kiddie collection?" he asked as he helped Jessica from the car.

186

"I didn't tell him that you have them, at least not exactly. I mean, I told him I'd seen you *looking* at them . . . " she trailed off as he turned to look directly at Jessica. She quickly turned her eyes to Jessica.

"You don't look like Lanni," she said, sounding puzzled.

"Oh, I do, but only on the inside," Jessica said, amused. Cutting off Denile's exasperated exclamation, she walked over to the young girl.

"I'm Jessica," she said, and held out her hand.

"I'm Monique," the girl responded, and shook hands solemnly.

"Perhaps you can introduce me to Lue and we'll see if we can convince him to spare Denile," she said, and was rewarded with a snicker. Denile pushed open the door and stood back so they could go in. A young woman in a flowing caftan stood in the foyer. Yards of pumpkin orange material swirled around her as she swayed to some unheard music. She turned to the door and drifted towards them.

"This is Sade, Lue's wife. Sade, this is Jessica," Denile said as she floated to a stop in front of them. She murmured something vague and proceeded to stare intently into Jessica's face. Jessica glanced uncertainly at Denile, but he didn't seem to find his sister-in-law's behaviour strange, so she simply stared back, though she didn't confine herself to the face. She stifled a laugh when she realized that the caftan was less than clean. It looked as if someone had used it as a cleaning rag over and over. There were smudges of every hue hidden in the folds of material, and the hands that slowly drifted towards her face were just as smudged.

"Good bones," she said, as she wandered back the way she had come. "She has very nice bones, Denile," she threw over her shoulder.

After Sade, the rest of the family was comfortingly normal. His mom enfolded her in a warm hug as if she had known her forever, and the evening became a blur of warmth, laughter and contentment. When dinner was finished, she helped clear the table, and in the kitchen offered to help with the dishes.

"Do you like doing dishes?" his mother asked.

"No," she replied. "I hate doing dishes, Mrs. Bentley, but I'll still help."

"Kind of you. But I hate doing dishes myself, so let's leave them for the boys and their dad," she said, tossing down the dish cloth.

"You boys have kitchen duty," she said as she passed through the living room. "Come along Sade, we're going up to my sitting room."

"You've been seeing my Denny for a while, haven't you?" she asked as they settled into chairs in a cozy little room beside her bedroom.

"Ye-es. A few months," Jessica answered uncertainly.

"I thought so. He's been different for a while, softer, and I thought there was a woman involved, but he never really said."

"He never brings anyone to a birthday dinner," Sade said, looking around absently as if she had misplaced something. She finally latched onto a piece of paper and started drawing quick lines.

"Sade's right. Denile will drop by with a friend for a casual hello, but he never brings females to any formal family function. So, you understand, we are very excited about this," his mother said.

"Maybe he's starting a new trend," Jessica said.

"Possible, but I don't think so," his mother replied, and reached across to take the paper Sade was waving at her. She looked at it closely and chuckled.

"No, I really don't think so," she said, passing the paper to Jessica.

It was a simple line drawing of the dinner table, but the only two faces distinguishable were hers and Denile's. They were looking at each other, and her face went hot when she saw the expression on her face. She was looking at him as if she hadn't eaten for days and he was her favourite meal. Then she focused on his face and her breath hitched. His gaze was smoldering. She wouldn't have thought so much could be conveyed in a few penciled lines, but the naked desire on his face was unmistakable. She closed her eyes in embarrassment, while his mother continued chuckling.

"Such amazing bones," Sade murmured. Jessica looked at Denile's mother and burst into laughter. Sade was once again staring at her face as if trying to memorize it.

Marrion took a discreet look at the other people seated at their table. Except for the mayor of DC and his wife, she recognized no one else. There was an attractive young couple who appeared to be completely engrossed in each other, which was a rare sight in the nation's capital. She didn't see a ring, but they were obviously beyond the dating stage. The other two occupants seemed to be unattached and had probably been placed there to even out the numbers. One was a young black man, the other an older woman. It didn't take long for the mundane and sporadic conversation to turn to politics.

"Bit of a shocker, wasn't it? That drug habit that was just uncovered," the mayor said. His jovial tone seemed to say it really wasn't such a shock after all.

Marrion lowered her eyes and prayed that her husband would let the comment pass. Her prayer was in vain.

"A shock, yes, as was the other one. And they almost made it to the primaries with those blots against their names. Suppose they had won? The American public would then be looking at an addict or someone who accepts bribes as a potential president. It is a cause for concern, isn't it?" he said grimly.

"Are you suggesting, Senator Welch, that there should be a system in place for officially checking into the past of potential presidential candidates?" asked the young man who'd only just managed to drag his attention from his companion. He had an odd mix of features, some Latino, some Black, some Oriental, some Caucasian. It was impossible to tell his nationality. The senator, who was on his fourth glass of wine, fixed his gaze on him. The gaze wasn't as alert as it should have been, bearing as it did the weight of the three double-martinis he'd swallowed in the cocktail bar before turning to wine at the table.

"I don't see why not," he responded somewhat belligerently. "A lot less money would be spent on campaigns if we had some checks in place. Why start out a campaign with seven candidates, if a thorough background check would take the number down to three? You mount a different kind of campaign when numbers are small. By all means, let's have everybody checked out before they run," he said with an expansive wave.

"And what would they find in your past, Senator Welch?" asked the young lady, who had been quiet until then.

"No wild parties where you smoked a little dope? Not even in college?" she said with a mischievous smile.

Barry J smiled hazily back at her.

"You forget—my father was a politician while I was in high school. I didn't have the option of smoking dope, even if I had wanted to. It would not have reflected well on the Senator. Luckily, I didn't want to," he told her.

"Oh. How horribly boring. No parties. How about girls. No offense, Mrs. Welch, but you must have had that one hidden girlfriend you knew your father wouldn't approve of. You know, sneak out to go snowmobiling with her when father was away. Skinny dipping, that sort of thing. Not that it would make good scandal material, but at least it would make you human, not half-saint," she responded with a light laugh.

The subject of girls seemed to sober the senator. When he next spoke, his words were measured with care.

"I'm from a political family, and I was taught early to always think of how my actions would affect the other members of the family. I wouldn't sneak around, because if someone found out and told my father, I'd have been grounded for years. It made better sense to find a mate early, and I did." He reached over and picked up Marrion's left hand.

"I not only married early, I entered public life early. I didn't have time to do anything foolish before I started my political career and had too much sense to do so afterwards. Of course, my father had instilled a deep sense of moral responsibility in me. There was just no room for the kind of character traits required for some of these appalling behaviours to take root," he said, sounding as if he was at a rally.

"No vices! Wow. Must be nice, and so unusual in the world of politics," said the young woman, before turning her attention back to her young man. The young black man looked up from the phone he had been checking.

"I'm not sure that I agree with you, Senator. People do sometimes do things that wouldn't stand up well to public scrutiny, but don't have any real bearing on their ability to lead. If you had been sneaking around and smoking dope with an unsavoury girlfriend at eighteen, I see no reason for that to stop you being a candidate for the presidency. We like to talk about the public's right to know. What about your right to privacy?" he asked.

"When you become a public figure, you forfeit your right to privacy," the senator admonished.

"Senator Welch, do you really believe the public needs to know about every mistake a politician made before he entered the political arena?" he asked, looking astonished.

"They may not *need* to know, but they have the right to know if they want to," Senator Welch responded, but beginning to sound unsure. He looked around as if trying to figure a way off the spike he had climbed onto.

"I'm glad there is one presidential candidate who believes in complete transparency. I don't agree with you, but it is good to hear. I rather liked the fellow who turned out to have a drug habit. I might not have voted for him after finding out, but I think it was a mean-spirited thing for someone to send that picture to the media. No doubt it was sent by someone who holds views similar to yours, Senator Welch, but there must have been a better way to handle the situation. If he's as unstable as the article implied, this scandal could end up pushing him over the edge into an overdose," the man said.

The Senator's words were measured, and a fine sheen of sweat glistened on his forehead. "It may have been mean spirited, but the person who sent that picture did the American public a very large favor," he said, reaching for a handkerchief.

"Well, right or wrong, the public knows now," said the mayor. "Do you also object to the bribery scandal then Sir?" he turned to the man with a twinkle in his eyes.

"No, not in the same way," he was told. "The bribe was taken to further a political career, and that would likely continue on a larger scale if he was in a position of higher authority. I just hope that whoever gave the information to the papers had the right motive."

The rest of the dinner went by without further reference to the scandals, and Marrion tolerated the senator's exaggerated gallantry as he held her chair and clasped her elbow in unnecessary solicitude as they exited the banquet hall.

She glanced at their table companions, also making their way out. They hadn't introduced themselves, and no one had asked who they were. She understood why her husband and the mayor hadn't asked. They would not have wanted to expose their ignorance if it turned out that they were people they should have known. Perhaps they were all acquainted and had not needed to introduce themselves to each other. But it was odd, if they knew each other, that they had not addressed one another directly even once throughout the evening. She couldn't recall the other woman saying a single word, but then, neither had she, was Marrion's final thought.

CHAPTER SEVENTEEN

Janelle Christy hurried through the doors of the Washington Post and dropped down at her desk. She was so tired she was almost shaking. For the second night in a row she'd gotten no sleep. Her five-year-old son was battling the worst asthma attack he'd ever had, and she had spent the entire night sitting by his bed with a nebulizer and prayers. As if that wasn't enough, the sitter was late, and her boy indulged in a pitiful, wheezy crying jag when she said she had to leave. She scrubbed at her eyes and pressed the heel of her palms against them. She just had to get through the next few hours, and then she'd head back home.

Her bleary eyes passed over the package without registering it. Then she backed up, and her heart started pounding. Another package! It didn't look like the last two, but she ripped it open as the effects of the sleepless nights wafted away like smoke. It was a USB key, and she stuffed it into her computer and leaned forward with

195

gleeful eagerness. If she kept getting these packages her career would be soaring before long. It was an audio file, and she was almost salivating as she plugged in her headphones.

"Senator Welch, do you really believe that the public needs to know about every mistake a politician made before he entered the political arena?" a male voice asked.

"They may not need to know, but they have the right to know if they want to."

She didn't recognize the voice of the person asking the question, but there was no mistaking the senator's well-known voice. She listened to the end. She was a bit disappointed that there was nothing incriminating on the recording, but it would make a great follow-up article on the other two. When she checked her emails, there was a picture of the senator and his wife, and the mayor and his wife sitting beside each other at a table. The caption said it was at an awards dinner at the Ritz the previous night, where the recording was made.

She made short work of the article, first calling the mayor to verify that he had attended the dinner and get his take on the senator's comments. Once he'd authenticated the recording, she took the copy to her editor. He approved it, front page for the next day. She submitted it and exited the building. She had done a full morning's work in under an hour. She spared a passing thought to the source of the material and the reason they were being sent to her, then gave a mental shrug. The mayor had been a bit concerned because no media personnel had been invited to the dinner. She had simply told him the truth. Her source was anonymous.

Senator Welch and his wife sat in silence at the breakfast table. She played with half of a grapefruit while he reached for the paper and a cup of coffee. He stared, stupefied at his image and the headline screaming at him: SENATOR HOLDS HIGH MORAL GROUND. He quickly swallowed the mouthful of coffee.

The Senator from Maine who holds the number one spot in the polls, thinks the government should institute a system that will automatically run a deep background check on everyone who enters the presidential race. This comes on the heels of the problems disclosed in the conduct of two other Republican candidates.

"When you become a public figure, you forfeit your right to privacy," the senator says. As one who has never done anything that would cause the public concern, this unusually virtuous politician would not object to having his earlier life put under an investigator's microscope. Our Mayor, who listened while Senator Welch aired these astonishing views, said that he is to be commended for his willingness to embrace transparency. It is not the most common thing here on the hill . . .

With a strangled sound he looked up at his wife, who was staring at the half-eaten grapefruit.

"Have you seen this?" he ground out. She looked up.

"No, I haven't read the paper yet." He threw it at her, and without a word she quickly read the article.

"Is there a problem? It seems to be quite well-written, and it sounds correct. Did they misquote you?" she asked in puzzlement.

"No, it all seems to be very disturbingly correct," he said as he got up and strode from the room. He had barely made it to the study when the phone rang.

"ARE YOU OUT OF YOUR MIND?" his father yelled at him. "This is the kind of stupid audacity that will cause someone to go scraping layers off your background. Why would you to do something so idiotic?"

"I don't know, Sir. One minute we were having a light chat, and the next we were talking about the candidates who'd dropped out. I don't know where any of the rest came from, and I don't know how this reporter got the information. As far as I know, there was no one from the media present."

"Are the quotes correct?" he demanded.

"Yes, I believe they are."

"You aren't sure?"

"Well, some parts are a bit fuzzy, but Marrion just read it and appeared to think it was correct. She'd have said so if there had been any errors."

"Drunk. You were drunk! You stupid sod! I've told you and told you. Don't take more than a glass of wine in public, but of course that means nothing. I've done everything possible to clear your way to the presidency, but if you choose to bury yourself with alcohol induced blathering, don't expect me to dig you out. I've bailed you out enough, and I won't be doing it again."

The phone slammed down, making the senator's ear ring. He slowly replaced the receiver and leaned on the desk. He reviewed the evening, trying to focus on the people at his table. Could one of them have been a reporter? He had assumed they were there courtesy of the mayor and had paid them little attention. Still, they had led him into the conversation, hadn't they? Or was it the mayor? Who had brought up the subject?

"Marrion!"

She walked into the study with a look of surprise on her face. The look was justified—he had never yelled for her in over twenty years of marriage.

"You called?" she asked in calm, quiet tones, the exact opposite of his agitation.

"Don't patronize me. Did you drink anything at that dinner?"

"About a quarter of a glass of wine. Why?" she asked, with open curiosity.

"I want to know how clearly you recall the evening. Who brought up the subject of background checks?"

"I believe you did, dear. The mayor commented on the two unfortunate candidates who'd just been ousted by the media, and you used that as the launching pad for airing your views," she told him.

"Why didn't you stop me? Why do you think I take you to these functions? It's obviously not for your rapier wit," he said with scornful disgust.

"Why would I have stopped you? You weren't exactly making a fool of yourself, were you? You have always taken a moral stand, so your comments can't be seen as unusual to anyone. What is your objection to the article?"

He waved an impatient dismissal, but his face tightened at the small, enigmatic smile on her face as she turned away. Could she have . . . ? No. Lars would have known if she'd had left home with a recording device on her—plus she would not have dared.

December the twelfth started out bright and sunny with temperatures in the low forties. Marrion left home to keep a hair dressing appointment and came out of the salon to face sleet. The temperatures had dropped below freezing and the drive home was nerve wracking. She pulled into the garage and entered the house with her teeth just about getting ready to chatter and was hanging up her coat when the doorbell rang. She let the FedEx driver into the foyer while she signed for the package. It was a small box, addressed to her, and she idly wondered if one of the kids had sent an early Christmas present.

"Here, I'll open that for you," Lars' syrupy voice came from behind her as she closed the door. She handed over the package without a fuss. She knew her kids would have sent something that would pass the Lars' test.

She stared in puzzlement at the small piece of metal that fell out. It was a police shield, reading "Chief of Police" on the front. On the back was a Fraizers Gap stamp. She picked it up and looked closely at it. It looked real. For perhaps the first time since she'd met him, she voluntarily addressed Lars.

In genuine bewilderment she asked, "Why would the Police Chief send me his badge? Isn't it owned by the department?"

He gave her an intense look.

"You should know that better than I would, I'd think," he said.

For once his sarcasm barely registered.

"I don't believe I've ever met the man, so why on earth . . . "

She turned the badge over in her hands and peered at it again.

"Is it real? It looks real enough, but it isn't exactly shiny is it? It looks like it was kept in a dusty drawer and the owner didn't bother to give it a rub before sending it off." She absently ran her finger over the surface, then glanced at the still bulky package.

"What else is in it?" she asked, marveling that she was having what could pass as a conversation with Lars. He silently reached in and pulled out something wrapped in layers of bubble wrap.

She stared in fascination at the intricate model yacht done in crystal. It picked up the overhead lights and sparkled in a rainbow of colours changing every time it was moved.

"It's beautiful," she breathed in awe. She cradled it gently and briefly scanned the paper that was still stuck to the bubble wrap. She left Lars standing in the hallway and took her crystal treasure up to her room. Only as she created a place for it on her dresser did she remember that she'd left the shield and the note in the foyer.

Over dinner the senator kept giving his wife sideways glances. He desperately wanted to bring up the package but thought it best to wait for her to broach the subject. He was getting agitated when desert arrived and she'd said nothing. Finally, he gave her a nudge.

"How was your day, Marrion? Did you go out at all? Nasty bit of weather we are having. Hope you stayed off the roads," he said, sweetness and concern dripping from his voice.

She looked up at him in open astonishment, and he coloured slightly. It had been years since he'd taken the time to ask about her day. Her shocked expression gave way to suspicion, but she answered with her usual equanimity.

"I went out for a bit earlier, before it started, but once I made it back in, I didn't go back out." She was tempted to stop there but thought it prudent not to make him have to ask outright about the package. He'd find some way to make her life difficult if she did.

"I got a package today. It had the shield for the Chief of Police of Fraizers Gap and a model boat in it. I'm not sure why he sent me a gift, but the boat is very pretty. Is he allowed to give away his shield? Isn't it town property?" she asked, reaching for her spoon.

"I believe it is. We might have to give it to Father to return. Why do you think it came from the Chief? Someone else could have sent it, you know," he said.

"True, but the badge was wrapped in a sheet of paper with the letterhead of the Fraizers Gap Police Department. There was a note, signed by the Chief."

"What did the note say?" he asked.

"It wasn't a note exactly, more a bit of prose. Something about the boats of the meek not springing a leak, but the boats of the proud going down in something or the other sound, and the badge should be worn with pride by those with nothing to hide. Do you have a new chief in the Gap? I never met the old one, but he never found it necessary to send me a gift. I was wondering if this is a new one and he's added us to his Christmas list. He did add a holiday wish to the note." She told him all this while applying herself to the superb torte Cook had prepared.

"Where's the note?" he demanded, ignoring her questions.

"On the table in the foyer, with the badge. Either that or Lars has them. The boat is in my room. It is really quite spectacular. Should we call to thank him, or will a card suffice?" she asked, deferring to his superior knowledge of how things should be done in his hometown.

"Don't worry about it. Either Father or I will take care of it," he said as he shoved away from the table. His composure started to crack as he hurried into his study. This time it was he who called.

"I think you'd best come to the Capitol," he said when his father answered. "We have a bigger problem than we originally thought." He hung up the phone and fingered the note that Lars had given him when he walked out of the dining room. The paper was new, yet the name of the Chief of Police was one who had left office years ago. Right letterhead, wrong name, and a signature that he would have sworn was authentic, if he hadn't known that the person was long dead. How did they get the paper? Could the current Chief of Police be involved?

CHAPTER EIGHTEEN

"Come on in and take a load off," Brandon told them as Denile and Jessica arrived at the door. Reena had decreed that it was time to have a party—but not just any party. This was no jeans and sweater do. She glided into the living room in a sparkling red jumpsuit that clung and flowed at the same time. She inspected Denile's immaculate sports blazer and sharply creased dress slacks and pronounced him passable. She turned her eyes on Jessica and moved in for a closer look.

Jessica grinned at Denile and turned a slow pirouette.

"Will I do, Madame?" she asked.

Reena continued to peer at her. Square neckline, long tapered sleeves and a simple box cut produced a knee-length dress that would not look like much on a hanger. On Jessica, it was a work of art. It was brown and brown and brown—three different shades in tiny alternating checks. Reena was trying to figure out if the shades were

204

the result of just colour or if some of them were textured. She finally gave in and gave the sleeve a rub.

"This material is the work of a genius. We'll have to talk later about where you find these little bits of niceties," she said as she finally allowed them into the room.

JC shook his head.

"What were you going to do if you didn't like their clothes? Send them back home? It isn't polite to treat your guests this way," he told her.

"They aren't guests. The guests aren't supposed to arrive until 8:30. You will note that it is only 6:20 now. If you don't stop complaining, I won't bring out the anti-pasta tray I prepared for us. The caterers are coming at 8:15, but I thought you might like something to nibble on while we talk about our beloved senator. Just so you know, I ordered some of your favourite olives for it, and some of that rank goat cheese you love so much. Think about that before you voice your next comment," she said and nodded her head when JC remained silent.

She plopped the platter down and eased her sparkles into a chair.

"So what's the latest on our dear senator?" she asked, flexing toes painted the exact shade as her attire, sparkles included.

"Both the Iowa and Wyoming Caucuses will be held in two weeks, and the New Hampshire primary the week after. The Welches plan to let his number one opponent go through the Iowa and Wyoming Caucuses, but he'll be instructed to withdraw the day after the Wyoming Caucus and endorse Senator Welch. Once he's removed, the senator will be guaranteed a win, and Super Tuesday will clinch his nomination as the Republican presidential nominee."

"How will they force him to withdraw?" JC wanted to know.

"A small matter of an illicit weekend with an old sweetheart while his first wife was still alive," Denile said quietly. JC made a face.

"Sex, drugs, bribes, rape, murder. What haven't these candidates gotten themselves involved in?" he asked with disgust.

"In defence of the former governor, this wasn't planned sex. It seems that he was going through a very rough time. His wife had been ill for several years, and he'd just been told that the end was imminent. He didn't leave home to spend a weekend with someone. He was away from home, possibly on business, ran into an old friend, and told her about the situation while crying into his beer. She comforted him, and he had no more contact with her until two years after his wife passed away.

"If fact, from what we can gather, old Daddy Welch has no proof that there was any actual sex. He can prove that they were there and can place them in the governor's room, but he has no way of knowing what happened once they closed the door. He's planning to appeal to the general tendency of people to assume the worst, and they certainly will."

He looked at their faces.

"Compared to the other contenders, I'd say he has the best morals, even if he fell once. It's obvious that he wasn't generally unfaithful, or they would have more material to use as leverage. As it is, they are going to have to put the right spin on this for it to have enough impact to force a withdrawal."

"What do we do about it?" Jessica asked.

"Very simple solution. If they can spin it, so can we," Reena replied. "I say we get to the man before they do and suggest a calculated risk. Go public before they do it for him."

"Will he believe us, though? They have evidence; we don't. Why would he believe that we know anything about his weekend with some unknown woman?" Brandon asked.

"Not unknown. His current wife," Denile said with a sly smile. "Wife number one was his college sweetheart. Wife number two was his high-school sweetheart. We have the same information that the Welches have, and it seems that over the years, our good governor has only had his name linked with two women."

Brandon gave him an incredulous look.

"Surely you jest. Two women? How . . . saintly," he murmured, sounding faint. "By all means, let's make him president. The man either has a will of iron and the morals to match or an unusually low libido. Either way, he has my vote," he said, dodging Reena's hand as it swiped by his head.

"Okay, that's settled then. Let's get this party started," Reena said, jumping up and giving Brandon a narrow-eyed glare.

"Oh, by the way, what exactly is Super Tuesday?" she asked, slinking and twinkling across the room.

Once again, JC supplied the information.

"It's a Tuesday when a large number of states simultaneously hold their primaries. I think it's planned for mid-February for this election," he told them absently as if he was thinking about other things. He shook his head and carefully selected an olive from the platter.

"It's a sad world we are living in," he said, popping the olive into his mouth. "Very sad."

Jessica collected the packages from the car's back seat and made her way to the Bentley's front door. She hesitated on the porch as tears stung her eyes. This would be the second Christmas without her mom. It promised to be more bearable than the last, but still, it hurt. Her mom had loved the holidays, and her throat clogged to think they would never share another. She took a deep breath and rang the doorbell.

Lue opened the door and pulled her inside. He passed her packages off to Sade—who looked as if she didn't quite know what they were—and pulled Jessica into his arms. The bear hug brought the tears closer to the surface, and she clung tenuously to her control. He released her, cupped her face, placed a gentle kiss on her forehead, then took her hand and led her to the kitchen.

"Here's Jess, Mom. She could use some hot chocolate," he said, and led her to a chair. Sade wandered past the door, arms still loaded with packages. With a loud sigh, Lue went to relieve her of them.

"My Lue. He's always believed that hot chocolate cures everything. Well, here's your chocolate love, but remember, it's alright to be sad. You loved your mom, and missing her is exactly as it should be. In time you'll know that it's alright to be happy without her, but till then, consider the pain a tribute to her. She was worthy of your love, and love brings pain."

Jessica wrapped her hands around the mug and let the tears drip off her cheeks. When the door chime announced more people were arriving, Mrs. Bentley passed her a wet paper towel.

"Mop it up, dear. You can cry some more later, but for now, go make sure that Sade has set the table with forks, not paintbrushes."

Jessica smiled as she wiped her face and started for the dining room. She stopped and stared in astonishment at the table. Extra leaves had been added, and it now had seating for eight. Sade had fashioned a remarkable centrepiece from pinecones, pine needles and holly. It flowed over the middle of the table, not taking up much room, but capturing the eye. The napkins stood up in perfect fans, and not a single fork was missing. Sade stood at one side, frowning at the table.

"Why are there so many glasses?" she asked.

"Ah . . . water, red wine, white wine, juice?" Jessica suggested uncertainly.

"Oh, I know what they are for, but why do we need so many? Nobody drinks red and white wine at the same time. Why can't we have just one wine glass, and whatever you drink, you put in that glass? And if you are drinking wine, you don't usually bother with juice, so why have an extra glass for that? Just pour your juice in the glass that other people use for wine. They crowd the table. Can't get any real symmetry with so many glasses."

She moved as if to start removing them, and Jessica hastily headed her off to the living room. She glanced back at the perfect table and smiled. An arm snaked around her waist and pulled her back. Before she could speak, she was in the den with the door closed and smothered in a hug. She clung to Denile's warmth as contentment seeped through her. It was going to be a wonderful Christmas.

The day after the Iowa Caucus, Milford Rube, former governor of California, took off his glasses and massaged the bridge of his nose. It was a small victory, but not bad. Of the thirty-four potential delegates, he'd won sixteen. Still second place, but a strong showing, almost a tie. It really came down to him or Welch. The two remaining candidates had not won any delegates and, realistically, were not expected to.

He leaned back and closed his eyes, trying to banish the mild headache that was throbbing behind his eyes. He slowly opened them when his wife walked in. He observed the worry on her face, and the headache intensified.

"What's the matter, dear?" he asked. His wife was not given to worrying. She held out an embossed invitation card, but it was not an invitation.

Former Governor Milford Rube and wife are cordially invited to an audience with Signorina Marcioni. In the interest of fending off potential gossipers, it is suggested that Mrs. Rube meet and escort Signorina Marcioni to your residence.

You want to be president, and my colleagues and I have no objection to that. There are some who do however, and intend to make public certain information regarding what appears to be an indiscretion with the current Mrs. Rube while the former Mrs. Rube was alive. There is evidence, there is what can be perceived as proof, and there is a way to nullify it.

We are willing to help take the teeth out of this particular shark so the public bite will be less damaging. Signorina Marcioni will be in the hotel lounge at 10:00 AM. We strongly urge Mrs. Rube to present herself there to escort her to your domicile.

The morning's vague throb was now an insistent pounding behind his eyes. He reread the card, noting the hotel's name and address at the bottom, and then read it again. The information remained the same. He raised anguished eyes to his wife.

"What should we do?" he asked, more to himself than to her.

"I'll collect the Signorina and find out what she wants. I don't see that we have much choice. At least it didn't just show up in the papers," she said with practical calm. He stood and held her tightly, seeing his dream disappear in a cloud of undeserved ridicule and censure. He didn't believe her when she whispered that they would be alright.

"Thank you for seeing me," the confident young woman said as she strolled into his study, her long black curls bouncing.

"I was not aware that we had a choice," he replied, facing her. She didn't offer to shake hands, for which he was grateful. He had an overwhelming urge to slug her, and he was not a violent man.

"I know," she smiled at him. "You probably want to knock my teeth out, but at least listen first."

He reddened at her accurate assessment of his state of mind. She pulled a sheaf of papers from the bag she carried and handed them to him. Copies of his hotel bill for that long-ago weekend. Copies of his wife's hotel bill for the same time. Although it was a bit grainy, there was no mistaking him and his present wife sitting at a table in the hotel lounge. Nor could the identity of the two people entering his room be doubted. The time at the bottom of the photograph said 2:52 AM. He closed his eyes and passed them to his wife.

Her eyes were clear, and her head high when she returned them to their guest.

"Why are you here, Ms. Marcioni? If you just wanted to shock us, and you have, you could have simply sent these to us. If you wanted to ruin Rube's campaign, you would have sent them to the press. I assume you want something else, but I can't divine what it could be."

"I want your husband to have a fighting chance at being his party's presidential nominee. I also want you to be prepared. What I just showed you are copies that have come into my hands by means I will not disclose. You will be receiving better copies sometime later today, with a threat to make them public if you don't voluntarily withdraw from the race. I want you to refuse to withdraw," she replied, her tone grim and determined.

"You want me to refuse? We'll be named in public as adulterers, my wife will be held up to ridicule, and no matter what we do, no one will believe we are innocent. And we are."

"No offence, Sir, but you are both guilty of appearing adulterous, even if, as you say, you are innocent. Unless you plan to give up politics entirely, you need to fight this. If you let this threat force you out now, whoever has this information will always be ready to use it whenever it is decided that you need to be checked in whatever you are doing. Don't fool yourself by thinking this is a one-time thing. It will forever be hanging over your head."

"She's right, Rube. I refuse to live with this over my head, and you should too. We are innocent, and we'll both suffer for it if we don't deal with it."

"Good," said the guest, not giving the former governor a chance to speak. "Here's what I suggest we do."

Janelle Christy pounced on the plain white envelope on top of her cluttered desk. She knew what every piece of paper in the untidy heap was, and this envelope was not there when she left the day before. She ripped it open, her excitement mounting. Whoever had singled her out to receive these little gems was doing wonders for her career. She vaguely wondered if she would be required to pay for it later, as she scanned the embossed invitation.

"How odd," she murmured as she started rearranging her day to accommodate an evening at a television studio. If the sender of her little stories said she'd be granted access to the interviewees and interview transcripts, who was she to say no? She would be there with camera and recorder, and hope for a juicy story. A nice scandal always boosts sales.

CHAPTER NINETEEN

"Amyotrophic Lateral Sclerosis. ALS. I can still remember the doctor's face when he told us. He hadn't yet seen his thirtieth birthday, young, fresh-faced, and worried. He looked as if he expected me to deck him as he went on about neurodegenerative disorders, but I didn't know enough about the disease to harbour that desire. Two days later, I was better informed and feeling murderous enough that I probably *would* have decked him if he'd been there," Milford Rube said with wry amusement.

"Wanted to shoot the messenger, did you?" asked the young woman doing the interview. She was as young and fresh-faced as the doctor he'd described.

"What did you learn about the disease?" she asked.

"A lot of people know it as Lou Gehrig's Disease. Lou Gehrig was a New York Yankees baseball player who was diagnosed with the disease in the 1930s. The disease destroys the motor neurons or nerve cells that control your muscles' movements. The neurons send signals to the muscles so they can move. Once there is no more signal, the muscles stop moving, and you become paralyzed. The really scary thing is that this doesn't just apply to muscles that you use to walk and lift things. It also affects the muscles you use to swallow and breathe, so after a while, it is truly debilitating."

"How old was your wife when she was diagnosed?"

"She was forty-seven years old, and had enough vitality to live forever," he said quietly.

"When did you first know that something was wrong?"

"We were slow to catch on. One of the things we did together was to take an evening stroll. No matter where we were, we always made time to walk together at the end of the day. It gave us a chance to catch up on each other's day and be together without interruptions for a while. One evening her right leg buckled. She said it just suddenly felt weak and wouldn't take her weight. Then she started dropping things. Then the other leg gave out one evening.

"You have to understand that this didn't happen one thing right after the other. Weeks would go by with nothing happening, then there would be an isolated incident. We were out with a friend whose wife was a medical doctor, and Lynda fumbled with her wine glass a few times. He must have mentioned it to his wife. She called the next day and asked a few questions, then gently suggested a series of tests. ALS became the focus of our lives when the test results came in."

"How long was she ill?"

"Three and a half years. She went from jogging three miles every day to doing a short ten-minute walk to slowly easing her way down the front walkway to the gate and back. She went from gripping a tennis racket and delivering a ferocious serve to having to concentrate on getting her hand to pick up a piece of toast. And once she had picked it up, there was no guarantee that she could get it to her mouth. She went from enjoying her meals with a healthy appetite to needing throat massages to stimulate swallowing the pureed foods that she was forced to eat because she could no longer chew. She bore it all with grace and stoicism that shamed me. I was barely holding it together." He shook his head, lost in memories.

"She could sometimes force words out, but most times she couldn't talk clearly, so we had to devise different ways of communicating. The day her breathing got so difficult that the doctor said we should prepare for having her hooked up to a ventilator, I lost it. Quietly, you understand. I couldn't curse and swear and rant and rave and kick things, but I did all those things in my mind," he told her, closing his eyes.

"And she knew," he continued, pinning her with a stark gaze. "What you have to remember is that we got married in our very early twenties. When she was diagnosed, we'd been married twenty-four beautiful years. Her response to the diagnosis was 'glad I got started on the good things early.' We'd been together for a long time, and she knew me well. She understood that I was slowly going out of my mind, so she sent me on a bender," he said with that wry smile.

"You're joking, right?" the interviewer asked uncertainly.

"Not at all. I didn't even qualify as a social drinker, so a bender for me would have been about three beers. But what she communicated was that I should go out and get drunk for both of us. It was a joke, because, as I said, I was no drinker, but she thought I needed to get away, so she convinced her sister to book me into this very quaint inn up in the Hamptons." His smile was vague and edged with pain.

"Once I got there, I didn't know what to do with myself, so I sat at the bar and nursed a beer. For six hours. Finally, the bartender reached over and took the mostly full glass of warm beer from me and led me to an alcove with a coffee table and a comfortable armchair. He brought me a non-alcoholic drink of some kind. I don't know what it was, but it was a strange green colour and fizzed a bit. I took a sip and closed my eyes. Only then did I realize that I was crying. I don't know how long the tears had been cascading down, but once I became aware of them, I also realized that I couldn't stop. I drained the glass and went to my room. I couldn't work up the energy to care that the people around thought I was drunk. I cried through the night and halfway through the next day." He paused briefly, then continued.

"That night, I ordered dinner, but couldn't eat it. I repaired to the bar. The same bartender from the night before looked at me and handed me an imported beer in a bottle. I downed it in one long drink, and would probably have had a dozen more, but he pushed the same green fizzy drink from the previous night in front of me. I swallowed that too. He followed with a glass of water. I drank it down in one long gulp. He kept me supplied with various liquids, and I drank them all, though I tasted none of them. Turned out, they were all innocuous because I was still distressingly sober at 11:30 PM, but I looked up and thought maybe I was drunk after all. I was sure I was hallucinating." He gave a quick smile.

"I'd loved two women in my life. One was a girl I dated all through high school, and the other was the only girl I dated in college. One of them was at home dying, and the other seemed to be standing in front of me. I squinted my eyes and blinked, but she didn't disappear. She ordered some kind of fruity looking drink, picked up my glass and waved it at the alcove I'd occupied the previous night.

"All right then, Rubiks, let's have it," was all she said when we sat down. The torrent of words poured out the way the tears had the night before, and sometime close to 3:00 AM, she took both glasses to the now-closed bar and said, 'You need to sleep.' She walked ahead of me to my room, took the key from me and opened the door." He was silent for a moment.

"Did I break my marriage vows? It depends on your interpretation. If you consider having someone undress you as if you were a child and tuck you into bed as breaking vows, then yes, I did. I wouldn't agree with your assessment, because I was asleep before she'd fully pulled the covers up to my chin, but there you have it," he said with that same vague smile.

"It wasn't until I woke up late in the morning that I started to wonder where she'd come from and where she'd slept. It turned out, she was booked into the same inn, for the same three nights, and had watched me cry myself out on the first night.

"Well, that's two nights accounted for, and yes, I spent the next day with her, assaulting her ears about the unfairness of life and my feelings of impotence and helplessness in the face of my wife's suffering.

"Did she spend the night in my room? A good portion of it, for certain. It was only fair to let her get a word in about her own life, after having spent an entire day and parts of two nights nattering in her ear about my problems.

"When we parted the next day, I felt as if my well of strength had been refilled. I could go on. And I did. For the seven months that my wife lived after that weekend, I coped. I died in small increments every time she had a crisis, but I coped. I don't think I would have been able to if it hadn't been for that weekend."

"Did you tell your wife about the weekend when you got home?" the eager young interviewer asked.

"Of course, I did. I might not agree with anyone who says I'd been unfaithful, but it didn't stop me from harbouring feelings of guilt. She would have known something was bothering me, and it would not have required an expert to deduce it had to be something that happened on the weekend.

"Rather than have her wonder, I told her. I was in the habit of telling her everything. Even if I had been unfaithful, I would not have been able to stop myself from telling her. Some habits are very hard to break," he said.

"Wasn't it a strange coincidence that your high school sweetheart was at the same inn you were booked into?" the interviewer asked archly.

"I've sometimes wondered about that, but whenever I asked her why she was there that weekend, she simply said she'd needed a rest," he answered in a low voice.

"Well, there it is, folks. An inside view of former Governor Rube's weekend in the Hampton's with his high school sweetie while his wife lay at home dying. Stay with us over the short break, and when we return, his current wife will join us and give her views on the subject."

She was calm and poised when she came in, and viewers marvelled that fifty-seven years could sit so lightly on anyone. She graciously shook hands with the interviewer and allowed her husband to seat her on the couch he'd been occupying.

"Tell us, Mrs. Rube, how did it feel to be the other woman?" the interviewer asked, pretending to joke.

"Having never occupied such an unpleasant position, I'm unable to speak about the feelings one may encounter in that state," came the serious and dignified reply.

"You have never told your husband why you were at that particular inn on that particular weekend. We understand that you needed a rest. Would you mind telling us why?" was the leading question.

"I have no objections. After personally looking after my mother for six years, I had just placed her in a nursing home. She had Parkinson's disease and some dementia, some memory loss, and it was a draining experience. I'd then spent a month trying to clear out the house she'd refused to give up. After sorting through papers that included every grocery receipt for the last forty years, I think you'll have to admit that I'd earned a rest," she answered.

"You certainly did. How did you come to pick that weekend and that particular inn?"

"I didn't."

Her husband sat up straighter, and the interviewer leaned forward with anticipation.

"Come now, don't keep us in suspense. Who made the choice for you?" she asked, voice tight with enthusiasm.

"I received a voucher in the mail. It included the round trip fare and three nights lodging, plus all meals at the inn. Attractive as the offer was, I did have other things to do, and I tend to distrust gifts like that. I would have ignored it had it not been for the note in the envelope."

"What did the note say?" The interviewer was almost bouncing in her seat.

"You can read it for yourself. I saved it in case he ever pushed for an explanation. He has asked once or twice, but he's never pushed." The interviewer took the paper and opened it with palpable excitement.

RC needs a shoulder he can trust. Though he hasn't seen you in many years, he considers you a true friend. I hope he's right because he needs one now, one who is not directly connected to our lives. Use the voucher, I beg of you. I fear for his sanity, and I can't help him. Will you? Signed Mrs. Lynda Rube, by the hand of her sister Laura, who, incidentally, objects to this plan.

"May I see that?" the governor asked, and slowly took the proffered paper. Instead of reading it, he slowly ran his thumb over it. He seemed more interested in the paper than the words on it. His voice was hoarse when he finally spoke.

"The paper is from the back of a daily devotional that Laura's daughter bought for Lynda. When she gave it to Lynda, she said, 'I prayed for God to make you better, Auntie, but even if he doesn't, you'll still be alright 'cause Jesus will watch over you.' She was six years old. Lynda cried when she left." He stared off into space, and the interviewer turned back to his wife.

"What did you intend to do when you arrived at the inn?" the interviewer wanted to know.

"Wait to see what developed. I really did need a rest, and if he wasn't there, or was there but seemed fine, I probably would have done just that—rested. I saw him at the bar when I arrived. I changed and had dinner, then sat in the lounge and watched him. He was hunched over his glass as if protecting it, but in over an hour of watching, I didn't see him take a single sip. I actually walked over to the bar intending to speak to him, but I realized that he was crying when I got close. He was just sitting there with tears running silently down his face. He didn't seem to be aware of them. I got a drink and returned to the lounge. When he left to go to his room, I followed. I wanted to know which room he was in, and I wanted to make sure he got there, alright." Her face became pensive.

"I was up early the next morning, and at mid-day, I started to wonder if he had left. He finally showed himself late in the afternoon and wandered around the place.

"When he decided to drown himself at the bar, I decided it was time. I'd had a word with the bartender, so he fed him non-alcoholic drinks. He was never able to handle alcohol, and I didn't want him drunk. When he started looking restless, I made my approach.

"The rest he's already told you," she concluded.

"Why did the note call him RC? Those are not his initials," the interviewer commented.

"Rubik's Cube. That's what we called him in high school, and it got shortened to RC. That's why I assumed the note was authentic. The name didn't follow him to college, so I figured they used it to show they were reaching out to someone from his past."

"Why did you wait two years after your wife's death to seek her out?" The question dragged the former governor back from the past.

"I didn't. I might have coped in the last few months of Lynda's life, but the coping didn't stretch to cover her death. Have you ever lost someone close to you? No? Pray, that you don't.

"No matter how much advance notice you have, you are never prepared. You can tell yourself that you are, but you aren't. I was convinced that I was ready to handle her death, but it still came as a shock. For months I operated in a fog of basic survival. I ate, not because I was hungry, but because I accepted that it had to be done. Taking a shower was a chore. Getting out of bed in the morning seemed a futile exercise, but I did them all because they had to be done.

"I didn't wait to get in touch with her or anyone else. The thought didn't occur to me. I was too busy trying to get through each day without shattering into a million little pieces," the former governor said.

"So when did you decide to look her up?" he was asked.

"I didn't. I took my granddaughter to see The Walt Disney World On Ice performance, and she was there with five kids. I remember thinking, 'what a brave woman.' I was having a hard time keeping up with one, but she seemed to be having no problems. I kept glancing over at the most well-behaved kids in the place, and

223

when the lights came up at intermission, there she was. I was visiting my son, and it turned out she lived in the area. We got to chatting, and here we are . . . " he trailed off. The interviewer wrapped up her segment, and a wide-angled view of the audience showed many wiping their eyes.

CHAPTER TWENTY

Jessica reached for the remote and turned off the TV.

"Well? Do we believe him?" she asked Denile. They had bunkered down in his condo to watch the televised interview.

"We have no way of knowing for sure if it's true, but there's no way to prove otherwise, which is our selling point right now. If we can't prove infidelity, neither can the Welches. I would want to bet that most of the nation watched this expo, and at least ninety percent of them believe they are telling the truth. Would you have believed them if you had simply tuned in to watch without any prior knowledge?" he asked her.

"I think I would have. As far as people know, he has no reason to tell any of this, and the women at least will be touched by the mothering that his current wife seemed to have provided without asking anything in return." She wandered to the kitchen and poured a drink.

"This will leave the Welches spinning in the wind. Anything that shows up in the press now will seem like sour grapes," she said, going to the huge picture window to look at the city lights.

"It will be even harder after tomorrow. The Washington Post will have a front-page spread on the story, we hope, and that will muzzle the senator for a day or two," he said with satisfaction. "He won't have time to do anything before the New Hampshire primary, and we'll have a little surprise for him after that."

"I don't want to talk about the senator. I always end up either depressed or angry when I think about him," she said, shaking her head at her petulant tone. He joined her at the window. Standing behind her, he gently rubbed his hands up and down her arms as she shivered lightly.

"So what do you want to talk about," he asked, nuzzling her cheek.

"Your mother. You said her birthday is coming up soon, right?" she asked, leaning back into him.

"Yeah. We always book a section of this great pub downtown. We crowd in and hang for a few hours. You are coming, of course?"

"A pub? What does your mom do in a pub?"

"Mostly, she watches us make fools of ourselves. We play pool and tell bad jokes. You know—guy stuff."

"Exactly. Guy stuff. Are you celebrating her birthday or using it as an excuse for a stag party?"

"It's not like that. She loves it. She likes the food there and says the atmosphere makes her feel young."

"Has anyone ever asked if she'd prefer to do something else? I mean, how long has this pub tradition been going on?"

"Since before I could drink. I wasn't allowed to go before then, and of course, Monique is still not allowed to go."

"Fine. Do your stag thing but do something else too. I'd like to do something just for her."

"What do you have in mind?"

"I want to take her and Monique out for a girls day. Go to the spa, get facials, manicures and pedicures. Waxing, eyebrows, full make up. Then hit the salon and get our hair done, and then we'll go shopping for the right outfit for the evening."

"And what's happening in the evening?"

"We are having dinner at the Royal York Hotel. Then we are going to listen to some jazz. Give her a chance to hear some of the stuff she has at home but never gets a chance to play. Then you are going to spring for a decent room at the Royal York with instructions for her and your dad to be served breakfast in their room the next morning. It's her sixtieth birthday. It needs to be different."

He was silent for so long she thought she had offended him. She turned in his arms.

"Did I upset you? I didn't mean to imply that going to a pub is bad. As you said, she enjoys the food and the atmosphere. I just thought . . . "

"Sshhh." He put a finger on her lip. "You're right. I was just thinking about how long we've been doing this without bothering to ask her opinion. Dad started the pub thing long ago, and we've just kept it going. She always wears a cowgirl outfit, right down to the hat. She has a new one all set for this year."

"Tell you what. I'll take her out the day before. Then she can wake up at the Royal York with her husband on her birthday and be served breakfast instead of having to make it. Then she can finish off the day in her cowgirl outfit with the snazzy hat. Start a new tradition and keep the old one intact. I'll leave it up to you to fix this with your family. You are all expected to show up at the Royal York for dinner and be properly amazed at her outfit. I'll let you know the time after I've booked."

"Yes, Ma'am," he said, giving her a mock salute. He just managed to dodge the cushion she laughingly threw at his head.

"Let's go for a drive," he said, pulling on her ponytail.

"Where would you drive to in the night?" she asked.

"Oh, we can go Downtown and cruise Yonge Street, look at the lights and stores. There's always something happening there, and if there isn't, we'll just look at people. All of Toronto's crazies come out at night," he said with a chuckle.

"If you don't wimp out on me, we can end the night with a nice stroll along the lakeshore," he told her and tossed her a jacket.

"Me. Wimp out? That is going to cost you. It is really, really going to cost you," she said, walking ahead of him to the elevator. When the doors opened, he crowded her in and whispered in her ear.

"Is that a threat or a promise?"

"Former Governor Tells All!!!" the headline screamed.

Senator Welch, his father and Lars were gathered in the senator's study. His father was pacing in short jerky steps from one corner to the other, unable to contain his fury. He threw the paper on the desk.

"How dare he! Who does he think he's dealing with? Does he really think the American people are so stupid that they'll buy a story like that? Ha! I've been in this game long enough to know. What he's done is the height of foolishness. All we need is one person to come forward and say he was at the same inn, and they were seen in a clinch. He can't prove otherwise, and we'll have an eyewitness."

"Do we have one?" the senator asked worriedly.

"Not yet, but it wouldn't take very much to buy one."

"What if the witness turns on us later? People you can buy will happily sell themselves to other people."

"Don't be a fool. I only need the person for a few days, and then he'll disappear. We just have to choose someone who doesn't have a close family to report him missing right away. Later we can point out that he disappeared right after he fingered the former Governor. Let him live *that* down."

"When do we do it?"

"After the New Hampshire primary. He can't win there, so we don't have to worry too much. After the primary, we bring out the witness and start a few rumours about other things—nothing libellous, just vague murmurings that could be true of any politician. Just get folks wondering if anyone could be as squeaky clean as he appears to be. Might even leak he came forward with this sob story

229

because he heard the witness was going to come forward. People have to be wondering why he's chosen to expose himself like that. They will take any reason once it makes sense."

"Why don't we just do it now?" his son asked.

"Because it will have all blown over by Super Tuesday. We want to release this info just a few days before Super Tuesday and bring his character into question when numerous people are getting ready to vote. It's how the game is played," he said, tossing back a quarter finger of Jack Daniel's.

"You need to take Marrion with you when you go out on the campaign route. I understand people are starting to question the absence of your wife and children. They might accept that the kids are in school, but you can't explain away not having your wife with you. She has no job that you can point to, so why isn't she with you? People want to see what the future first lady will look like. Give her some money to get the right clothes, and for heaven's sake, let her choose them herself! She has better sense than you when it comes to what is appropriate. You don't want her at a rally in one of those pasted on dresses you like to pick out for her."

His father swept from the room, and the senator grabbed the glass he'd left on the desk and threw it against the wall.

"So now he's telling me how to run my house?" he growled.

"He is right, you know. You choose her clothes for their sex appeal. She chooses them for elegance. The public will prefer elegance to sex in their First Lady," Lars replied.

"Instead of wasting time analyzing my family, you might want to put some effort into sorting out this mess. If I lose and he thinks you could have prevented it, your life will become as fragile as the glass I just tossed," he told him as they left the study.

In her room, Marrion was so surprised by her father-in-law's comment that she wasn't paying attention to the rest of the conversation. By the time she realized that they had left the study, she could hear footsteps coming to the room. She barely had time to disconnect the device and plug the headphones into the stereo built into the headboard.

"What are you listening to?" her husband asked as he walked through the door. She was so rattled that it took her a second to recognize what she was hearing.

"Spanish. I'm listening to a Spanish lesson," she told him, although it was as much news to her as it was to him. She had bought the 'Learn to Speak Spanish' package more than a year ago and had never used it, except to test the first disc. She'd obviously left it in the stereo.

"You're learning Spanish?" he asked in surprise.

"Not much yet, but I thought I'd give it a try," she answered, knowing that she'd have to actually start on the lessons now. He'd be sure to check on her. He gave her a speculative look and turned towards the closet.

"I'm taking part in a national debate tomorrow. You're coming with me. What will you wear?"

She feigned shock and looked at him in puzzlement.

"You want me to pick out something to wear to a campaign debate?"

"For the love of heaven. You are a grown woman. There's no reason I should have to spend time choosing your clothes," he said testily, as if she had been requesting his assistance all this time.

"Where is this debate to be held?" she asked, voice neutral and calm.

"In New Hampshire, so we aren't talking tropics here. Saint Anselm College. Some of the big networks will be there, so you need to look right."

She strolled to the closet and pulled out a severely cut forest green, knee-length dress with a high neck and long sleeves. Attached to it was a light brown scarf with green accents.

"Here you go. Team it with high heeled, light-brown long boots, and it should work just fine," she said, knowing he would never have picked out something like that. He looked longingly at the array of clingy outfits he had insisted on over the years and glanced at her. She kept her eyes purposely averted. He frowned at the dress.

"Where did this come from? I don't remember seeing it before."

"I've never worn it. Actually, your dad bought it about a year ago on one of our visits to Fraizers Gap. I took him into town, and while he looked after his business, I visited a little boutique that I'd parked in front of. When he came back to the car, he saw me coming out and asked if I'd seen anything I liked. I told him that I had but would get it another time. He insisted on buying it," she told him, hiding her glee as he stalked from the room. She'd get as much mileage as possible out of her father-in-law's unexpected support of the clothing issue.

Senator Welch arrived in the small northern New Hampshire town of Dixville Notch at 11:49 PM the night before the primary. He could have stayed in the car but preferred to stand in the biting wind and greet the residents strolling by. The polling station would open its doors at midnight, and he intended to greet the voters as they entered or exited. The state law said that municipalities with less than one hundred people could vote early, and Dixville Notch had been exercising that right for years. He wanted to be there when the ballots were counted. He was number one in the polls and was confident that he would hold that spot after the last ballot was cast in the state. He'd had a gruelling few weeks, going to each of the fourteen cities, and he was looking forward to a few days rest in Fraizers Gap.

When the results were announced in his favor at 12:06 AM, he gave a short impromptu speech, introducing his lovely wife, who was with him to show solidarity and support and headed to Manchester. He would be there when the polls opened at 7:00 AM.

Decades later, at least it felt like it, Marrion dragged her sore feet up the steps of the Welch's Fraizers Gap mansion. She would have preferred to head straight to the section of the house they liked to pretend was theirs, but her father-in-law was waiting in the foyer. He was beaming.

"Sixty percent of the delegates! Not bad at all, not bad. Now we have to get through Michigan, Nevada, South Carolina, Florida, and Maine before Super Tuesday. You don't have to worry about Maine, but you'll have to put in some time for the others.

"Marrion, my dear, how do you like campaigning? You look a bit tired, but you'll get used to it. It is a good thing you are doing, deciding to join Barry J on the road," he all but shouted.

She struggled not to flinch when he threw an arm across her shoulder.

"Come, we'll have a drink to celebrate before you turn in." It would have been futile to resist, so she asked for a glass of white wine and took tiny sips as they rehashed the day. The doorbell startled them, but Barry J recovered almost instantly.

"That should be Lars. I thought he might be a bit later, but I guess he got started earlier than planned," he tossed over his shoulder as he headed for the door. He flung the door open in time to see the receding tail lights of a vehicle, and Marrion followed her father-in-law to the door.

"Who is it, then?" his father asked.

"I don't know. The person left," he said, waving his arm in the direction the car had gone. The two men seemed oblivious to the box on the porch, but Marrion's eyes were fixed on it.

"Maybe it's a present . . . you know, to say congratulations?" she said in her best timid voice, pointing at the box. The men looked at each other but made no move to pick it up. She nudged it with her toe, and it moved a bit.

"For such a big box, it's not very heavy," she said, nudging it again.

"Stop pushing that," her husband snapped, and she hid a smile in her wine glass. Suddenly she wasn't so tired after all, and the wine had taken on a new mellowness. They held their breath when a car pulled up in front of the gate.

"Why are you all out here?" Lars asked as he unfolded himself from the bucket seat. He sprinted up the steps and stopped when he saw the box. Without a word, he grabbed it and headed for the study. Barrington J. Welch II hurried ahead of him to open the door, and he put the unwieldy box on the floor. Reaching into his back pocket, he pulled out a lethal-looking switchblade and attacked the box.

"Let's hope it's nothing fragile," Marrion thought, but prudently kept silent. She wanted to see what was in it, and anything that reminded them that she was in the room could lead to banishment.

She stared, baffled, at the old bicycle wheel that came to light. It was very old, rusty and twisted. The spokes were bent, and some broken, but jammed in at an impossible angle was a brand new piece of wire. It stood out incongruously against the rusty spokes, and she would have kept staring at it if it wasn't for the continuing silence among the men. She glanced at her husband. He was pasty white, covered in sweat and seemed to be swaying on his feet. She grabbed his arm and led him to a chair so he wouldn't topple.

"I think Barry J is going to be sick," she said loudly enough to penetrate the concentrated silence of the other two. Neither man looked her way, but her father-in-law waved a dismissive hand.

"You can go on to bed, Marrion. I know you're tired. Don't worry about Barry J. It's just a reaction to the stress of the past few weeks. He'll be fine." She slowly backed out of the room, taking her glass with her and wishing this was happening at home so she could listen in. She couldn't even pretend to need something from the library so she could try her old listening spot. She went to bed with

235

the uncomfortable knowledge that something important was happening, and she wouldn't find out what it was.

CHAPTER TWENTY-ONE

Reena was on her back, long, fleece covered legs pointing straight up into the air. She was stretching her back, she had told them when she'd walked in and dropped to the floor. For a while, they glanced at her every few minutes. After fifteen minutes, they ignored her.

"Where's JC?" the question floated up from the floor.

"On his way. He had to officiate at a funeral, and he's a bit behind. You know JC. He's not the type to hurry off if any of the bereaved wants to talk. He'll be here when he can," Denile told her.

"Are we going to start without him then?" she asked, slowly bending and straightening her legs.

"I told him we'd start at five, and we will. But that's still seven minutes away, so feel free to keep stretching," Brandon replied.

At exactly 5:00 PM., Denile walked over to the television and switched it on. A few clicks of the remote and an image sprang to life.

Senator Barrington J. Welch III was sitting in an armchair looking pale and ill. His father walked towards him, a shot glass in his hand. For a second, it looked like it was for his distressed son, who reached for the glass. His father merely looked at him and took a slow sip.

"Perhaps, Barrington, you would care to tell me why a busted up old bike wheel is having this effect on you? You see, this package was delivered to my house. It was addressed to me. Yet I can't seem to put my finger on the reason. But *you* apparently can." He drained the glass.

"I don't care to be in the dark, so I'd advise you to enlighten me. NOW!" He'd been speaking in a quiet, fatherly voice, and when he roared the last word, even Lars flinched. He walked back to his desk and slammed down the glass. Barry J's mouth was working, but no words came out. Finally, Lars spoke up.

"That's how he stopped her," he said almost inaudibly. "He shot a piece of wire through her back wheel. Some of the spokes bent. Some broke. The bike stopped, and she tumbled over the handlebar."

"Is that the actual wheel? From that afternoon?" Barrington J. Welch II asked.

"I don't know. The police picked up the bike, and I never checked what was done with it," Lars replied.

238

"Not that it matters," the older man mused. "Someone somewhere knows about that bike. That is way too much information to have floating around. Lars, find out where this package came from. Tonight." His voice was down to a hoarse whisper when he turned to his son.

"Alright. Who did you tell?" he asked, turning to his son.

"Lars. The only person I have ever mentioned it to was Lars," he said with a shudder. His father looked over at Lars, eyebrows raised. Lars simply shook his head.

"Then the girl or her sister talked. They are both gone, so you will have to start back there and find out who the sister was friends with. You said you checked before, and the girl didn't mention her experience to anyone at school, so it has to be someone in her family that talked. They didn't have relatives, so it would have to be a friend that someone told. Anyone from her parents' generation is probably dead, and I can't see their progeny going to such lengths over a second- or third-hand story from back then," he mused.

He started pacing around the room.

"You can ignore the girl. She was gone soon after this happened, and even if she talked, there is no reason anyone should have connected it to you. Someone in the Gap suspected, and that's who we have to find. Lars? I need to know who it is. And I need to know now." It was a command, even if delivered with quiet calm. Lars gave a quick nod and walked out of the study.

Senator Welch had not moved from his trance-like position in the armchair. Now he slowly extended his hand to his father, holding a small white square. His father grabbed it as he paced by.

Tell your son to withdraw from the primaries and to stop interfering with the other candidates' campaigns.

"Where was it?" he snapped.

"On the outside of the box. It fell off as Lars was bringing it in."

"Lars!" His bellow reverberated through the house.

"Put a watch on Rube and his wife. This is a political move. Someone has given him some information, and he's using this to try to get Barry J out. I want to know everything they do. Who they talk to, when and what about. I want to know what they have for breakfast, who shines their shoes, how many times they empty their bladders. If it happens, whatever it is, I want to know."

Reena lowered her legs and sprang up from the floor.

"That does not sound good," she said. "I think we just turned him loose on the Governor."

"Not really," Denile replied. "He already has a bug on the governor's phone, a bug in his study and a tracking device on his car. The governor knows about them, so he's already careful. We'll have someone watch them both when they leave home, though, and we've planted security persons, a male and a female, among their household staff. With their permission, of course."

"So, what now?" Reena wanted to know.

"Nothing," Denile told her. "We are going to let the good senator stew until Super Tuesday. He'll win a lot, but I suspect that Rube is going to keep pace. The senator won't be in any primaries after that."

"Happy Birthday!"

Mrs. Bentley blew out the lone candle stuck in the slice of chocolate cream cake and sat back with a glow.

"I've always heard the saying 'once a man, twice a child', but aren't you all pushing the onset of my second childhood rather quickly? I mean, now I'm a year old? Good thing I still have my teeth, or you might have gotten me a teething ring!" she said as she dug into the cake, face alight with laughter.

"Don't worry, dear. I'll make sure when the time comes that you get one that you can chill. Get it nice and cold to soothe your gums," her husband said.

"Watch it, old man. Just remember that you were born before me. I'll still be gadding about town while they're changing your diapers," she replied.

"If you know how to gad about, why are you waiting until I'm in diapers to do it?" he asked. "I wouldn't mind doing some gadding about with you," he said, with an exaggerated wiggle of his eyebrows.

She went bright red and nudged her plate closer to him as he grabbed a fork and reached for her cake.

Jessica leaned back and closed her eyes as they pulled out of the driveway.

"Thank you," Denile said softly. She opened one eye.

"You're welcome. But for what, exactly?" she asked, turning sideways so she could see him.

"Taking the time to do this for Mom. It's something a grown-up daughter would think of, and she only has grown-up sons. Sade doesn't count. Most times, she wouldn't remember that there are differences between the genders if Lue didn't remind her."

She started laughing as she remembered his brother's wife. She had shown up to dinner in a gorgeous dress that had to have cost more than most of Jessica's wardrobe, but had stopped to wash out her paintbrushes after getting dressed. She looked great but smelled strongly of turpentine, her hair was uncombed, and there was a purple smudge on her forehead. She smiled vaguely at her mother-in-law, who hustled her off to the ladies' room, frantically searching for a comb.

"She may not be your typical daughter, but she is definitely sweet. And just so you know, she isn't as flaky as she comes across," she chuckled.

"I've never thought she was flaky. Lue wouldn't have married her if she was. But she is rather absentminded unless it has to do with her painting," he replied.

"Did I tell you that she got the dress your mom wore tonight? I told her about the day I was planning, in case she wanted to join us. Of course, she didn't want to come, but she told me not to worry about shopping for an outfit for your mom. She just told me where to show up and what to say when I got there. The dress was already picked out and altered to fit your mom. It was perfect. And pricey!"

"Sade got involved in buying a dress?" he asked in amazement. "Does Lue know?"

"I'm sure he does. If he doesn't, he soon will. She billed it to him, I think. I told your mom, though. She was starting to worry about me footing the bill for the day but was tickled at the thought of Sade choosing her a dress, even if she did it remotely. It was a fun day. I hope she enjoyed herself."

"She did. We went over the breakfast menu and placed her order before she went up, and dad got a special bottle of champagne sent up to their room."

"Good. Monique ordered her flowers to be delivered in the morning. I'm going to see if I can convince Sade to come out tomorrow night. She makes me laugh," she said, remembering the bemused look on Sade's face as her mother-in-law steered her back to the table, hair neatly combed and smelling less pungent.

"You have a very nice family," she told him softly, as sadness washed over her.

"Lanni would want you to be happy," he said. His voice was gentle, and he covered her hand with his where it rested on her knee.

"I know, and she'd be happy that you are sharing your family with me. It's not as if, having discovered the senator, I'd want to share him with anyone!" she said wryly.

"True. We need to be careful, you know. I don't want that man to ever find out about you, so we have to be careful how close you get to him. This next move we have planned is giving me some uneasy moments," he told her quietly.

"Don't worry. Reena's already got everything we need to manage a quick appear and vanish scenario. It will be fun," she said, even though her stomach had become a giant knot.

"But once he has seen your face, what's to stop him finding you?" he wanted to know.

"Oh, we aren't going to show him my face. We are going to show him his daughter's face. Trust me; it will work," she said, patting his knee.

CHAPTER TWENTY-TWO

The air in the Welch household was pulsing; you could almost see the excitement. Marrion dressed with care in a well-tailored skirt suit that screamed elegance. She had spent Barry J's money buying clothes that suited her and that she had every intention of keeping. He was grudging with his praise, and she knew he hated most of them, even if he was forced to admit they suited the purpose.

She walked to her daughter's room and waited while she undid the lock. Lars had barely glanced at her when she arrived, and Marrion was thankful for whatever issue was occupying his mind. Maybe they could get through this week without any incidents.

Jordana looked young, vibrant and very beautiful in the pantsuit her mother had bought for the occasion. She smiled at her mother and hooked her arm through hers as they descended the staircase she had climbed earlier for the first time in over two years.

Senator Barry J. Welch III looked up as his wife and daughter entered the living room. You couldn't tell that the two were related. One tall and blond, the other shorter and dark. Their mannerisms were similar, but you had to observe them over time to know that. His daughter looked like him. They would make a good-looking family on stage. If only his son wasn't so unsightly, he would have ordered him home with his sister. He'd decided that Justin's pimply face would ruin the picture he expected to see on the front page of the next day's paper.

"I've asked Cook to prepare some finger food. I know you said we'd have dinner afterwards, but since we don't know how long that will be, I thought we should eat something before we leave," Marrion said quietly.

Her father-in-law looked up from the laptop balanced on his knees.

"Smart girl. Can't have our next president fainting on stage. Might cause the public to think he's sickly and not be able to serve out his term." He put the computer aside as a maid entered with a loaded tray.

"Fix me a drink, Barry J," he told his son as he heaped a plate with food. "Well, the numbers are still coming in, but as of a minute ago, it was 597 Welch and 461 Rube. He's keeping pace for now, but we'll leave him behind. We'll get the delegates we need to win before long. He must realize that he's just delaying the inevitable and taking up time that would be better used to launch the presidential campaign." He gave a huge belch and downed the drink Barry J had made him. He gestured for another.

"He'll soon see reason. It might be a bit later than we wanted, but he'll withdraw. Met a chap today who thinks he remembers him from a few years ago. Met him in the Hamptons, he thinks." He lifted his glass and saluted his son with an evil grin.

"Wonder if the former governor will remember him?" he murmured as he drained his glass. Jordana looked at her mom, who shrugged to show she knew nothing about the conversation going on around them.

"Friends, ladies and gentlemen, well-wishers—thank you all for coming out tonight. With your votes, I can confidently say that we are moving ahead to great things. We have garnered the largest number of delegates so far and will continue to do so. Our opponents will soon become our supporters as we work together towards a national presidential campaign. My family and I are grateful for your support, and we will continue to work towards maintaining the core values of our country and . . . "

Senator Welch was just hitting his stride when a young woman walked in the door at the back of the room. Ever conscious of the television cameras, he struggled to control breath that was starting to come in gasps, and just managed to keep talking. He stared at the woman in confusion, then swung his eyes quickly to his right to confirm that Jordana was still on stage with him. The woman glanced briefly at him before her eyes moved on as if he was of no consequence. She was standing directly in front of the door, making no attempt to find a seat. He searched frantically for Lars and, when he found him, tried to direct his attention to the woman, using the movement of his eyes. When he looked back, the woman was gone.

His father's hand on his shoulder was bruising, and he used the pain to stay focused, as he supposed his father intended. He quickly wrapped up the speech and didn't wait for questions. He had too many himself. He gave Marrion a quick look as they shook a row of hands on their way out. She was calm and polite and very confident. He was wrong, he decided. She would make a very good first lady.

She didn't say anything as they made their way to the car. Cameras flashed, and a few reporters hurried behind them with questions as he hustled his family into the car. He leaned his head back as Lars pulled into the traffic.

"Cancel the reservation, Lars, and take us home." The command came from the ultra-authoritative father. His son made no objection, and the ride home was completed in silence.

"Find something for you and Jordana to eat, Marrion. We'll take care of ourselves. We have some business to discuss," her father-in-law told her as they walked into the house. She nodded and took her daughter's hand. In her mother's room, Jordana opened her mouth, questions at the ready. Marrion put a finger to her lips, and Jordana's mouth closed impatiently.

"With the number of delegates he has won, your father has a good chance of becoming the Republican presidential candidate. How would you like to live in the White House, love?" While speaking, she adjusted the door to a particular angle and then led Jordana to the dressing table.

"Watch," she whispered, pointing to a corner of the mirror.

"I hear they have a bowling alley," Jordana answered, staring at the spot her mom had indicated. "Would be nice not to have to wait for lanes." Although she was watching closely, she almost missed the movement as Lars carefully peeked in. His head didn't come around the door, but obviously, he was listening to them.

"Did you see the girl who was dressed up to look like you? Your dad's not even president yet, and you already have a groupie!" Marrion said with a light laugh.

"Yeah, that was weird. I thought Dad would try to find out who she was, but maybe it was normal for him. I don't normally go to political rallies, so who knows, maybe they have look-a-likes showing up all the time," she said and started cleaning off her make-up.

"Is there a pool at the White House?" she asked, glancing at her mother. When she turned back to the mirror, Lars' reflection was no longer there. She jumped when her mom touched her shoulder.

"Come," she mouthed, leading her to the bed. She locked the bedroom door and sat beside her daughter. Almost cheek to cheek, she tucked one side of the headphones into Jordana's ear, the other side into hers. Lars had just entered the study.

"What are they saying?" Senator Welch asked.

"They think it was a joke, someone dressed up to look like Jordana. Your wife was teasing her about having a groupie before you even became president. Jordana wants to know if there's a swimming pool at the White House," he answered.

"Good. Best if they think it's a joke. That way, they won't ask any awkward questions, although Jordana won't be able to help saying something about it. I'll pretend its common-place," Barry J said.

"That may work for your daughter, but I want to know who this woman is. If Jordana hadn't been on stage, I would have sworn it was her. It's an ingenious disguise. She had to get a face mask done up with Jordana's face. That means a special order. Probably the same one she wore to the Gap, so it isn't new. Find out who she is, Lars. She was there for one reason only, and that was to rattle Barry J. I want that woman found, and so help me, when I get my hands on her, she'll pray for death," Barrington J. Welch II vowed.

Jordana shuddered at her grandfather's voice, and slowly removed the headphone from her ears. She watched, bemused, as her mother packed them away and locked up the listening device.

"What's going on, Mom?" she whispered.

"I'm not sure. A while back, someone went to Fraizers Gap, pretending to be you and broke into your grandfather's study. That's the person we saw tonight. She's taunting your dad about something, but I'm not sure what. If they don't bring up the subject in the morning, you might want to make a brief comment or at least ask if anyone knows who she is. Your dad will think it odd if you don't."

At her desk, Janelle Christy plugged a USB into her computer. A close-up shot of Senator Welch, his wife, daughter and father popped onto the screen. They were grouped on stage and looked like an ideal first family. She planned to get the story out before the paper was put to bed. It was a big enough story. The senator, having the most delegates so far, looked like he'd be the presidential candidate for the Republican Party. She wondered where the son was. Maybe she could find out what was up with him and use it as a sidebar. If that wouldn't work, she could make it into a regular piece sometime later when things were slow. She made a note of it.

"You've got mail!!!" chimed her computer. She kept scrolling through the pictures from the rally. They were all focused on the stage and showed only a few people in the front row.

"You've got mail!!!" She was tempted to continue ignoring it, but it wouldn't stop annoying her if she did. She impatiently clicked on the icon, planning to cache whatever bit of junk was clogging her system.

It's Jordana Welch. Or, is it????

The subject line caught her eye, and she couldn't resist opening it. There were five pictures. One was similar to the one she had been looking at before the email notification, Senator Welch and his family on stage at the post-Super Tuesday rally. Picture number two was a wide-angle shot of the room, showing the stage and the door. There was a woman standing directly inside the door. Picture number three was a close-up of the woman. Picture number four showed the senator's family looking towards the door. Picture number five was a close-up of their faces.

With a few keystrokes, she had two of the pictures side by side. Wearing different clothes, Jordana Welch was standing in two different places in the same room, at the same time. Janelle Christy hunched over her keyboard and went to work. She would have a sidebar, but it would be the story that most papers would be carrying as headlines.

CHAPTER TWENTY-THREE

"Well, it has hit the fan and is being blown all over the room," Brandon said as he pulled out a chair. They were at the Bentley and Spade table at Cartiers.

"Check out the 'deer in the headlights' look on our senator's face." He unrolled a copy of the Washington Post and spread it on the table. It had made the front page. The centre picture showed the senator and his family on stage looking at his daughter's clone standing at the door. Jordana seemed puzzled. Marrion Welch looked with interest and a hint of amusement. Senator Welch appeared to be awash with fear, and there was no mistaking the anger on the face of his father.

The next picture was a close-up of Jordana at the door staring at the stage, seeming to issue an amused challenge. The third picture was a side by side comparison. Jordana at the door and Jordana on stage. The faces were almost identical. Only the clothes were different.

Senator's Daughter Has Double

Who is the mystery clone of Senator Welch's daughter? That's the question we would like to have answered. The woman, who could be the identical twin of Senator Welch's daughter Jordana, seemed vastly amused by the situation. The look of puzzlement on her face gives the impression that the real Jordana had never seen her double before. Former Senator Welch looked like he would have given the imposter a good hiding if he'd been closer, and Mrs. Welch appeared to find it a trifle humorous that someone looked so much like her daughter. But perhaps she would have been less entertained if she could have seen her husband's face. I'll happily accept correction if necessary, but dare I ask, isn't that open fear on Senator Welch's face?

Now tell me, why would the senator be afraid because someone had gone to the trouble to dress up like his daughter? Of course, we are speculating about the disguise, and it is a superior one, but . . . is it? After all, Jordana Welch is not so well known that there are masks of her face rolling around the city. Someone would have to go to an awful lot of trouble to get one made. So it begs the question. Did someone really go to that trouble, or is it that woman's natural face, and she simply decided to show it? Just a speculative question, but it will be interesting to see what the senator, our strongest advocate of family values, has to say.

When they had all taken a look at the pictures, Brandon put the paper on the empty chair between himself and Denile.

"From the look on his face, I wouldn't want to be in that woman's shoes if old Daddy Welch ever meets up with her," Brandon said grimly.

"No reason he should," Reena answered. "Jessica looks a lot like Jordana, but they are not identical. We recreated Jordana's face for impact value, but once you do it, you realize how different they are."

"Did you have any problems getting out of there?" he asked, turning to Jessica.

"None. I walked into the ladies' room, took the padding out of my cheeks and peeled off the stuff around my chin. The hair changed from a blond page boy to shoulder-length black curls. The black jacket turned inside out to become a tan one, and the long black skirt ripped off, leaving sleek black pants. Whole thing took about two minutes. The skirt material was so light it took up no room in my purse when I wadded it up and tucked it in beside the wig.

"No one gave me a second look when I walked out, but I kept my head down as I passed Lars. He was on his way to the ladies' room," she told them.

"I don't believe we can let the senator involve himself in any more primaries. It would be a shame to have him win the candidacy and then have to drop out, not for him, but for the public. I say we stop playing and finish bottling him up," Brandon said.

"Oh, he's bottled. We've just left the stopper off so he can breathe. Now we put the lid on and let him decide if he wants to punch air holes or suffocate," Denile said, smiling resignedly as JC began to lecture him on human kindness.

"What I felt wasn't fear in the sense that you understand it. Seeing that woman gave me a nasty shock, and I admit that for a moment, I thought I was hallucinating. I had to check to make sure my daughter was still on the stage with me, and I was almost sorry to see that she was, because that meant I had to find a reason for someone to be made up to look so much like her. Whatever reason I come up with, it spells trouble, and not necessarily for me.

"I've kept my family away from the media for years, and as you can see, it was a wise decision. I urge the young woman to come forward and let us talk about her situation. If it's a cry for help, we will certainly listen. If it was just a joke, then I'd like to share it.

"I want to think my family is safe, and it is hard to convince myself of that when there is someone walking around out there with my daughter's face, and I don't know why!"

The senator oozed sincerity as he gazed at the camera. He had invited the same young host who had interviewed Former Governor Rube to his house for an exclusive TV interview, shared only with Janelle Christy of the Washington Post. Janelle had engaged her recorder and pulled out her camera to take pictures at convenient intervals, but otherwise stayed out of the way of the TV crew.

The Welch charm worked its magic, and a satisfied crew left his house firm in their belief that his apparent fear and his father's anger on seeing his daughter's face reproduced were justified. He watched them leave, consciously keeping his hands from fisting at his side. When their tail-lights had disappeared, he walked back to his study. He grabbed the short, squat glass his father handed him and drained it.

"I think we managed some effective damage control," the older man said as he refilled the glass. "Where did the Christy girl say she got the pictures?"

"She didn't. She just looked at me and reminded me that she was at the rally and could take whatever pictures she needed. I thought it best not to push the issue," Barry J said wearily.

"Doesn't matter," his father replied. "We'll let this story hit and then wait a day or two before we send our pigeon to them. Once he makes a liar of Rube, it will be a sure win for you. He'll be out within the week."

Barry J roused himself after a brief rest. "Where's Lars?"

"I assume he's somewhere following your wife. Don't know why you bother. The woman has not taken an incorrect breath for over twenty years."

"Yeah? Didn't you watch your wife for over twenty-five years? And didn't she leave as soon as you eased up the surveillance? That is one mistake I don't need to repeat." He pulled out his cell phone and called Lars, who arrived thirty-five minutes after the call.

"Who is she?" Barry J's father asked as soon as Lars walked into the study.

"We are still working on it. No one saw her enter the building; no one saw her leave. I didn't see her clearly myself, because I was watching the stage, and when I figured out what Barry J was signalling, she had already turned to leave. I got out as fast as

I could, but she had disappeared. I even checked the ladies' room. There was no one there."

"You already told us that. We need results, Lars, and I'm trying to believe that you are capable of handling this. We are removing Rube from the race in two days, and I want that woman by then. Two days, Lars. You disappointed me years ago when you chose men who let my wife slip past them. You don't want to disappoint me again," Barrington J. Welch II said in a rasping whisper.

Morning found Marrion at the breakfast table listening to her husband and father-in-law talk in codes.

"Once the bird is out, we can relax for a bit. He's well trained and will fly off when we decide it's time. He has no reason to connect this to us, so even if he should—"

The doorbell interrupted him, and he waited with his fork suspended until the maid walked in.

"It's a FedEx package, Sir, and they need a signature," she said with appropriate servility. Barry J climbed to his feet. He ripped the seal flap off a FedEx document envelope as he walked back to the table. He pulled out a sheet of paper and gave it a quick glance. Every drop of blood drained from his face, and he swayed on his feet. His father jumped up and grabbed him and led him out of the room to the study. Marrion neatly dabbed her lips with her napkin and pushed back from the table. In her room, she reached for the headphones.

CHAPTER TWENTY-FOUR

JC moved slowly from one picture to the next, murmuring approval as he stood in front of each one. Denile leaned against the breakfast counter and watched him, a slight smile playing around his lips.

"Well bless me," the reverend muttered, turning a disapproving eye on Denile. "What was the person who took that photo thinking? Was no thought given to the fright in store for that poor young boy?"

The picture in question showed a boy about ten sneaking up on a boy about eight years old with a garter snake in his hand. His intent to drop it on the younger boy was evident.

"Don't turn that look on me JC. I'll have you know that the young boy about to be terrorized is none other than your humble servant here, and that was my brother Lue about to commit the crime. If you think the true crime lay in the hand holding the camera, then

259

I'll let my father know that you wish to have a word with him. I remember that day quite clearly, and he laughed as hard as Lue at my screams. It would give me great pleasure to have you inform him of the dangers of fostering tyranny in the bosom of his family," Denile told him.

"I'm more concerned about your reason for displaying the picture," JC said musingly.

"To remind me to watch my back. Just because you know the person behind you doesn't mean you should let down your guard," Denile replied. JC gave him a narrow-eyed look and shook his head.

"That's a sad philosophy, especially since the incident doesn't seem to have had any lasting effects," the reverend returned mildly.

"Not unless you call an unnatural fear of snakes a lasting effect," Denile replied. Before JC could venture another comment, a brief knock and the opening of the door interrupted him. Reena, Brandon and Jessica arrived and thwarted his plan to talk Denile into changing his way of thinking.

"I need to be out of here in about an hour, so let's get to it," Reena said as she grabbed a bunch of grapes off a fruit platter. Without speaking, Denile turned on the television, and Barry J. Welch's study sprang to life.

The door crashed open, and Barrington J. Welch II steered his son towards an armchair. The senator clutched a piece of paper in his left hand, which was shaking as if he was in the throes of a seizure. He dropped into the chair and lowered the paper to his lap. His right hand held a FedEx envelope.

His father reached out and plucked the paper from Barry J's trembling hand and read it aloud.

"The next primary will be in nine days. You have that time to withdraw voluntarily from the race. If you don't, we will release certain documents in our possession to the media. And before you decide that this is an empty threat, let us remind you. August 23, Fraizers Gap, about twenty-eight years ago. We have the facts."

"Stupid, arrogant, bumbling ass. You better pray they are bluffing, because if one hint of evidence is presented, you will withdraw. It's enough that you short-circuited my political career. I will not watch my family name go down in disgrace because of you as well," Barry J's father said, his tone completely conversational.

He dropped the paper on Barry J and began rapidly pacing across the study, hurling invectives at Barry J each time he passed him.

"Lars!" The bellow shook the house, and Lars hurried into the study.

"Give him the paper," he commanded his son.

"Well?" he demanded when Lars had read it. "Truth or Bluff?"

"Bluff at zero and truth at ten—I'd say a seven," Lars answered.

"Why so high?" Barrington J. Welch II tossed at him.

"This, on its own, would stand at four and a half, maybe five. The bike wheel pushes that probability over fifty percent. Someone knows what happened. Exactly what happened, though I don't believe they can prove it. There are no documents out there for them to release," said Lars, and lobbed the paper back into Barry J's lap.

"Alright. We'll sit tight for a few days and see if anything develops. In the meantime, go and have a long talk with Jordana. She's involved in this in some way. I don't know how or why, but she's involved, and she will tell you what she knows," her grandfather said grimly.

"How do I get her to talk to me? She won't voluntarily go someplace where we can be alone, and the kind of conversation we need to have will require privacy," Lars said.

"She'll meet with you because I'll tell her to," said the older man.

"No, she won't," Barry J spoke for the first time. "No one can talk her into meeting Lars anywhere. You'll have to make her think she's meeting her mother. For that, she'll go anywhere, no matter how remote."

"Can you manage that, Lars?" his father asked.

"No problem. Barry J will have to tell Marrion that he's arranged for her to spend some time with Jordana. We'll book a room for Marrion in some hotel and tell her to wait there for Jordana. Jordana will be told to wait for her mother in the hotel dining room. There will be a miscommunication, and they won't meet," he answered.

"Get it done. I want to know everything she knows within the next two days."

"Even if you manage to meet with her, what makes you think she'll tell you anything?" Barry J asked, mildly curious.

"She's going to be waiting for her mother in the dining room. She'll sip cranberry or grape juice while she waits. That's what she always does. Someone, probably the waiter, will spike it with the most tasteless vodka I can find. She won't notice the taste, but she'll feel the effect. You know she can't handle alcohol, and since she doesn't usually drink, she'll feel it even more," he said with suppressed excitement.

The older man turned a hard stare on him.

"Keep your hands off her. Whoever got her involved in this is probably watching her, and I don't want any additional problems. If you find out that she's helping to railroad her father, I'll personally deliver her to you at a location of your choice. But for now, hands off!" he commanded.

In Denile's living room, the group looked at each other.

"Poor girl," sighed JC. "To be saddled with a grandfather and father like that . . . "

"If he gets her alone, he's gonna try something. He won't be able to resist, especially if she is drunk," Brandon said.

"No worries. He won't be getting her anywhere alone," Jessica answered.

"Her mother agrees with you, Brandon. She was concerned enough to risk calling. She wanted to be sure we saw this in time," Denile told him. Jessica turned to Reena.

"Seems like we'll be testing your artistic skills again. I think you'll have to accompany Signorina Marcioni on a quick trip," she said with a tight smile.

"It will be my pleasure," Reena answered with a mocking bow.

"I don't have to tell you to be careful," JC said softly, giving Jessica a hug.

"No, you don't. My life is good, and I have no wish to cut it short. I'll be safe," she said, her eyes on Denile.

Lars swaggered into the hotel lobby and checked in. He'd stood with Marrion and watched her go through the same process half an hour before. Her instructions were clear. She was to stay in her room until Jordana arrived. She could order anything she wanted from room service, but under no circumstance was she to leave the room before her daughter arrived. Lars was used to giving Marrion orders that didn't always make sense, so he wasn't worried about her disobeying. Just in case, though, he assigned someone to watch her door.

Jordana strode through the main doors right on schedule and walked hesitantly to the dining room. She took a quick look around and walked back out. Lars tensed, then relaxed when she went into the ladies' room. He waited for what seemed like a long time and was starting to get worried when she came out and went straight back to the dining room.

A waiter hurried to her table, and Lars gave a slight nod when he glanced at him. He settled down to watch. She downed the first drink very quickly, and with the second glass of cranberry juice, she also asked for water. Again, the waiter looked at Lars, and again he gave a nod. Even the water wouldn't escape. It was bottled and had its own unique taste. She wouldn't notice anything amiss.

Three glasses of cranberry juice and almost two glasses of water later, Lars walked to her table. If the waiter had done what he'd been seriously overpaid to do, she'd just had the equivalent of five double shots of vodka. He was surprised she could still sit up straight, although her head was drooping dangerously close to the tabletop.

He didn't sit down, just reached out and picked up her bag.

"Come. Your mother asked me to bring you to her room," he told her.

Like her mother, she was used to strange commands from him, and although she looked a bit confused, she didn't question his being there. She'd understood since childhood that wherever her mother was, he was not far away.

"Why's she not here like she said?" she asked, her voice thick and slurred. He didn't bother to answer. He boosted her out of the chair and grinned when he realized she would have toppled over if he hadn't been holding her. She stood, swaying slightly, and didn't seem to have any plans to move. He nudged her, and after a second prod, she began a weaving walk towards the door.

In the elevator, she slumped against the wall with her eyes half shut, and he began to worry about her falling asleep before he could get her to talk. She looked around the room, vaguely as if she couldn't quite remember why she was there. He ran a finger down her cheek. She sluggishly batted his hand away.

265

"Mom?" He wasn't sure if she was calling her or questioning her whereabouts.

"She'll be here in a little while," he told her, and gently pushed her into a chair. He spent a frustrating half an hour trying to gouge information out of her and finally concluded that she really knew nothing about the situation. She seemed to have forgotten about her mother.

He pulled her out of the chair.

"Don't like you," she muttered. "Got snakey eyes." He grinned. She was well and truly drunk. A sober Jordana wouldn't have dared to say something like that to him. He put his hands on her waist and slowly moved them up, stopping just under her breasts.

She blinked up at him as if processing what was happening. He stared into her eyes, which seemed to be focused somewhere on the inside of his head. His hands moved up to cup her breasts, and everything went black.

CHAPTER TWENTY-FIVE

"Tell me again how you got to your mother's room," her grandfather said to Jordana. She frowned in concentration.

"I'm not sure. I think Lars took me to her room, but she wasn't there. Then he went somewhere. I don't know when. The time is fuzzy. But I waited, and he never came back, and Mom didn't come either. Then I went to the front desk and asked, and they called her room, and she said she was there, though I don't know how she could be since I'd just left there. Someone took me up to her room. Her room seemed turned around, somehow, like the furniture was all in the wrong place, but I don't really know," she answered, sounding miserable.

He looked at Marrion. She looked back at him with open anger, the first time in her years as his son's wife.

"I'm not surprised that she can't remember. When the bell boy brought her to my room, she was totally intoxicated. How she

267

got drunk is a mystery. The bartender said she ordered cranberry juice, and that's what he poured for her. Why was she in a different room with Lars when he knew quite well which room I was in? He'd booked it and stood at my elbow while I checked in. Then he followed me to the room and walked through it, checking for I don't know what before leaving. So how did he manage to take her to a different room to wait for me, when he knew exactly where I was?" she asked, incensed.

"But my dear, are you sure that happened? Jordana herself can't remember if she was in a different room or not. She can't remember Lars leaving her in the room. She can't remember getting to your room. We don't know how much of what she's thinking really happened. In time, she may remember enough to tell us how she got drunk, but I wouldn't give her recollection of what happened while she was under the influence too much weight. No harm's been done. You got to spend a day with her, she's here, and she's safe," he said, waving a dismissive hand.

Marrion, far from satisfied, opened her mouth to protest. One look at both her husband and father-in-law staring at her with identical glacial eyes, and she led her daughter out of the room.

"Do you believe her?" Barry J asked his father.

"Not much choice. We got her drunk, so we can hardly complain about the consequences of her inebriation," he answered.

"But what about Lars? Where is he?" Barry J asked, voice laced with worry.

"He'll show up. He did take her up to the room. We don't know when he left the hotel, but Jordana did go to the front desk to ask for her mother. When she showed up at her mother's door, the fellow watching it tried calling Lars. He couldn't get him on the phone, so he checked the room. The door was left open, which makes sense if a very drunk Jordana was the last one out. Lars had no one watching his door, so the fellow had no way of knowing when he left or why. But he'll be back. People like Lars never disappear," Barrington J. Welch II told his son.

"Don't mean to sound like old Daddy Welch but tell me again how Jordana got to her mother's room," Brandon said, breaking the silence in Lanni's living room. The Welch father and son were frozen on the television screen.

"I'd rather know where Lars is," JC said. "Please tell me we had nothing to do with his disappearance."

"I can honestly tell you, JC, that I have no idea where Lars is," Denile responded, and JC prudently didn't pursue the question.

"How did Jordana get into her mother's room without being seen?" Brandon asked.

"Oh, the man watching the door saw the maid delivering extra towels—he just didn't know who it was," Reena said.

"But didn't he wonder when the maid didn't leave?" JC asked.

"The real maid was a tiny little Mexican girl with a flair for the ridiculous. She was well paid to tuck herself down into the empty hamper and climb out inside the room. If the man had been observant, he would have noticed that the maid was a lot taller going into the room than coming out, but we banked on him only seeing a uniform when he saw the maid. A dark-haired maid in a uniform went in, and a dark-haired maid in a uniform came out," Reena told him.

"What happened to Lars?" Brandon wanted to know.

"That I can't tell you. I do know that he started to get fresh with "Jordana" before he had a small accident. She left him passed out on the floor, and that's as much as I know," Jessica said.

"Must have been some accident," JC mused. "Did he sustain any serious injuries?"

"If he did, it was after Jordana left the room," was the firm reply.

"Mom, who is the woman who took my place with Lars? I know it's the same one who was at the rally, but who is she?" Jordana asked her mother.

"I don't know, love. She's trying to upset your father, but I don't know why."

"She's either really brave or really stupid. Which do you think it is?" Jordana asked.

"Probably both," her mother answered. "But remember, she doesn't know your father and Lars the way we do, so she doesn't understand the danger she's in."

"Why did she agree to go with Lars?" she asked her mother.

"Because the little session with Lars was arranged because she'd made herself up to look like you. Her actions made your grandfather think you were involved in her scheme."

"But how did she know about the meeting with Lars?" she asked.

"Oh, she's spying on your father. I think she may even have planted a recording device in his study. Anyway, I got a note telling me that she was willing to switch places with you and told me what to do. It was easy for me—all I had to do was follow Lars' instructions. Did you have any problems turning yourself into a brunette?"

"No, but I didn't do it. She did all the work before she walked out wearing my face. It was a real shock to see her up close. Her face looked so real; it was like looking into a living mirror. And she didn't seem worried about Lars at all."

"I know. When I tried to warn her about Lars, she laughed. Said there wasn't enough alcohol in the bar to get her drunk, and she has a black belt in karate. Lars would mess with her at his own risk."

"Where do you think Lars is?" Jordana asked her mother.

"I don't know, but I hope his tiny, shrivelled, black soul is on its way to hell. Not that we'd ever be so lucky. People of his ilk usually live until they are dried up husks. But that's enough. Years ago, I promised a good woman that I wouldn't let them make me bitter."

Lars struggled into a sitting position. He was cramped and cold, and the darkness was absolute. He moved his legs, testing for bonds, but they were free. He got stiffly to his feet and did a quick inventory of his person, hoping to find his switchblade.

He hunched his shoulders when he realized he was naked, and shuffled forward, hands extended in front of him. He felt nothing and shuffled forward some more. He kept going for what seemed like a long, long time. The darkness still remained, but he met no obstacle. He didn't know where he was or how long he'd been there. He sidled to the left and touched a wall. He hugged the wall and shuffled forward. Rested. Shuffled. Rested.

A tiny white dot appeared. He shuffled forward. The dot seemed to move. He stopped. The dot stabilized. He shuffled. The dot moved. He gave up shuffling and hurried forward, keeping one hand on the wall. The dot got bigger. His fast walk became a trot. The dot got bigger. The dot became a window, and the trot became a sprint.

It was big enough for him to fit through but was sealed shut. The dim light showed a smooth floor, and he felt around for something to pry it open. Nothing. Not a piece of clothing on his body, no knife. He started clawing at the window with his fingers and kept at it till they bled. He sat down in frustration, every muscle aching. He must have fallen asleep, for a slight noise woke him.

He scrambled to his feet and looked in astonishment at the window. It was open, just a crack, but open. He marshalled his depleted strength and pulled. It opened all the way. After trying a few times, he managed to climb part-way out and shut his eyes at the sun's merciless assault. He opened them a slit and glanced around. He was only a few blocks from the Welch house, and if clothed, he could have been home in a few minutes. He was in the basement of an older apartment building that had been rezoned. It was sitting empty, awaiting the decision of those in power. The cold was rapidly turning him blue, and he hustled back through the window and into the darkness. He'd barely made it back in when something fell on him.

"Hey!" he yelled. "Who's there?"

No one answered, and he picked up the things that had been thrown in: a lady's skirt—very, very short—a large pair of high heeled lady's boots, and a very short jacket. He sat down. He was close to home, but it may as well have been miles away. Walking there naked was not an option. He would likely get arrested for indecent exposure, and some body part would be sure to freeze off. Wearing the skirt was almost as bad. If anyone saw him, he'd be laughed out of town. Staying in the basement was not to be considered. He trekked back to the other end of the basement, feeling around in the dark. He found nothing. Back at the window, he waited. He'd call to the next person that passed. Maybe he could get some help.

He waited. And waited. He heard footsteps, but no one passed. He couldn't understand it. Finally, he donned the jacket and stuck his upper body out. Each person that approached was stopped and directed across the road. He couldn't see who was stopping them. He looked in the other direction. The same thing was happening there too. He slithered back down, fury burning in his gut.

CHAPTER TWENTY-SIX

Jessica climbed out of the perfumed bath, feeling pampered and relaxed. She slathered on the scented lotion that matched the bath salts and bubbles she had just soaked in, and took a deep, appreciative breath. The set was a gift from Denile, and the scent was light enough to be layered without becoming overpowering. She spent fifteen minutes on her face, and when she was done, she looked as if she wore no enhancements. A blue contact lens covered her green eye, her lips were fuller, and her cheekbones defined, but only a trained eye would be able to detect what her expert hand had applied.

The dress was the exact shade of her eyes. In deference to the cool temperature, she had chosen the hundred percent wool ensemble with an eye on comfort. It was a simple dress: calf-length, no sleeves, and a row of gold and blue buttons ran down the front to the hem of the flared skirt. A small bolero jacket provided warmth

274

and covering. She pulled on flesh-coloured stockings, and when she stepped into the strappy gold sandals, she crossed her fingers that her feet would not completely freeze before she got back home. Denile had said 7:30, and it was 7:24. A quick waft of perfume and she made her way down to get out her long coat.

He was right on time. Her eyes widened when he walked in, wearing a superbly tailored black suit. He took his left hand from behind him and presented a simple bouquet of violets with a deep bow. She gave a quick laugh and, with an equally deep courtesy, accepted them and went to the kitchen for a vase.

"Our reservation is for 8:30, and we are going downtown, so let's head out and give ourselves some time in case we run into traffic," he said lightly and helped her into her coat. They stepped outside, and she looked around for his car. He took her elbow and led her to a Cadillac with a chauffeur holding the back door open.

"What's going on?" she whispered as he slid in beside her.

"Let's see. One, I wanted to do something special. Two, there's a game at the Roger's Centre and a concert at the Air Canada Centre, so parking will be a nightmare. Three, it's cool, so I didn't want to risk having parking problems and end up freezing your tootsies," he answered.

With a contented smile, she settled into the luxurious seat to enjoy the ride.

When the driver pulled up in front of the steps leading to the Rogers Centre entrance and the CN Tower, she looked at him in disbelief.

"You better tell me that we are getting out here so we can go up John Street to some trendy little restaurant," she said with forced calm.

"That's the other reason for the car. If I had driven and dropped you off to go find parking, you might have bolted before I got back," he said, taking her hand. "You might not enjoy getting there, but I promise you will love it once you are. The 360 is one of the restaurants in this city that you shouldn't miss."

"Their food can't be good enough for me to go that far into the air to eat it," she insisted.

"The food might not be worth the ride up, but the view is. You'll never be treated to a more complete view of this city at night than you'll get here," he told her as he hustled her along. When they got to the entrance of the CN Tower, he pulled her inside the door and stopped.

"I've muscled you this far, but I won't force you to go up if you really do not want to. I'd like you to go up with me. It's one of my favourite spots, though I don't come here often. Will you trust me enough to try this for me?" he asked with quiet intensity.

"Oh, I trust you. But you didn't hitch those elevators onto the outside of this building. It's them I don't trust. Have you ever listened to the spiel they give when you get on? '..one of the world's tallest free-standing structures, a gazillion feet high and blah blah blah . . . ' Why do I need to go that high in the air without an airplane, or at least a parachute?" she demanded.

"Alright, we'll eat somewhere else," he said. She could sense his disappointment and cursed herself for a fool even as the words tumbled from her mouth.

"No, no. We are here already. We may as well go up. But I expect big bonus points for this, and I won't let you forget it." She tucked her arm into his and let him lead her up the ramp.

She walked to the back of the almost empty elevator, and he effectively blocked her view by standing directly in front of her. Even so, she didn't breathe normally until they were seated at their table. He smiled at her and nodded to the window.

"OK, you're off the hook. I agree. This is the best view I've seen of the city at night, except when coming in to land." Her entire being softened as she told him, "I'm glad you made me come."

She divided her attention between him and the view and couldn't remember what she ate. While they waited for desert, he reached into his pocket and brought out a box.

"I got you a present," he said, pushing it across the table. Her stomach jumped as she reached for the small rectangular box. She opened it and raised shining eyes to his when she unearthed the beautiful crystal curio. It was a pair of hands clasped as if in prayer. It glistened in hundreds of different colours as she turned it this way and that.

"Oh, there's a little button on the side. What does it do?" she asked and pressed it without waiting for an answer. The hands slowly opened. Nestled inside was a diamond solitaire in a platinum setting. She stared at it, her breathing shallow, and the hands reclosed, hiding the ring. She stared at the clasped hands for a long moment, then finally looked at him.

"Will you marry me, Jessica?" he asked. It was a quiet question, unaccompanied by any of the words he could use so well. The knot in her gut eased, and for the first time, she acknowledged the tension that had surrounded him all evening. His face was expressionless as he waited for her to answer. He didn't urge, didn't prod, just waited.

"Yes," she said, voice hushed. "Yes, I'll marry you." Her heart squeezed when he closed his eyes and took a deep breath. The tension rolled off him as he gently took the ring from the crystal hand and put it on her finger. It was a perfect fit.

Lars gulped the drink Barry J handed him and walked in jerky steps across the room.

"Let me see if understand you," Barry J's father said, his quiet tones hinting of storms to come.

"You took Jordana to the room, you talked to her and decided that she knew nothing about this woman masquerading as her, and then you woke up a few blocks from here."

"That's right," Lars said, his voice an open challenge.

"And you're sure you remember nothing else?"

"Yes, I'm sure."

"Jordana thinks you went to talk to someone at the door and left with that person," the older man told him.

"I wasn't expecting anyone, and only an emergency would have caused me to leave her unattended in that room. If I'd had to leave, I would have called my man off her mother's door to watch her," was Lars' response.

"Are you saying you didn't leave with anyone?" Barrington J. Welch II asked.

"No. I'm saying it is highly unlikely that I would have done so without making some arrangement about Jordana. I can't say I didn't leave with someone, since I can't remember, but I think it is not the most likely explanation."

"And the most likely explanation would be what?" was the mild question tossed at him.

"I don't have an explanation, likely or otherwise," Lars returned tersely.

"And you are quite sure that you remember nothing else?"

"Yes, I am quite sure," came the impatient response.

"What condition were your clothes in? They might offer some clue as to what happened," Barry J suggested.

"No, they don't. Other than being dusty, they were in perfect shape, except that my jacket seems to have disappeared," he told them. He had no intention of having them find out what he'd arrived home wearing. He'd be having nightmares about that tiny skirt for a long, long time.

Marrion picked up the envelope from the passenger seat and looked carefully around. She didn't bother wondering how it had gotten into her locked car. Her eyes almost popped out when the bright, glossy photographs spilled onto her lap. Although the surroundings were in darkness, there was no mistaking Lars sneaking up to the house. He looked angry, furtive and cold. His mini skirt was neon green, and the short black boots showed off his athletic legs to perfection. The black jacket stretched taut across his shoulders and was too small to button in front, leaving his midriff and a good portion of chest bare.

All in all, he made a very good advertisement for a cross-dresser. A note was attached to the last picture.

If it becomes necessary, these may help to keep him in check.

She laughed out loud and gathered them up. She tucked them in the waistband of her pants and pulled her shirt down over them. She couldn't risk putting them in her purse. She had no doubt that Lars would kill to retrieve them if he ever found out about them.

JC stared at the pictures, shuffling them absently. When he finally lifted his head, he pinned Denile with a penetrating glare.

"I thought you didn't know what happened to him?" he asked.

"I didn't, and before you ask, I didn't orchestrate this either," Denile replied, aggrieved.

"I think you'd better tell me exactly what your instructions were," JC said quietly.

"When Jessica called and told me what had happened in the room, I asked that he be removed from the hotel and be kept quiet for a day or so. I explained the problem of him being a constant threat to Jordana, to the point where she wouldn't even visit her own home. I didn't ask for these pictures, but I'm told he'll likely leave her alone if the alternative is to have these pictures made public," Denile told him.

"Is his sexual orientation in question?" Brandon asked.

"No. He is completely heterosexual. In fact, he's an open homophobe, which is why these will be so effective," Denile said.

"I can't like exposing anyone to ridicule, but it may well keep Jordana from being assaulted, so I'll say no more," JC said with a troubled sigh.

"You have to admit, it couldn't happen to a more deserving person," Reena said with a savage grin. "The man is a viper, and as such, does not rate your sympathy, JC, although I know you can't help giving it. And don't worry. He'll never know about these pictures unless they are required to keep him away from Jordana."

Jessica said nothing, only looked at the pictures with a mysterious smile on her face.

Four of the nine days he'd been given were gone, and he'd heard no more. Barry J relaxed and agreed with his father that it was a last effort by the Rube campaign to create a clear field for himself. He'd relaxed so far that the sight of a plain brown envelope beside his breakfast plate didn't cause him undue anxiety. He was used to getting business envelopes with his morning paper, and his tormentors had been using FedEx.

As always, he pushed the envelope aside and dealt with his meal. His father had eaten early, and he barely spared his wife a glance as he sat down. He certainly didn't waste a greeting on her. Next, he did a quick scan of the paper while he had a final cup of coffee. He was still the favourite in the polls, and everyone was predicting a win for him. He'd have to start thinking about how best to organize his presidential campaign.

He reached for the envelope almost absently, basking in the glow the accolades in the paper had created. He withdrew the sheaf of papers and laid them on the table but didn't focus on them. His mind had wandered to the day when he would officially launch that campaign. He even had the skeleton of a speech ready. He was adding bits to it in his head as he picked up the first sheet of paper.

The victim is a fifteen-year-old Caucasian female. She is a visitor, often seen around town with her sister, who is a teacher in the local school. The incident happened between 2:00 and 3:00 PM yesterday, August 23rd, on an empty lot owned by a local businessman. The bicycle the victim was riding has been taken into custody and is being examined by the forensics team. The victim did not see the face of her attacker, who wore a balaclava and hence she cannot give a clear description. The victim claims to have bitten a piece out of the base of the perpetrator's thumb, and describes him as white, possibly blond with blue eyes . . .

Barry J stared in confusion. He might have been reading a foreign language, so complete was his incomprehension. He read it a second time before he recognized it as a police report. He'd never seen it before, but it was from Fraizers Gap, dated August 24, almost twenty-eight years ago. His eyes wanted to roll back in his head, and waves of nausea washed over him. With no warning, he was suddenly soaked with icy sweat.

Silence hung over the house. The servants didn't know what the problem was but sensed that any disturbance would be unwelcome. Marrion had watched Barry J stumble from the breakfast table, clutching the envelope and surrounded by almost palpable fear. She went straight to her room, where she remained vigilant at her listening post. In the study, father and son were silent, awaiting Lars' arrival.

He was greeted by the hoarse, scratchy voice the Welch patriarch used when he was trying not to shout.

"You told us there was no evidence out there. You were wrong. I want an explanation," he rasped.

"Evidence? What evidence?" Lars asked. Without answering, Barry J handed him the stack of papers on top of the envelope. He slowly went through them. They were photocopies, and not completely clear, but legible enough to be recognized. The police report, the hospital record, the brief account in the newspaper, the contract offered to the Chief of Police, the contract with the school vice-principal, the report of the boating accident that killed Constable Downs, and the report of the speculation about his newly acquired wealth. There was even a brief piece on the possibility of his death not being an accident.

"Only two possible explanations. Someone copied the originals before you asked me to retrieve them, or someone copied them after they were delivered to you. Either way, there is nothing I could have done to prevent it," Lars said.

"It wasn't done after they came to me. I took the precaution of marking each paper before putting them in my safe. None of these copies carry my mark."

"That doesn't mean anything. All they had to do was remove your mark from their copy and make a second copy. Of course, someone may have made copies before we got to them. I retrieved the original police report and hospital records the same day you instructed me to do so. The rest is public knowledge, so anyone could have copied those," Lars returned.

"You promised me that there was no evidence left out there," Barry J said, his voice petulant and tinged with anger. Lars turned around slowly and faced him.

"Do I look like a psychic? I collected the evidence, and I didn't leave any out there. You got the police report. You got the hospital record. You got the rape kit. And you'd best thank Downs, dead as he is, for giving up the kit. It would have been pretty hard to find out where it was being stored if it hadn't been for him. I retrieved all the information the social worker had recorded. I cautioned both Bribank and Downs and removed Downs when his behaviour started to bother you. I finally iced the sister, even though I didn't believe that she knew anything, because you wanted a senate seat and she made you nervous.

"I didn't realize I was supposed to look into my crystal ball and tell if someone had copied any of the documents before I got to them. If you have a way of finding that out, perhaps you should share it with me," he said in a dangerously soft voice.

Barry J shrank from the menace on his face, surprised and frightened. He had swatted a house cat, and it turned out to be a cougar.

"I've been holding your hands and wiping your nose for nearly thirty years, and I don't ask anything of you. I cover up your mistakes, I clean up your messes, and I watch your wife and kids. All of it is by choice. I don't ask anything of you because I don't need anything from you." He walked to the window and continued speaking with his back to the room.

"I accept my mistakes when I make them. It might be too late for you to start doing that yourself but have the sense not to try to pass them off as mine. It will only annoy me. And Barry J?" He whirled around and advanced on Barry J.

"Friend or not, you really, really don't want to do that. While you're at it, you might want to remember this. I didn't touch that kid. You did. Try, try very hard to remember that, because if you ever again imply that any of this mess is my fault, I'm going to be just a bit upset." His smile was grim, and Barry J flinched when Lars gave him a comradely slap on the shoulder.

"You boys can fight with each other later. Right now, we need to decide what to do," Barry J's father said. "Is there enough here to force a withdrawal? The documents are damaging, but they don't prove anything. There were lots of blond men in the Gap back then, just like today. Some of them must have had blue eyes. And they only mention blue eyes. Why should anyone think these documents finger Barry J?"

CHAPTER TWENTY-SEVEN

"Good question," Jessica said, looking at Denile. "Those documents don't really prove anything, so how do we convince my beloved father that we know it was him?"

"Simple. We send him some DNA evidence. We have a sample of his DNA, and he has no way of knowing when we got it," he answered.

"When did we get it?" she asked, curious.

"Recently. I'm not sure when, exactly, but we do have it, and we already had the DNA fingerprint done. We held off sending it because it requires a bit of fudging. We will have to imply that the sample was obtained back then, and I didn't think JC would like that. As it is, I'm going to have it delivered without his knowledge. I don't think the senator will withdraw without more proof than he currently has."

"We could always send him my birth certificate and mom's name change information. That way, we wouldn't have to fudge, and JC wouldn't have to worry about anything," she said, leaning on him.

"Yes, he would. We all would. If they find out about you, we will spend the rest of our lives worrying about them coming after you. Believe me—this way is better. If there was enough time, I'd sit down with JC and figure out an alternative. He's usually good at that, but we gave the senator nine days, and this is day five. I want him to decide today, so I have to convince him today," he said.

"Do you know anything about rape kits?" she asked.

"Not a lot. The original name was the Vitullo Kit. A Sergeant Vitullo from the Chicago Police Force developed it. The idea was to have a standard kit holding specific items for collecting physical evidence in sexual assault cases. I read that he worked with someone from the Citizens Committee for Victim Assistance. This was sometime in the 1970s, so they've been around for a while," he told her.

"Would a DNA sample from 28 years ago be any good today?" she asked him.

"According to our source, yes, it would. Here, this is what was sent to me," he said, handing her a single sheet of paper.

"DNA can be extracted from any cell found in a sample. This sample can be from a variety of sources, including saliva, sweat, blood, feces, urine, hair or skin cells. DNA is found in a cell's nucleus, and every cell in a person's body contains the same DNA, hence the possibility of using samples from a wide range of sources. Depending on how detailed the DNA test is, the probability of having

287

two individuals with the same DNA fingerprint can be up to 1,000,000 to one, unless they are identical twins. That statistical probability suggests that DNA typing can distinguish beyond doubt between any two people. The conclusion? If they have any of your cells, they can identify you. DNA can remain stable for years, but even badly degraded DNA can still be used due to scientific technology advances."

She read it slowly, and when she finished without saying anything, he reached for the phone.

The timid knock startled Marrion. She'd been sitting in the same position for so long that her legs were cramped. She pulled off the headphones and shoved them under her pillows.

"Come in," she called, knowing it was neither Lars nor her husband, who, she knew, had not left the study.

"Please, Ma'am, there's a delivery man at the door. He wants a signature, and we were told not to disturb the senator in the study," one of the maids said.

Marrion followed her down the stairs. She looked at the envelope. It was bigger than the one from the morning, and she debated whether to leave it on the hall table or risk the anger of the trio in the study. They had been quiet for a long time, no doubt contemplating how best to circumvent the current situation.

She suspected that the envelope would nudge them into further speech, and she was tired of listening to silence, so she tapped lightly at the door.

Lars jerked it open and stared at her in surprise. In all the years he'd lived there, she had never disturbed them once they closed a door. She thrust the envelope at him.

"This was just delivered. I don't know if it is campaign material that he needs, but with the next primary so close, I didn't want to risk leaving it out here," she said by way of explanation. She didn't wait for a reply but went straight back to her room and her waiting headphones.

Lars gave the envelope to the senior Welch instead of Barry J. He pulled out a long piece of paper and looked at the horizontal lines running down its length. They meant nothing to him. He handed it back to Lars, who took a quick look before passing it on to Barry J.

Only when Barry J held it up did his father notice the folded note taped to the back. He struggled out of his chair and ripped it off. The sound that escaped him when he opened it was a cross between a strangled moan and a gurgle, and he collapsed into the chair he'd just vacated.

"What is it, Dad? What's wrong?" Barry J asked in alarm. Thoughts of heart attacks and age crowded his mind, and the strange strip of paper fluttered to the floor unheeded as he heaved himself up from his chair. Before he could reach him, his father rallied, waved him off, and then gave him the note.

In case you don't know what this is, let us explain. It is called a DNA fingerprint. They tend to be pretty good at identifying a specific person. This one belongs to you, Senator Welch. We went the extra mile and paid for the most detailed test available, so there is no mistake. Of course, we know that you stole the rape kit from that police station, or rather had it stolen since appearances seem to indicate that you would not have had enough guts to do it yourself.

But what makes you so sure there was only one? Just a thought. But I wonder, did you or your saintly father look at the kit before you had it destroyed? I bet you didn't. If you had, you might have paused to think. Wasn't something missing? Yes, it might be that you and your accomplices overlooked one vital piece of evidence. Remember that indentation at the base of your thumb Senator, the one you often rub your middle finger across when you get nervous? What do you think became of the chunk of flesh that poor young girl bit out?

Unfortunately, the medical personnel who collected the evidence for the kit were a bit remiss and didn't check her mouth very well. Don't think badly of them. The kits were fairly new, and the girl suffered so much trauma that it isn't surprising something was missed. That hunk of flesh didn't make it into the original kit, Senator, and therefore never made it into the hands of your corrupt officers.

As I said, why were you so sure there was only one kit? You should have checked her mouth before you dumped her, Barry J. We can call you Barry J, can't we? After all, we are going to be such close acquaintances. Yes, you should have checked her mouth. The good news is that she didn't choke on it and make you a murderer. The bad news is, they preserved it, and a piece of flesh that size would have provided more than enough DNA to identify the perpetrator. Isn't that what your friends, Constables Downs and Bribank called him? The perpetrator?

That's you, Barry J! The DNA sample proves it.

Don't take our word that this DNA profile is yours. Go to a reputable lab and give them a sample. It won't hurt, we promise. Give them a single strand of hair or a bit of spit. They'll do a profile and compare it to this one. See! We have even included the name and location of the lab that did this profile, to make the comparison easy. You could go to them. We were considerate enough to use one close by so you can access it without too much inconvenience.

Do the right thing, Senator.

We are confident that you will withdraw in the allotted time. Enjoy the rest of the day, Barry J.

Barry J collapsed on the floor in a shuddering heap. The roaring in his head drowned out his father's litany of abuse, and he curled into himself, sobbing and broken. His father stepped over him and walked to the sideboard to pour a drink. His voice was whisper soft and hoarse when he spoke.

"Twice. That one stupid incident has robbed this family of a presidency twice. I have a mind to kill you myself and make sure you don't hang around to damage my family name after I'm gone. I might as well go ahead and die now. Who knows what else these people will want." He stood over his son, staring at him in disgust.

"Get up and stop that blubbering!" he finally yelled, pushing him with his foot. "Get up, you blundering idiot. This is your mistake, and I'm damned if I'll try to fix it for you. Get up. There's work to do and precious little time in which to do it. If you didn't have my name, I swear I would just leave you there for the media vultures, but I'll not have my political career smeared by your misdeeds. Get up off that floor before I give in and kick you like the dog you are," the older man said viciously.

Lars edged around him and lifted Barry J to his feet. When his legs refused to hold him, Lars dumped the limp form into a chair. His head lolled to one side, and his father reached out and dealt him a stinging slap.

"You will pay attention, and for the first time in your life, you will take a hand in fixing a problem you created. I have been bailing you out for years, and that was my mistake. Well, that's about to stop. You will fix this, and I'll help you, but after that, you are on your own."

"Lars?" As was their custom, Barrington J. Welch II turned to Lars for the first step in resolving Barry J's problem.

"If he is going to withdraw, it has to be for a reason the people will understand and sympathize with. There can't be any room for speculation, and it has to be something provable that he didn't know about before. He'd best have a heart attack," was Lars' laconic reply.

"Alright, but how do you prove a heart attack?" the elder Welch asked.

"He'll have to fake one. I read someplace that a bunch of lawyers ran a scam to bilk insurance companies years back. The lawyers would get some john to take a drug, get some kind of heart test and then put in an insurance claim after the test showed abnormal results. Scam worked for a long enough time. They were using a drug called digitalis that they say will cause a heart test to look like you've had a heart attack.

"I could get some. We'll have to figure out how much to use and when, so it doesn't wear off before the ambulance arrives. He needs to do the test not too long after he takes it; at least, that's what these lawyers figured. Maybe we should have him collapse at a rally or some public function, then no one will wonder about it," Lars told him.

"Alright. Seems like a good idea. That's what we'll do. You start thinking about where to get the drug right away, and I'll find the right event for him to go to tomorrow," the now desperate father decided.

Barry J said nothing as he listened to his father and friend plan the death of his dream.

Up in her room, Marrion listened and weighed the odds, then decided that the possible gain was worth the risk. She straightened her clothes and headed for the study. She knocked lightly on the door but didn't wait for an answer. She opened it and stuck her head inside.

"Father, may I speak with you for a minute?" she asked.

He was so surprised he didn't answer, and she withdrew her head and closed the door. Had she asked to speak to her husband, Lars would have been out to find out what she wanted. He wouldn't try it with her father-in-law.

"Yes, Marrion. What can I do for you, my dear?" He sounded concerned, but she could sense his underlying impatience.

"Nothing. I don't need you to do anything for me. I thought you should know that you and Lars are speaking loudly enough to be heard. And having heard the plan, I also thought you should know that there's a flaw in it that will be difficult to circumvent and may eventually lead to the speculation you are trying to avoid," she said quietly.

Her voice was confident, and she looked directly into his eyes. She refused to let him know just how scared she was.

"You've been listening to our plans?" he said ominously.

"No," she replied. "I didn't need to listen. I could hardly help hearing the plan. And if you don't want every servant in the house to hear as well, you and Lars might want to modulate your voices." She paused for a moment.

"I usually stay clear of whatever plans my husband and Lars are involved in, but I also bear the Welch name, and I don't want to be held up to ridicule along with Barry J if you all attempt to carry out this plan you and Lars have agreed on," she said with quiet dignity.

He looked at her with incredulity, but curiosity won out.

"What's wrong with the plan? He'll fake a heart attack, Lars will slip him enough digitalis to give a satisfactorily abnormal ECG reading, and we'll be able to work the attack to our advantage."

"Did Lars tell you that there is a possibility that Barry J could end up with real heart problems after taking digitalis? But that's not the flaw I was referring to. One of the first things they'll do once he gets to a hospital is a take a blood sample. When the heart is damaged, as it would be in a heart attack, certain enzymes leak out and enter the bloodstream. They'll test his blood for those enzymes. How do you plan to fake that?"

"A blood test? Are you sure?"

"Yes, I'm sure. I went with Mrs. Kerr, you know, our neighbour on the left, when she had a heart attack, and that's what happened. They did the ECG while asking questions, and the blood test right after."

"How long was she in the hospital?" he wanted to know.

"Three days. It was a mild attack, or so they claimed," she responded.

"Alright. Thank you for telling me," he said and disappeared back into the study. Marrion went back to her room in time to hear his first comment to Lars.

"You didn't tell me that Barry J could end up with real heart problems from this drug!" he hissed.

"Why would I know that? I'm not a doctor. I told you that I had read that the drug can mimic some heart attack symptoms well enough to fool doctors. Other than that, I don't know anything about it," Lars' replied carelessly.

"We need a new plan. The digitalis option won't work."

"Fine. When you come up with one, you let me know, and I'll do what needs to be done," Lars said, sliding into a chair.

The silence stretched, broken only by Barry J's laboured breathing. He sounded like he wouldn't have to fake a heart attack after all. His father eyed him with disgust.

"Ruddy fool," he muttered and walked out of the room.

Marrion was at the top of the stairs when he got to the hallway. He beckoned her down.

"Tell me. Do you have any suggestions on how we can accomplish this?" he asked abruptly. She hid her amazement.

"Am I allowed to know why we need to do this?" she asked.

"Not now," he replied.

"Okay. Take him off somewhere tonight. Somewhere far from here, but not too remote because you want to have multiple choices for hospitals. He can have his attack there. Do it in a hotel or restaurant and have him picked up by a fake ambulance. I'm sure Lars can arrange that. No one needs to be told where the ambulance took him.

"Have him brought back to Washington for observation after he has been treated elsewhere. He'll need to come back with all the medical records already in place. You need ECG results, blood tests, maybe an echocardiogram. Lars should be able to procure some.

"Just make sure that they show only mild irregularity. That way he can refuse any further testing here in Washington. He should be back to normal before he arrives, so hospitalization here would be just a precaution and last no more than twenty-four hours.

"He can hold a press conference from his hospital bed and play on the public's sympathy. Between him and Lars, they should be able to pull this off."

He looked intently at her, nodded and left. She hurried back to her room. In the study, he faced his son and Lars.

"Alright. Listen up," he said with authority. "This is what we are going to do."

Denile pressed a button, and the senator's study and its occupants disappeared.

"Do we assume that he got that plan from our very helpful Marrion?" Reena asked.

"Yes, we do. It was suggested to her some time ago, but I didn't think she'd be called on to use it. It does make life easier for us. It means we'll be able to monitor the senator's heart attack, Lars' procurement of the appropriate medical documents and use that information if it becomes necessary," Denile answered.

"Okay. The senator is settling into his bottle nicely, and we have the stopper ready. What have we done about the son?" Brandon inquired.

"He is no longer registered at Georgetown University, and according to records, never has been. The money the senator paid for his tuition and board has been replaced in his account, and there's no record of it ever being paid to the university," he was told.

"And the young man who was taking his place?" JC asked.

"Legally registered in school, living in the same room, but looking nothing like the person who is supposed to be in the room. We have removed everything that Justin Welch brought with him and had the young man remake himself into his original self, so Lars would not recognize him as looking anything like Justin. The transformation was gradual enough that we don't think his watcher noticed. At least he hasn't been suspicious enough to try to contact Lars.

"I think the young man will be fine for the time being, and it clears the slate for Justin," Denile told JC.

CHAPTER TWENTY-EIGHT

Janelle Christy pulled the single sheet of paper from the envelope as she cleared the doors to the newsroom. She had fifteen minutes to get to her son's school, which was twenty-five minutes away. She had to find a way to make up the ten minutes. She raced to her car, glancing at the paper as she unlocked the door.

Senator Welch will be admitted to hospital this afternoon. He'll be there for observation only, following a mild heart attack while visiting family out of town. You might want to present yourself for an interview at about 5:30 PM.

A heart attack? Why hadn't she heard anything about it? And where was she going to find a babysitter on such short notice? Who was sending her these things? She screeched out of the parking lot, questions crowding her mind, and mentally mapped the fastest route from home to the hospital.

Marrion walked down the hospital corridor and pushed open the door to the private room. Her husband was propped up in bed, hooked to a machine that gave off occasional beeps. She was not entirely successful in hiding her shock. He was pale and ravaged, and if she hadn't known otherwise, she would have sworn he was really ill.

Her resolve wavered until he opened his eyes and glared at her.

"So, you've decided to drop in. Most concerned wives would have been at the hospital to meet the ambulance when I arrived. But not you. I expect you to make a proper public show of support. You are my wife, and—"

"And I will make a public show of support," she interrupted him. "Let's not paint this with too high a sheen, Barry J. You and I both know that there's nothing the matter with you that a little restraint years ago would not have cured," she said tersely, causing him to look at her in surprise. She had never used such a tone with him in all their years together.

"What are you talking about? What do you think you know?" he asked with just a hint of unease.

"You would be amazed at the things I know, my dear husband. I've been thinking about our life together, and I've concluded that it isn't one that suits me. You are about to make a major change in your life, and I've decided that it is time to make one in mine.

"I have some papers for you to sign, and it would be best if you don't quibble about them. Right now, I'm feeling generous, but that could change. Here," she said, shoving a few sheets of paper into his hands. He gave the top one a quick look and laughed. It was a grim sound. "You actually believe that I'll let you divorce me?" he asked incredulously. "Have you lost your senses? You don't leave a Welch! No woman leaves a Welch, and any who try it don't live to tell about it. You are not getting a divorce. But you will get a handsome reward for even thinking about it," he told her.

"When we get through with you, you'll think you've been living in paradise all these years." His voice was quiet and reasonable as if they were discussing what to have for dinner.

"You seem to think I'm *asking* you for a divorce," she replied, in equally reasonable tones, masking her terror. "Have you forgotten why you are here trying to fool the public? Oh yes! I know that there's nothing wrong with you, and I even know why you are doing this," she said, smiling at him.

"It doesn't matter what you think you know. I understand you've been listening at keyholes, and we've been too busy to deal with it, but don't think anything you overheard will make a difference to you. You aren't going anywhere, and the more you talk, the more you'll have to pay for your insolence," he said with mounting fury.

"Please, don't agitate yourself. Remember your heart," she said with fake sweetness. Then she pinned him with an icy look.

"You've been receiving a lot of packages lately. It's been a very busy time for Lars, so don't hold this against him. It must have slipped by him that I also received a package," she told him with a slight smile.

"Now, when would that have been? Oh, right—it doesn't matter. The only thing you need to know is that it included many things you are familiar with. A police report. Some hospital records. A few newspaper clippings. Ah! I see you are beginning to comprehend the complexity of the situation," she said, pulling the chair forward and dropping into it.

"And before you instruct Lars to try to pry them from me, please note that I have given sealed copies to a few lawyers, all with the same instructions. If they don't hear from me at agreed-upon times, they are to send the envelope to certain news reporters," she said lightly.

"Father will never let you get away with this," he said, voice tight.

"I wouldn't be too sure of that. He's so upset with you right now that he'd probably divorce you himself if he had the choice. So yeah, I think he'll let me get away with it. After all, you are sitting here in splendid health pretending to have a wonky heart because he doesn't want anyone to see those papers," she reminded him.

"What do you want?" he ground out.

"A quiet, uncontested divorce. I've worked out all the details. We'll do it in Las Vegas for a variety of reasons. The residency requirement is only six weeks. You haven't spent much time campaigning there, so you aren't as well known there as in some other places. It should be easier to get your name through without it

301

sending up any flags, especially since they tend to have a fairly busy schedule. I've found someone to get the papers through with minimum exposure, so there's a good chance that we can do this without any national repercussions. I assumed that would be your preference," she finished.

"And you think I'll let you go to Vegas to fulfill the residency requirement?" he asked, faintly amused.

"Oh, I've already taken care of that. I've been a resident of Clark County for over two months. Now all I need is for you to sign these papers," she said, tapping her finger on the papers resting on his thigh.

"As far as I know, the state of Nevada has community property laws. If I grant you a divorce in that state, you are entitled to half of everything I've acquired during our marriage," he said.

"You were barely old enough to drink when I married you, and now you want half of what I own?" His anger was palpable.

"I don't know Barry J. I'm sure there are some who would think that I'm entitled to that, and maybe more, for the years I've had to put up with you and Lars. But I'm not about to get into an asset war with you. One of the papers in that stack renounces any claim on my part to all your property and assets. I don't want anything from you," she said quietly. He looked at her, perplexed.

"How do you plan to live?" he asked. "Or are you renouncing assets in a bid for bigger alimony payments?"

"That would be the logical thought progression, but, no. I don't want anything from you, including alimony. I want only two things. One, that you sign the papers, and two, you agree to keep Lars away from me and my children."

She looked on without expression as he laughed long and hard.

"And you really believe that I can make Lars do anything he doesn't want to do?" he asked, still chuckling.

"It doesn't concern me overmuch whether you think you can make him listen or not. I'm simply telling you that you had better try. And not just try. You would do well to succeed.

"How you manage that is your concern but understand this— the first time he comes within three feet of Jordana, the papers go straight to the press. You have sat back and allowed him to terrorize us for years, and I don't intend for it to continue." She looked at his uneasy face and took pity on him.

"If you have any problems with him, tell him I said I once saw a picture of a friend of his in a neon coloured miniskirt, and from the lighting on the picture, it was late at night. I'll happily suggest that the photographer send a copy to a lurid tabloid if he so much as walks into the same room as my kids," she said with a smile. "I believe he likes his friend too much to let that happen."

"And the kids, when will I see them?" he asked, more for form than any desire to know.

"They aren't kids anymore. I won't tell them where to live. If they want to go home to you, they can. They can decide who they want to spend time with. I won't attempt to influence them. You get to decide whether you have the kind of relationship with them that will make them want to see you," she told him with quiet satisfaction.

"Leave the papers. I'll talk to father about the best way to go about this, and we'll work accordingly," he said.

"No," she replied, shocking him. "I'm not married to your father. I'm married to you. You sign the papers now, or I call the first lawyer and tell him to go ahead and send out the envelope. I want these papers submitted tomorrow, and I don't intend to give your father any more say in my life. You and I are finished, so he and I are finished too. He can see his grandchildren when they choose to see him. Otherwise, he has nothing to do with us.

"Sign the papers, Barry J, or I'll go ahead and file for a very public divorce right here in Washington D.C., citing your recently divulged past criminal activities and the resulting fear for my life as the reason. Sign the papers." Her voice was almost whisper soft.

"You're trying to blackmail me?" he asked, his face a mass of conflicting emotions.

"If you choose to call it such, I can't stop you. But I'll go ahead and do what I have to do because I will not live this life anymore," she told him quietly.

He called her a nasty name and scrawled his name in the appropriate spots.

"See, that wasn't so hard, was it?" she asked with a syrupy smile. "I'll be here to stand decorously by your side, showing full support when you call your press conference. I'll come in tomorrow so the watching world will have no reason to doubt that we are the wonderful couple they have known us to be all these years.

"In the meantime, it would be best if you told Lars to leave me alone. I am tired, very, very tired of his constant presence."

As soon as the door closed behind her, he reached for the phone. He had signed the papers because he had no intention of letting her get to Vegas with them. Lars would take care of them and her until he got home.

Marrion walked by the nurses' station, rummaging in her bag. In the elevator, she ignored the only other occupant, but when she emerged, she no longer had the envelope that had been too big to fit in her purse.

CHAPTER TWENTY-NINE

We are shocked and saddened by the news that Senator Barrington J. Welch III suffered a heart attack two days ago while away from home.

Although the attack was a mild one, the senator is being held for observation in hospital. With no prior cardiac problems and no history of heart disease in his family, the senator expressed surprise at the tragic occurrence and dismay at the timing.

When asked what effect this will have on the campaign, the senator was noncommittal. He would make no decisions without appropriate medical advice.

At present, he is unsure of the prognosis but will inform his beloved public as soon as any information is available . . .

Senator Barry J. Welch III swallowed the bile that was threatening to rise up and choke him. With a petulant flick of his

306

wrist, he hurled the newspaper to the ground. The story had covered the points he wanted covered, but the need for the story was a roiling mass of fury burning his insides.

"Stupid dolt!" he exclaimed. "How much clearer do I need to be?"

He'd just spent two hours explaining to his campaign manager why he felt his health was more important than the presidency. And how unfair it would be to the American people to have them elect a president who might have to resign before the end of his term.

Without opening his eyes, his father, reclining in an armchair, answered. "You weren't too convincing, you know. He tried talking you out of it because you sounded as if you didn't believe what you were saying yourself."

"Of course I don't believe it! I'd happily run for president from my death bed," he replied.

"True, but only you and I need to know that. If you are going to convince the public, you will have to do a better job than you managed this morning. If you can't convince your own people, how do you expect to convince people who'll only be seeing you on their television?" his father asked.

The campaign manager was not as sympathetic as Barry J had expected him to be. The man was so sure of a presidential win that it felt almost sacrilegious to withdraw from the race. Almost as sure of a win as his campaign manager, Barry J tamped down the anger threatening to overwhelm him.

The presidency was his; he could feel it! He was highest in all the polls, and the Democratic candidate was no competition.

Never again would the field be as open to him as it was at this time. He was poised and ready to assume the nation's leadership, and he was being robbed of the chance by these people, whoever they were.

"If I ever get my hands on these people, there will be no mercy," he murmured.

"Since you mention them, I should give you the latest delivery. Just a note, this time. Came last night, almost at midnight. The delivery man said the sender paid extra for the late delivery. Funny how there was no one but the servants there until 11:30 PM. Whoever they are, these people are keeping a very close eye on us."

He pulled a carefully creased piece of paper from his shirt pocket and leaned over to give it to Barry J.

This will be our last correspondence with you, assuming, of course, that you follow the instructions. If not, we will send notice of our condolences when your family name has been submerged in a tide of public disgust. I'm sure neither you nor your father wants that.

The instructions are simple, and you should have no problems following them.

1. Withdraw from the primaries and endorse Governor Rube.

2. Resign from public life and never accept another political appointment. We are sure that a talented, youngish man like yourself can find some other occupation.

It has come to our attention that your wife has made two unexpected requests of you, and we have decided to endorse those, hence instructions 3 and 4.

3. Grant your wife her wish for an uncontested and quiet divorce.

4. Keep Lars away from your wife and children.

5. Don't come looking for us.

6. Remember, WE ARE WATCHING YOU!

He ground his teeth in frustration and started to crumple the paper. His father stretched out his hand.

"I'll take that," he said with quiet authority. "I got the DNA profile and comparison back from the lab. The profile they sent to us is identical to the one the lab did from the sample you gave them. I'm taking no chances. You will follow the instructions," he told Barry J.

"Yeah? How do you expect me to keep Lars away from Marrion and the kids? I can tell him to leave them alone, but I can't make him listen. He's obsessed with Jordana. He'd have snapped her up long ago if Marrion hadn't been watching so closely. It would take more than my request to keep him away from her," was his weary reply.

"Yes, I'm aware of that. It would be best for everyone if Lars was no longer affiliated with this family. He's been very useful to us, but right now, he's a liability. We can't afford any more liabilities," the elder Welch said thoughtfully.

"He's been living with my family for over twenty years. Plus, he knows more than these people who are jerking our strings. What's to stop him telling everything if we ask him to leave?" Barry J demanded.

"We will not be asking him anything," was his father's amused reply as he heaved his bulk out of the chair and headed for the door.

"You work on your press release, and I'll work on building our assets and removing our liabilities," he said as he left.

Barry J sank into the bed. What would his life be without Lars? Still, with or without Lars, he would find out who that woman was. And if it turned out to be his final act in life, he would die happy if he could take her with him.

EPILOGUE

Lanni's living room was quiet as they focused on the television. Every network would be carrying the live broadcast, and CNN was rehashing Senator Barrington J. Welch III's political career as they counted down the minutes. Ten minutes. There was footage of the senator with his parents when his dad was a senator. His parents made an arresting couple, holding hands and striding confidently onto the stage at a rally.

Five minutes. Jordana hurrying into a building at Cornell University and a summary of her years there. Three minutes. The pimply, scarred and unsightly face of Barrington J. Welch IV at some high school event. One minute. Footage of the senator and his family on stage after his Super Tuesday win.

"Ladies and gentlemen, we are here in front of the room of Senator Barrington J. Welch III, and it is rumoured that he has decided to withdraw from the presidential race. He has agreed to issue a statement, and we are here to bring you that live broadcast from Senator Welch's hospital bed."

The senator was pale, with dark purple shadows under his eyes. Hooked to a machine and reclining in the narrow hospital bed, he could have been at death's door, but his voice was strong when he began to speak.

"Good evening, friends. As you know, I was the victim of a heart attack a few days ago, which has left me wrestling with a dilemma. The attack was a mild one but having spent some time gathering information on heart disease and talking to health professionals, I have come to the conclusion I am about to share with you.

"I have no doubt that as your elected president, I could do a competent and credible job of leading our country. I have no doubt that I would have the support of you, the voters, and all the staff that surround the office of president. I have no doubt that I could and would make a valuable contribution to our great nation.

"I do, however, doubt that I could serve the term of the presidency without being forced to resign because of health reasons. The final word from the health professionals is that I need to adopt a relatively stress-free lifestyle, and you must agree that the job of the president does not fall into the stress-free category.

"It would be unconscionable on my part to continue my bid for this most important office, knowing that I may be unable to fulfill the term of office. It is, therefore, with deep regret that I announce the resignation of my campaign.

"Though saddened by this necessity, I am happy to acknowledge I have a competent and able colleague I am confident will provide you with inspiring leadership. As I withdraw from this race, I urge you to give your full support to Former Governor Rube. I will be doing everything I can to aid his campaign and have no doubt that he will win our party's nomination to be the presidential candidate. He will be a worthy adversary in the presidential race, and when elected, a noble and efficient president.

"I thank you all for your support during my campaign and implore you to lend your support, as I will, to my friend and colleague, Former Governor Rube. Thank you again, and God bless you."

The final shot was of him and his wife holding hands as the picture faded. There were tears in his eyes.

The silence lengthened as their eyes stayed glued to the now blank screen.

Pop! The sound of the cork exploding from a champagne bottle jerked them back to the present.

"There you have it, folks. The perfect bottle for the little weasel. We measured him, fitted him, and stuffed him in," said Brandon, doing a tango with the champagne bottle.

"And JC should be happy. We left the cover off, so he can breathe. The worthless twerp still lives, but I bet he wishes otherwise," a gleeful Reena said, grabbing a glass.

"I admit the man is not fit to lead and had to be stopped. I've ignored some of your less than palatable methods and resisted the urge to lecture you on your unseemly enjoyment of someone else's misery, but Reena love, I don't think I want to join you in a toast to that man's downfall," JC said quietly.

"That's not what the champagne is for JC," Jessica said, rescuing the still dripping bottle from Brandon.

"I am satisfied with the outcome of our little campaign, and I must say I fully approve the size and shape of the senator's bottle. But you are right. It would be just a bit indecorous to toast his downfall.

"We are celebrating, but it has nothing to do with the senator," she said, smiling slightly as Denile walked over with glasses.

"So? What's up? I refuse to be robbed of a toast since this lovely wine is here, and if I can't toast Daddy resigning his presidential candidacy, this had better be good," Reena said, just a bit peeved.

Denile handed her a glass. "Patience, patience," he said, as he passed out the full glasses. He faced them and raised his glass.

"The senator is a twerp. He is a weasel and he deserved to be bottled. However, twerp or weasel, he inadvertently gave Lanni the most precious gift of her life. Had it not been for the twerp, the weasel, I would not be making the best decision of *my* life. Reena, you can help me toast the future, Mrs. Denile Bentley," he said, waving his glass in Jessica's direction.

"Married? You're getting married? Whoopee!! Do I get to be a bridesmaid? When is it going to be? Can I—?" Jessica's laugh stopped her.

"No, you can't be a bridesmaid, but I'd be grateful to have you as my maid of honour. As for when? All I can say is soon. I have to finish fighting with Denile's mother about the size of the wedding. I want small; she wants big. Once we iron out the number, we can start looking at things affecting the date, like the hall and things. Till then, drink your wine!"

After all the hugging and congratulations, Jessica looked at the picture of her mother smiling down at them and her eyes misted with tears. JC gave her hand a squeeze.

"I know, love, I know. This is a moment for mothers. But I do know that she would have approved of your choice. Denile was one of her favourite people," he told her.

Jessica unashamedly let the tears fall and leaned into JC until Denile came and gently took her in his arms.

THE END